Pucking My Next-Door Enemy

A Brother's Best Friend Second Chance Romance

Livvy Stone

Have More Bookish Fun with Livvy Stone!

Snag *thousands* of freebies, bargains and sneak peeks (or only freebies, your choice!), get the scoop on the latest releases, and be the first to dive into upcoming stories. Oh, and did we mention your welcome gift? Say hello to 'Pucking My Brother's Best Friend,' a free Enemies to Lovers Fake Marriage Short Romance crafted by Livvy Stone just for you! Scan the QR code to join 'Bookish Fun with Livvy Stone' now!

Trigger Warning

Hello Dear Reader,

This book is a spicy standalone hockey romance with no cliffhanger, but in their journey to a HEA, Mike and Eve do face some violent characters.

Please be mindful of your comfort level before reading it.

Enjoy!

Livvy Stone

Contents

1

Eve

"Is this seat taken?" a voice asks confidently.

I turn on the bar stool and look the man up and down slowly. Tall, blonde, not bad looking, wearing a designer suit and tie.

He looks like a douche.

"Yes, I'm waiting for someone," I reply as I look away.

Two weeks ago, I bought a new car, loaded it down with some of my personal belongings, and Diesel and I started a trek across the country to return to my hometown after some men from the Tambov Gang, the Russian Mafia, showed up at my house.

My Pitbull, Diesel, is a trained military/police dog. I had a similar incident a few years ago and my mentor at the time hooked me up with a rescue group who trained dogs as service animals. Diesel quickly became my protector and best friend.

I don't want to be found, so Diesel and I drove from California up and crossed the border into Canada before dipping back down to the United States by way of Michigan. I'm using cash and burner phones, my regular phone has as much advanced security protection on it as it can have, but when dealing with these types of people, you can never be too careful.

I am about eight hours from my hometown of Legacy right now and that's where I'm headed to stay with my brother for a bit. Our parents died in a car accident when I was sixteen and my brother took care of me until I turned eighteen. We used to be really close, but life took us away from each other. I have been here in Detroit for the last few days. I started talking to a guy named Mark on Bumble and he is supposed to be meeting me here.

Because of my background and job, I tend to get to dates at least thirty minutes earlier. In doing so, it gives me the opportunity to pick my seat with a view of all entrances and exits, while also scoping out the place and the people in it. I can never be too careful when it comes to meeting someone online, for obvious reasons as a woman, but also because the Tambov Gang isn't the only group of derelicts who would love to get a hold of me.

This man is not him. Not even close.

I like my men not in the douchebag flavor and he screams it.

"I'm that someone."

"No, you're not."

"I could be."

There's a lot of chaotic noise behind us as a group of six men walk into the bar. I glance back briefly noticing they're rowdy and annoying.

The blonde man in a suit takes a step forward, putting his hand on me.

"I'm sorry," I purr as I grab his wrist. "Did I say you could touch me?"

He laughs awkwardly, clearly thinking I'm playing hard to get.

"You don't have to say the words, babe, when you wear a dress like that. It's obvious you're looking to be touched in all the right places."

Entitled. Douchebag. Creep.

I laugh as I tighten my grip on his wrist, about to engage him in a wrist lock when someone knocks into me hard from behind.

The douchebag rips his arm away. He takes a step toward whoever bumped into me and puffs up.

I turn around and fall into a pair of light, intense blue eyes.

Holy Hell, are those real?

He kind of looks like my Bumble date. Damn, that's good timing.

My stomach flips and I suck in a breath as he puts both hands on my arm. Electricity shoots through me.

"Oh man, I am so sorry," a deep baritone voice says, barely audible over the noisy bar.

"Are you Mark?"

"Yes, how are you? Again, I'm sorry. We're a little wild today."

"No problem," I smile. "Have a seat."

The blonde in a suit shoots me a dirty look, removes his grubby paw from my arm, and walks away in a huff.

"Who was that guy?"

"Someone who didn't understand the meaning of the word no."

"Let me buy you a drink, gorgeous," he smiles as he gestures toward my almost empty beer.

"Sure, but only if you promise to make it worth my while."

"Oh, I have no doubt that it will be worth your while."

"I love a confident man."

This man is way hotter than his profile pictures online. He's like a six-foot-four wall of muscle. He's got amazing blue eyes, dark hair and a stubble.

"What brings you in here tonight?" he asks before he hails the bartender and orders us both drinks.

"You," I reply flirtatiously.

He glances back at me and chuckles. "Lucky me."

"Are you and your friends celebrating something or are you always the life of the party?"

"Both. You look like you could be trouble."

"I am."

Our eyes lock onto each other and I get lost in his sexy, soft blue eyes. A smile tugs at the corner of his mouth.

"I can handle that challenge."

"That's what I'm hoping for."

"You're absolutely breathtaking," he says as he turns toward me and takes a long pull from his beer bottle. "Can I kiss you?"

I laugh as I lean toward him and kiss him instead. "Asking ruins the mood," I reply as I pull away from him.

He pulls me right back into another kiss. This time, I can feel the warmth flooding my core as his hands go up to my face.

"I have a room upstairs; do you want to continue this there?"

"Lead the way, Romeo."

I stand, he takes my hand and leads me out of the bar. We go to an elevator and as soon as the doors close, he's pulling me into a hot kiss.

The elevator dings softly as we reach his floor, and he leads me down the hallway to his room. As he fumbles with the key card, I can feel the anticipation building in the air between us.

The door swings open, and he pulls me inside, not wasting a moment before pressing me against the wall in another searing kiss. The room is dimly lit, the only source of light filtering in from the city outside, casting long shadows across his face.

His hands are on my hips, firm, but he's hesitant to explore anymore.

Guess I'll take charge then.

My hands go down to his pants, unbuttoning them quickly. He takes the hint and his mouth moves down to my cleavage, exploring hungrily while his hands move down to grab my ass cheeks.

Atta boy.

I moan as I unzip his pants and yank them down. He removes them the rest of the way while also continuing to kiss me.

That's talent.

He hikes up the hem of my little black dress and reveals that I'm not wearing any panties. His eyes find mine before he grins back at me. He drops to his knees in front of me before he spreads my thighs apart.

Yes!

He buries his face in between my legs, moaning as he gets his first taste of me. The vibration sends tingles all over my body and I gasp.

My hands find their way to his hair, tugging gently as he licks and sucks on me, driving me wild. The feel of him is intoxicating.

My breathing quickens as he explores further, his tongue darting in and out, teasing me to the brink.

"You taste so good," he groans into my wet folds, making my heart race. "I could spend all night down here."

The heat between my legs is building, and I know I won't be able to hold back much longer.

He stands up, kisses me, and cups my butt, lifting me up. I wrap my legs around his waist as he guides himself inside me, filling me.

"Yessssss," I breathe.

I grip his shoulders tightly as I grind down on him.

His eyes lock with mine as he thrusts slowly, our bodies moving in perfect harmony.

A low groan escapes my lips as he picks up the pace, each thrust deeper than the last. My breath catches in my throat as the pleasure builds, the tension within me coiling tighter and tighter.

He leans down and kisses me softly, his breath warm and ragged against my lips. His touch is electric, and his hands roam over my body, sending shivers down my spine. He knows exactly where to touch with his hands, and his mouth, it's like he's the conductor of my body.

He carries me to the bed.

"Spread your legs," he commands, his voice low and gravelly. I comply, eagerly opening myself up to him. He takes a moment to take in the sight of me, lying there naked and exposed, before he crawls up my body, his eyes never leaving mine.

His lips meet mine in another passionate kiss, his hands exploring every inch of my skin. I arch my back, wanting to feel more of him against me, and he complies, positioning himself at my entrance.

He enters me again, this time slowly before he hits my G-spot.

"There it is," he breathes.

I don't know that I've ever had a man know when he hits that spot, at least not that they've voiced.

Fuck.

I let out a gasp as he hit just the right spot, my entire body trembling with pleasure.

"Take it, baby, take it all," he urges, thrusting into me deeper and harder with each word.

He pumps his hips faster and faster, sending electric sparks through me. I can't help but moan, my body responding to his every touch.

"That's it, take it, take it all," I whisper back, my voice barely recognizable as my own.

His hands grip my thighs. His body moves with a power and intensity that sends shockwaves of desire through me. I want him to take me higher, to push me over the edge and into the abyss of pleasure.

He picks up the pace, his thrusts becoming harder and faster, hitting my sweet spot over and over again. The room is a haze of sensation, the city lights dancing in the shadows as the sounds of our passion fill the room.

Then, suddenly, everything comes to a head as I cry out, arching my back and clinging to him as the most intense orgasm of my life takes over. He continues to thrust into me, his own release building.

With every swift thrust, he takes me to the edge, and I can feel it coursing through me. My orgasm is building up within me, like a volcano about to erupt. I cling to him, my nails digging into his back, unable to control myself.

"Oh, God," I moan, my voice trembling as I surrender to the wave of pleasure flooding over me. The whole world fades away, and all that exists is him and me, connected in the most intimate of ways.

He keeps thrusting, riding out my climax, pressing into me with every powerful stroke. It's intense, it's beautiful, and it's ours. His eyes stay locked with mine, the heat of them burning into me, reflecting my own desire.

He lets out a primal growl and collapses on top of me, spent and panting.

"That was incredible," I whisper, finally able to catch my breath. He kisses me softly, tendrils of warmth still pulsing between us.

"Are you okay?" he asks, his voice soft and concerned.

I smile up at him, a warm feeling spreading through me. "Better than okay," I reply. "I've never felt so alive."

"Good, we're feeling the same vibe."

He slowly pulls out of me, moves to the side, and pulls me into him.

Normally, I would bail after sex. I'm not the cuddly type at all.

I can't be, especially now. One night stand with a hot guy that I'll never see again, that's all this can be. But for now, I'm going to pretend like I didn't write a computer program for the military that has caused the Russian Mafia to come after me so that they can get classified information.

I'm putting this sweet man's life in danger by even being with him tonight.

I used a fake name on the dating site, so hopefully he doesn't suffer for this one night of sweet release.

I feel so safe right here.

Damn it, it's that really good orgasm afterglow that has me feeling like he'll protect me from dragons.

You can protect yourself, girl. Get out of here.

"Damn, I am worn out," he chuckles. "Usually, I have way better stamina than this."

"That's what they all say," I giggle.

"Is that so? Let me get a ten-minute power nap and then I'll make your legs shake even more than they already are."

"All talk."

He chuckles and pulls me into him. "It's a promise."

He closes his eyes and within a few minutes, he's sound asleep.

It's really annoying how men can do that.

My phone buzzes with a notification. I have a new message on Bumble. I open the app to see that Mark has messaged me.

What?

> Hey, I'm really sorry I missed our date. I think I have COVID, I've been asleep for the last twelve hours. Raincheck?

Who the fuck is this man if he's not Mark?

Shit, Eve, shit. How did you let this happen?

I move and when he doesn't notice I remove myself from the bed. I straighten my clothes quietly leaving his room.

I immediately go to the shower, and turn the spray on as hot as it can go before, I climb in.

Was he one of Ivan's guys?

No, if that were the case I'd be dead. He'd have taken the many chances I'd given him to catch me off guard.

Was that just dumb luck that I ran into a hot guy with an incredible dick?

That guy seemed pretty great, he definitely knows what he's doing with that dick and mouth, but it can't be anything else.

I have to get to my brother's house and hide out. Ivan, the man chasing me, won't know to look for me there and it's my only chance at staying alive.

The only chance Mark, or whatever his real name is, has at staying alive.

I can't bring him into this no matter how bad my body wants to go back to him.

2

Mike

I OPEN MY EYES the next morning and smile.

Damn, that woman was incredible.

Bumping into her wasn't an accident. Luca saw her and told me to go for it.

"Be her knight in shining armor and rescue her from that douchebag," he had said.

It worked.

We'd just walked back into the hotel after winning our game against the Detroit Redwings. It had been an intense game, and we were still pumped afterward and none of us wanted to call it a night.

I instantly spotted this gorgeous woman with jet-black hair in a short bob at the bar, sipping a Bud Light and looking extremely annoyed at the suit hitting on her. She was wearing a tight black dress that hugged every luscious curve of her full body. Both of her arms were sleeved in colorful tattoos.

My tongue must have hit the floor. It's rare that I even notice women, let alone go up and speak to them when we're out.

I'm much more of a reserved, hermit type of man. I'm a professional hockey player, so sometimes it's hard to tell if a woman is interested in me or the celebrity and money that comes with what I do.I reach to my side and keep reaching. I sit up.

I didn't imagine her, right? She was really here last night.

I glance around my hotel room, but there's no sign of her anywhere except the pillow next to me smells like lavender and vanilla.

Shit.

It's another day of travel with the team, and we're heading back home to St. Louis. The thought of being back in familiar territory fills me with a sense of comfort.

Traveling is necessary for my job, but I'm a homebody through and through. I love what I do, but I'd rather if all games were at home. I'm not much of a people person, I guess you would say.

Throwing off the covers, I swing my legs over the edge of the bed and plant my feet on the floor. The coolness of the carpet grounds me, awakening my senses. With a quick glance at the clock, I realize it's time to get moving if I want to catch the team plane.

I pad across the room to the bathroom, splashing cold water on my face to shake off any lingering drowsiness. As I brush my teeth, I mentally run through my checklist for the day. Flight home, then straight to the rink for a workout – just another day in the life of a puckster.

After a brisk shower, I towel off and dress in my team gear, ready to tackle the day ahead. Grabbing my bag, I head downstairs to meet the rest of the guys in the lobby. The buzz of excitement is palpable as we gather together, eager to get back home.

The journey to the airport is smooth, and before long, we're boarding the team plane. I settle into my seat, exchanging greetings with my teammates as we prepare for takeoff. The atmosphere is light-hearted, filled with banter and laughter.

As we ascend into the sky, I can't help but feel a sense of relief wash over me. The pressure of the game is momentarily lifted, replaced by the anticipation of returning home. I lean back in my seat, closing my eyes for a moment of quiet reflection.

I can't stop thinking about the woman from the bar.

What a creep I am. I didn't even get her name. I treated her no better than a damn prostitute.

The hottest woman I've ever met in my life and I don't know her name.

What an idiot.

But my moment of peace is short-lived as my teammates start ribbing me about last night's escapade. The memory of the beautiful woman I met at the bar flashes through my mind, and I can't help but chuckle at their teasing.

"Hey, Mike, you sure know how to pick 'em!" Georgie says with a playful grin.

"Yeah, I gotta hand it to you, man. That one was hot," Blaze calls out.

"I'm glad you finally got out there bro," Luca adds. "It looked like it worked out in your favor. What was she like?"

"Hot," I chuckle. "She seems really cool and down to Earth."

"The artwork on her arms was intense. I bet she's kinky," Drake interjects. "Tell me she was freaky."

I shake my head and roll my eyes. I shrug off their comments with a good-natured smile, knowing that it's all in good fun. After all, what happens on the road stays on the road – at least, that's the unwritten rule among us.

The flight passes quickly, and before I know it, we're touching down in St. Louis. The familiar sights and sounds of home greet me as I step off the plane, filling me with a sense of belonging.

Without missing a beat, I make my way to the rink for my scheduled workout. The familiar scent of sweat and ice greets me as I step inside, invigorating me with a sense of purpose. I head straight for the weight room, eager to get started on my routine.

As I begin my lifts, I can feel the burn in my muscles, a satisfying reminder of the hard work I've put in over the years. My teammates join me, offering words of encouragement as we push each other to new heights.

But amidst the grunts and groans of exertion, the topic of last night's rendezvous resurfaces. My teammates can't resist teasing me once again, and I find myself laughing along with them, grateful for their camaraderie.

"Looks like your girl has got some competition, Mike. That blonde is eying you," one of them jokes, nodding towards a group of attractive women entering the rink.

Puck bunnies.

No, thank you.

“Why are they here?”

“Because dudes like Drake give them attention,” Luca rolls his eyes.

I think it’s thirsty when these women, who are not attached to any player, show up at our practices just with the hope that they’ll hook up with a player. I’m not sure how some of my teammates don’t see it the same way.

I focus on my workout tuning out all the other noise. It's all part of the game—both on and off the ice.

After a rigorous session, I hit the showers, relishing the feeling of hot water cascading over my tired muscles. As I towel off and get dressed, I feel a sense of accomplishment wash over me.

With my workout complete, I make my way back to Legacy, my hometown just thirty minutes outside the city. The familiar sights and sounds greet me as I drive through the streets, filling me with a sense of nostalgia.

Legacy is a town like something out of a movie. Cobblestone streets and white picket fences. Everyone knows your name and your business. It used to feel like a cage, but now, it's home.

Pulling into my driveway, I exhale deeply, grateful to be back home once again. Staying in my hometown is great because I'm still connected to my friends from kindergarten. I try to help them out whenever I can.

My best friend and agent, Damon, texts.

Where you at?

Almost there.

Game starts in twenty.

It's our tradition to spend Sunday together watching whatever games we can find and ESPN recaps.

I pull into the driveway, half expecting my Blue Heeler, Piper, to bound out the front door. She doesn't because she's at my friend Miranda's house. I glance at the house sadly.

I should go get her now.

I shake my head and laugh. I can go another day without picking up my dog. We're trying to breed our dogs together, and that takes time, according to Miranda.

But as I step out of the car and glance over at Damon's house next door, something catches my eye—a sleek, unfamiliar car parked in the driveway. Frowning slightly, I wonder who could be visiting at this hour. But then again, as a sports agent, it's not uncommon for Damon to have meetings at his house or to invite others over for our weekly Sunday dinners.

Shrugging off the thought, I make my way to his front door, my mind already drifting to thoughts of home-cooked meals and catching up with my best friend. Without bothering to knock, I push the door open and step inside.

And that's when I see her—the woman from last night, standing in the living room wearing a tank top and shorts, her hair pulled back into a messy strawberry blonde ponytail. Her face turns white as she sees me, and for a moment, we both stand frozen in place, caught off guard by the unexpected encounter.

It's her. Her hair color is vastly different, but it's her.

A gray and white Pitbull comes charging out of nowhere, barking and growling at me.

"Holy shit!"

"Diesel, sitz!" the woman says in a low growl.

The dog stops immediately as he gives me an evil glare before he retreats to his owner.

"Hey, Mike," Damon's voice breaks the silence, pulling me back to reality. "Do you remember my sister Eve?"

Oh shit. That's Eve?

I manage to plaster a smile on my face, my heart pounding in my chest as I struggle to maintain my composure. Internally, I'm freaking out—how could I have slept with my best friend's sister without even realizing it? But outwardly, I keep my cool, nodding casually as if it's no big deal.

"Yeah, of course," I reply, trying to sound nonchalant. "Nice to see you again, Eve."

She gives me a tight-lipped smile, her eyes betraying a hint of discomfort. I can't blame her—I'm sure she's just as shocked by this turn of events as I am.

"That's her guard dog, Diesel. He's not friendly at first."

"I see that."

"He's a trained killer," she states as she shoots her brother a dirty look.

He rolls his eyes and laughs. "Only if you're an asshole."

"As I directly remember he fits that profile."

"Eve, come on, it's been like ten years since you last saw him."

"Not much has changed, I'm sure."

Eve Carlisle did not look like that the last time I saw her ten years ago. She's always been known as a wild child, the girl who went against every direction she was ever given.

In high school her hair was always dyed wild colors, her makeup always extremely dark matching the clothes that she wore. She had her nose and lip pierced back then too. She'd always been a little on the heavier side as well.

She's a curvy woman now and her body is banging.

Did she know who I was? She called me by my name at the bar. She had to know. Why didn't she say anything?

I look the same other than my hair is longer, and I have a goatee. We were in Detroit rather than close to Legacy, maybe she didn't put two and two together.

Taking a deep breath, I focus on the present. After all, there's no use dwelling on the past—I'll just have to make the best of this awkward situation and hope that Damon doesn't hold it against me if he ever finds out. Though I'll make sure he doesn't.

"She's visiting for a bit. Hopefully long-term," Damon explains. "She's in between jobs."

"What is that you do, Eve?"

"Computer stuff."

"You always were so smart," I say as I remember that she was a borderline genius but made herself look dumb a lot. She made herself small to fit in.

"I wasn't," she snaps.

"You once wrote my entire paper on 'Great Expectations' and I got an A. You did every single one of your brother's science fair projects and made him look like a genius."

"Oh God, remember that douchebag Kevin that you used to date?" Damon interjects. "You're the only reason he was able to play football because you did his homework, so he passed Trigonometry."

"I don't know what either of you are talking about," she rolls her eyes and walks into the kitchen.

"Why does that bother her so much?" I mouth to Damon.

He shrugs his shoulders and shakes his head. She comes back from the kitchen carrying three bottles of beer. She hands one to her brother and then another one to me. Her eyes lock onto mine and I can't tell what she's thinking.

I take the bottle and she immediately walks away and plops down next to Damon.

"So, you're staying here for a bit?" I ask as I sit down in a recliner nearby.

"For now," she shrugs.

"My sister doesn't stay anywhere long," Damon laughs. "Her job has her traveling a lot."

"I feel that."

She shoots me a weird look. "What do you do?"

"I play hockey for the St. Louis Blues," I laugh.

Damon pulls back and looks at her in surprise. "How do you not know that? He's like my first-ever client."

"I don't know. I guess I forgot," she shrugs. "Why would I remember what your asshole best friend does for a living?"

"Why am I an asshole now?"

She turns and gives me a pointed look. "You were the biggest douchebag to me growing up."

"I don't remember it that way."

"Of course you don't," she rolls her eyes and leans back into the couch.

I never understood why she fought to not be so different from everyone else. I couldn't fathom why she was so smart and pretty but chose to play dumb and play down her looks. I said it to her often too, is that what she's talking about?

"Tell me what I did."

"Did someone buy the old house finally?" Eve asks, dismissing my question as though I hadn't even spoke.

"Yeah, I transferred you money when it sold," Damon laughs. "A few years ago."

She shrugs her shoulders. "I didn't remember."

"Why?"

"I drove by and saw a pink bike out front and had a flashback. Are the neighbors still there too?"

"Mrs. White is. The Pinkards moved a few years ago and they've had two new people in there since, I think," Damon answers her. "Mrs. White asks about you all the time."

"She's the sweetest. I don't know what we would have done without her and Mr. White when Mom and Dad died," Eve murmurs as she looks down at her dog.

He whines and nuzzles into her. She absentmindedly starts petting him.

"She's pretty incredible," I interject. "She's fostered a few kids in the area. She's always a big help at the humane society and the Catholic church."

"How would you know that?" Eve snaps.I shrug my shoulders. "I just do."

"Because he is the biggest donor for the humane society and whatever other charity happens here in town," Damon replies. "He gives back to Legacy a lot."

"As do you."

"Isn't that sweet?" she says sarcastically.

"Why are you being so snarky?" Damon asks.

"I need to make a phone call," she says as she stands up and walks out the back door.

Her demon dog follows behind her quickly, but not without giving me a dirty look again.

Is that possible? Do dogs give dirty looks?

My eyes flit to Damon's quickly. He chuckles and laughs as he shakes his head.

"You don't want to go down that road, bro. You know how stubborn she is."

"I don't know why she always hated me."

"I don't think she ever really hated you. When Mom and Dad died she kind of shut everyone but me out. You fell into that category."

Eve had just turned sixteen when their parents passed away. Damon and I were living it up our junior year when they're whole world crashed around him.

He'd had plans to play football at college, but dropped everything to join the Marine Corps so that he had someone to support his sister. They had gotten really close after losing their parents. A family friend halfway stayed with Eve when Damon went to bootcamp, she was really just there for appearances.

I tried to check on her, look out for her as much as I could but she was adamant that she didn't need anyone else's help. Constantly. We got into a lot of arguments when I'd come back from college to visit.

"I tried to be helpful," I shrug.

"Let her get to know you now. As much as I want her to stay, I have a feeling that she'll be gone within the week."

Not if I have anything to do with it.

3

Eve

How in the Hell did I not realize that man was Mike Hunter?

Why did he tell me his name was Mark?

How did I not remember those eyes?

Fuck. This is not good.

He's all I thought about on the drive here and now he just appears in my brother's house less than an hour after I get here?

No fucking way.

I need some space, so I grab my phone and walk out to my brother's expansive backyard. He lives in a really nice neighborhood where every house has a wrought iron fence surrounding it, a pool and hot tub in the backyard, and all of the lawns look like they're actually turf from a golf course.

I should go inside and get my bathing suit and take advantage of the sun.

I shake my head.

"Go potty, Diesel," I command as he takes off past the cement that surrounds the pool and goes out into the yard to do his business.

I blow out a breath and look up into the sun, closing my eyes and letting the warmth hit me for a few seconds.

I have got to clear my head and get Mike Hunter out of my thoughts. I don't have time for distractions and he's definitely the best kind of distraction.

Remembering how much of a dick he always was to me growing up is helpful. Instead of wanting to rip his clothes off, I want to punch him in the face.

My phone vibrates in my pocket, interrupting the tranquility with its insistent buzzing. With a sigh, I pull it out, glancing at the screen to see an unknown number flashing back at me. I answer the call.

Shit. Why did I do that? I never answer calls, especially without engaging my tracker. Damn it, that asshole has me distracted.

"Hello?" I say, my voice is tentative as I wait for a response.

"Eve, my love," comes the reply, a thick Russian accent sending a shiver down my spine. "Ivan here. I believe we have some unfinished business to attend to."

Ivan.

The name alone is enough to send a chill down my spine, memories of our last encounter flooding back with painful clarity. I swallow hard, steeling myself for whatever he has in store.

"What do you want, Ivan?" I ask, trying to keep my voice steady despite the fear gnawing at my insides. "How's your bestie doing?"

"I think you know exactly what I want, sweetheart," he says, his tone dripping with malice. "Your mangy mutt made a mess of my guys, and now it's time to pay the price."

I can't help but laugh at his words, a bitter edge to the sound. "Your guys looked like a bunch of pussies," I retort, unable to resist the urge to taunt him. "Maybe they should learn to pick on someone their own size. Five guys were sent to take little old me out and they couldn't even get the job done. You need to rethink your hiring process."

"Laugh now, my love, but you will pay."

“Doubtful. Diesel got the taste of blood, he wants more.”

There's a moment of silence on the other end of the line, followed by a low, menacing growl that sends a shiver down my spine. "You may have run and hid Eve, but I will find you," Ivan says, his voice laced with fury. "And when I do, you will give me what I want—your secrets, your loyalty, everything."

I scoff at his words, the bravado masking the fear that threatens to consume me. "Good luck with that," I say, my voice dripping with sarcasm. "You'll have better luck catching a unicorn than getting anything out of me."

His frustration is palpable now, his voice rising with each word. He’s yelling so loud that I have to move the phone away from my ear.

"You won't be laughing for long," he threatens his words a chilling promise of things to come. "I will make you and your dog pay for what you did to my guys. Count on it, bitch. I will gut you in front of your precious pup and let him eat you from the inside out.”

“You bastard,” I hiss just as the phone is ripped out of my hands.

“Listen, I don’t know who you are or where you get off calling my fiancé a bitch, but if I ever find you, I’ll rip your throat out and let her precious pup have it as a snack.”

Fiancé? What the Hell is he doing?

“Fiancé?” Ivan bellows with laughter. “Eve doesn’t have a fiancé.”

“Shows what you know. Don’t ever call her again. I will find you and I will kill you,” Mike growls, his voice is low and menacing like nothing I’ve ever heard before.

“Who is this?”

“Mi...”

I rip the phone out of his hand, end the call, and power it off.

“You idiot!” I shriek.

“What?”

What the fuck? What kind of idiot is this man?

"What gives you the right?" I snap. "Do you have any idea what you just did?

I slam the phone down on the concrete as hard as possible.

"What are you doing?"

It doesn't break.

Damn, these new phones for being indestructible.

The anger coursing through me is like fire, burning bright and fierce as I stare down at the burner phone. Ivan's threats echo in my mind, his voice dripping with malice and intent. I refuse to be intimidated by him, but the fear gnaws at the edges of my resolve, whispering doubts and uncertainties that I can't ignore. I can handle myself; Damon can handle himself as he spent four years in the Marine Corps. I don't know if Mike can handle himself and his mouth just opened Pandora's Box for him.

"How dare you grab the phone out of my hand and take over like you're someone. How dare you tell anyone that you're my fiancé? In what world does that even make sense? I wouldn't touch you if you were the last man on Earth."

"You didn't seem to have that problem last night."

"Bastard," I hiss as I slam the phone down again.

It bounces and barely has a scratch.

Break you stupid thing. I need the freaking GPS out of you now.

"Eve, are you okay? What are you doing?" Mike repeats. "Why are you trying to break your phone? Give it to me, I'm stronger."

I will punch this man in the face for that comment. He will not rescue me from anything.

I glare back at him. With a growl of frustration, I pick up the phone again and I grip it tighter, my nails digging into the plastic casing as I try to break it. But it refuses to yield, stubborn and annoying in the face of my fury. Without thinking, I stride over to the hot tub, the water bubbling and steaming.

I hurl the phone into the water, watching as it sinks beneath the surface with a satisfying splash. But when it resurfaces moments later, still intact and mocking me with its resilience, I see red.

“Go back into the house and don’t worry about what I’m doing,” I hiss.

Grabbing the phone out of the water, I slam it against the concrete edge of the hot tub, again and again, until my knuckles are sore. But still, it refuses to break, mocking me with its unyielding strength.

“This is not normal behavior. Who was that guy? Why would you allow someone to talk to you like that?”

Panting with exertion and frustration, I drop the phone to the ground, my chest heaving as I try to catch my breath. And then, I finally see a good break in the casing, I reach into the phone, my fingers fumbling for the tracking device inside.

“Yes!”

And then, I find it—a small, inconspicuous chip hidden inside the casing, blinking with a faint green light. With a triumphant smirk, I pluck it out, holding it up like a trophy of my victory.

But my triumph is short-lived, shattered by the sound of Mike's voice behind me. "What the Hell are you doing, Eve?"

Diesel is finally done doing his business and comes charging toward us. He doesn’t like the anger in Mike’s voice right now and he places himself in between the two of us.

“Sitz,” I hiss at Diesel.

I pull out a lighter, hold the chip above the flame, and let it start melting it until it’s too hot and I drop it on the ground. I put it out with my shoe, destroying it further.

Finally, Ivan won’t be able to trace that anymore.

I whirl around to face him, my blood boiling with rage and frustration. "Mind your own damn business, Mike," I snap, my voice sharp with irritation. "This doesn't concern you."

But he isn't backing down, his brow furrowed with concern as he steps closer. Diesel growls. Mike looks down and makes a face.

"I heard you talking to someone on the phone, I'm not going to allow someone to threaten you," he says, his voice tinged with confusion. "Who was it? What's going on?"

"I don't have to explain myself to you," I say, my voice cold and distant. "You don't know anything about what's going on, so just stay out of it. I am not some damsel in distress that needs to be rescued, I've never been, so leave me alone."

"Why won't you tell me?" he asks, his voice tinged with frustration. "Why would you allow someone to talk to you like that?"

"What gives you the right to speak to me in any way right now?"

"I'm worried about you. That man was threatening your life."

"Through a phone," I laugh dismissively. "Do you think I'm worried about someone who is threatening me from across the country? Also, it was a wrong number, so get your panties out of the bunch that they're in. Go back into the house with my brother and forget about it."

"Wrong number? What kind of idiot do you take me for? He said your name. He called you love. Is he an ex? Did you come home because you left an abusive ex?"

"Oh my God, no! Get over your fucking hero complex, dude," I sigh with a forced laugh. "You and I had sex, we are nothing... It meant nothing. That doesn't give you any sort of right to swoop in here and make up stories about my life or try and rescue me from invisible threats. Do you understand? Back. The. Fuck. Off."

He stares back at me in surprise. Diesel is still sitting on my feet, knocking his nose against me because he feels my anxiety. I grab the pieces of the phone and storm into the house.

"What just happened?" I hear Mike say.

"I'm going for a run," I hiss to my brother when I get back inside the house. I grab Air Pods, put on my tennis shoes, and grab Diesel's harness and leash.

"Good to see you and Mike still get along swimmingly."

"Who says the word swimmingly?"

"Me, it's fitting since you were by the pool," he laughs.

"Have another beer, bro," I snort. "I was right by the way, he's still an asshole."

I roll my eyes then Diesel and I go out the front door. I need to clear my head so that I don't rip Mike's head off.

***

When we return from our run, Mike is sitting in the living room while Damon is sound asleep on the couch.

"What is this, a sleepover now?"

"No," he chuckles. "I was waiting for you to come back."

"Why?"

"I wanted to make sure you were okay. Legacy is a small town but it doesn't mean it's always safe."

"I'm surprised you weren't following behind me in your Range Rover making sure I was safe."

"Who says I wasn't following?" he teases.

I laugh and roll my eyes. "I would have known."

"Maybe not. How was your run?"

"It was good."

I walk into the kitchen just as he stands up and follows me. I go to the refrigerator and grab a bottle of water.

"Did you just run around the neighborhood?"

"Yeah, where else would I have gone?"

"Why do you hate me so much?"

"I never said I hated you."

He blows out his breath and leans against the wall, crossing his arms in front of him and leaning his head against the wall.

Why is he so damn hot?

"How have you been?"

"Great."

"What have you been up to?"

"Stuff."

"One word answers, huh?"

"I'm not interested in making small talk with you, Hunter. We have never been friends, us having sex doesn't change that in the slightest. It was a mistake."

"A mistake, huh?"

I nod.

"Everyone needs an itch scratched every now and then."

He inhales and nods slowly, his eyes roam over my body and I feel as though his hands are running over me at the same time.

I swallow hard as I shift slightly.

I want his hands to run over me again.

"I can scratch that itch again, if you'd like."

He pushes off the wall and crosses over to me.

"No thanks," I say as I move away from him. "Besides, Damon will kill you."

"Doubtful."

"Then I will."

I walk away and go into my bedroom. I need to get away from him quickly before I do something stupid like sleep with him again.

It takes everything in me not to turn around and grab him in a kiss right now.

Cold shower it is.

4

Mike

Maybe I overreacted.

Damon's kitchen window had been open so I could hear the man on the other end call her love, I couldn't not listen after what happened between us last night. The way he was talking to her, threatening her I reacted without thinking.

I'm not going to let someone talk to her like that. I'll stand up for her if she won't stand up for herself.

I don't remember her having such anger issues.

What was that all about?

Why would she allow anyone to threaten her like that? Why was she lying about it?

I walk back inside the house and look at Damon. He laughs and shakes his head.

"What happened out there? She was so pissed when she came in."

"I overheard a phone conversation and took control of it."

"What does that mean?"

"Why did she come home suddenly after ten years? Did she tell you?"

"Just that she needed a change of scenery," he replied looking at the television quickly.

He's lying, he rarely looks away in a conversation.

"A change of scenery?"

"Yeah. I need another beer, do you?"

"Damon, some man was threatening her on the phone. He threatened to find her and kill her and her dog. He called her love, too. Is she running from an abusive ex?"

"No," he hesitates.

"Why are you lying to me?"

"Why do you think I'm lying?"

"Whoever it was, I told them I was her fiancé. He asked my name and she ripped the phone out of my hand and freaked the fuck out."

Damon laughs and shakes his head. "Why would you say you were her fiancé? Where did that even come from?"

"I don't know. She's your little sister, man, I think I was just reacting and protecting her because of that," I lie.

He shakes his head again. He inhales and exhales slowly. He glances at the front door before he walks into the kitchen and goes to the refrigerator. He pulls out two beers, hands one to me, and then opens his. He takes a long pull before he leans against the counter.

"I'm only telling you this because you're my best friend and I know you won't blab it to everyone else. Eve cannot ever know that I told you though."

"Okay." "Most people don't know that Eve went into the Marine Corps when she graduated from high school, just like I did. They immediately realized that she was a tech genius and used her to their advantage. She has one of the highest security clearances you can have."

"I never understood why she downplayed her brains. So, the man on the phone is not an ex?"

"No."

Why did that realization make me smile on the inside?

"Then who is he?"

"I don't know. She gave me the bare minimum information to keep me safe, she says."

"Safe from who? From what?"

He shrugs his shoulders and takes another long pull from his beer bottle. "I didn't ask questions because I knew she wouldn't answer them. I also knew that asking questions or pushing her for information would make her run."

"Run?"

"She'd go somewhere else to hide out and I'd never know if she was safe. This way, I know where she's at and that she's safe. If she came home, it's bad."

"Why didn't I ever know she went into the military?"

"Eve is a secretive person. I didn't even know she joined until I got a letter from her in boot camp while I was at Camp LeJeune. As I said, she has one of the highest security clearances you can have, so she has always asked that we didn't tell many people she served."

"What can I do?"

"Nothing," he laughs. "Do you know why you two have never gotten along?"

"Because I hold her accountable?"

"No," he shakes his head and snorts. "Because you're too overprotective of her. I get why you are, and I appreciate it, but she doesn't."

"Overprotective? I've never..."

He cocks an eyebrow and gives me a funny look.

"How many fights did you get into because of Eve?"

"None."

"Bullshit. You punched Kevin in the face and got benched for a week because of it."

"He came at me."

"No, that's what you told everyone. That's what the story was, but RaeLynn Peters told me and had a video of it, that Kevin was telling everyone he used Eve to do his homework and that she was a freak. As soon as you heard the word freak, you swung."

"I don't remember that."

"Of course you don't. You got into a fight with a rival hockey player because Eve dated him, dumped him, and he called her a bitch in front of you."

"He..."

"It's why you've always made comments like, why do you pretend like you're not smart? Why do you allow people to treat you like that? You think you're holding her accountable, and she sees it as an attack that she's not good enough."

"I have never thought she wasn't good enough, she's so much smarter and..."

"I know, bro. You have always protected her because she's my little sister. You've always looked out for her and beat me to most fights. That's not what she needs, especially right now. She can protect herself."

"I didn't..."

I never realized I was doing those things. Maybe I did but I always did them because Damon's the only family I have left.

My parents got divorced when I was very young. My little sister went to live with my mom and I stayed with my dad. When I was around eight, my mother began dating a bastard of a man who put her in the hospital numerous times until he walked into the house and shot my mother, my little sister, and himself while my dad and I were at a hockey tournament when I was ten years old. My dad spent most of his time working after that, trying to keep himself busy to not think about the massive loss we had.

Damon and Eve's parents took me in most of the time. I was always at their house. They were my family. When their parents died it was like losing my mom all over again.

"I get it, bro. I do. Eve doesn't though. She's always been self-sufficient. She's always been on her own path, and no one could tell her otherwise. You're not going to do any good by going back into those patterns. She will leave and I don't want that."

I blow out a breath as his words rattle around in my head. He's right.

"I'll back off."

"Thank you. I always kind of thought she had a crush on you, but she acted so hateful toward you because she thought you only saw her as my little sister."

"Crush on me?"

"Yeah. I'm sure that's not the case anymore but if it were, don't go there. I want my sister to stay in Legacy for good, but she's not good at relationships or feelings. If you two were to get together it wouldn't end well, and she'd run from here for good."

Shit.

"She's your little sister, that's the only way I see her," I lie again.

"Good."

I apologized when Eve returned from her run, but she isn't going to make this easy on me, that's for certain. Damon is snoring on the couch and I can hear Eve turn the shower on in her room. I could wait in the living room for her to come out, but that's creepy.

I head home for the night. As soon as I'm in the solitude of my massive home I fire up my laptop and put Eve's name in the search engine.

There's nothing about her, not even an address or social media. It's like she's a ghost. That would make sense with what Damon told me.

***

The piercing sound of my alarm clock jolts me awake, dragging me from the clutches of sleep. I blink away the remnants of dreams and stretch, muscles protesting the early hour. It's another day, another chance to push myself harder, to strive for perfection on the ice.

With a groan, I roll out of bed, feeling the familiar ache in my limbs. The rink awaits, a second home where I find solace in the cold, smooth surface beneath my skates. It's where I belong, where I feel most alive.

I quickly pull on my workout clothes and grab my bag, filled with the tools of my trade. As I step out into the crisp morning air, I feel a surge of anticipation. Today, I'll push myself to the limit, leaving everything I have on the ice.

The rink is quiet when I arrive, the only sound is the echo of my footsteps against the concrete. I make my way to the locker room, nodding to familiar faces along the way. This is my sanctuary, where I come to escape the chaos of the outside world.

I start with lifting, the weights heavy in my hands as I push myself to the brink of exhaustion. Each rep brings me closer to my goal, the burn in my muscles a welcome reminder of my dedication.

Next comes conditioning, a grueling series of drills designed to test my endurance. I push myself harder, and faster, knowing that every second counts. Sweat pours down my face, mingling with the chill of the air as I push my body to its limits.

Finally, it's time for practice, the ice beckoning me like a siren's call. I step onto the surface, the familiar glide of my skates sending a thrill through my veins. This is where I come alive, where I feel most at home.

As I skate, I lose myself in the rhythm of the ice, each movement fluid and precise. I push myself harder, faster, and determined to be the best. With each stride, I feel the weight of the world lift from my shoulders, leaving me free to soar.

But amidst the flurry of activity, there's one thought that lingers in the back of my mind.

Eve.

How do I get her to let me in, to not hate me?

Luca sidles up to me during a water break, his easy grin lighting up his face. "Hey man, you hear from your one-night stand yet?"

I sigh the weight of my uncertainty pressing down on me. "Can we not refer to her as a one-night stand?"

"Does that mean you heard from her?"

"I saw her last night, Luca. It didn't go well."

He raises an eyebrow, his curiosity piqued. "Wait, you met her in Detroit. How did you see her last night? Is she crazy and showed up? What happened?"

"I didn't recognize her at the time, but she's my best friend's little sister. She hasn't been home in ten years. She's back home now. Aaaand... She hates me."

Luca laughs a sound that echoes across the empty rink. "Come on, Mike. You're kidding right? You hooked up with a girl in Detroit, who also happens to be Damon's sister? And now she's in St. Louis?"

"Yeah, wild, right?"

"Beyond. Maybe give her a little space. Does she know that you didn't know who she was?"

"We didn't talk about it."

"Maybe you should."

"Yeah, you're right."

We return to the ice and my focus is directly on practice. Whatever happens with her, I know one thing for certain: I won't let it distract me from my dreams.

When practice comes to an end, I make my way to Miranda's house, to pick up Piper.

"How was she?"

"Perfect angel as always," Miranda grins. "The kids love having her and so does Thanos."

"I'm sure he especially enjoyed it."

"She's not in heat yet so no puppies."

"It'll happen."

Piper and I head to my truck. She jumps in the front seat and settles in for the ride. We make our way back to the house. As soon as we park and I let her out, she starts running around the yard sniffing everything in sight.

My eyes dart next door and see Eve's car is still in the driveway.

Hey, I have to go to Texas for a few days. This new kid Blake I just picked up is already causing me trouble. Keep an eye on Eve and the house for me without her knowing, please.

Got it.

I smile to myself as I glance at Damon's house again.

I'll keep an eye on her. She may act like she hates me, but the woman I met Saturday night didn't hate me in any form and I'll get her back to that.

5

Eve

I GAZE AROUND MY brother's house, taking in the opulence of the grandeur that surrounds me. It's extravagant, the kind of place that screams luxury and privilege. And yet, it's exactly what I need right now. Hidden in plain sight, I know Ivan won't think to look for me here. Not in this sprawling mansion nestled in a good neighborhood, where the police response time would be quicker than anywhere else.

As I wander through the spacious rooms, Diesel right behind me, a sense of calm washes over me. It's been a whirlwind few weeks. But here, in Damon's house, I feel safe. I am protected from the chaos of the outside world, if only for a little while.

My thoughts are interrupted by Damon's voice, breaking through the silence like a ray of light. "Hey, Eve, I need to talk to you."

I turn to face him, a smile tugging at the corners of my lips. "What's up?"

He sighs, his expression grave. "I have to leave for a few days. I've got another athlete/client who needs my help."

My heart sinks at the thought of being alone, but I nod, trying to hide my apprehension. "Okay, no problem. Who's the client?"

Damon's face lights up as he launches into an explanation. "He's a fairly young MLB player who skyrocketed to the top quickly. He's struggling with fame and making good choices. He needs a little mentoring."

I listen intently as Damon outlines the details, a sense of admiration swelling within me. Despite his busy schedule, he always finds time to help those in need. It's one of the things I love most about him.

But as he bids me farewell and heads out the door, leaving me alone in the vast emptiness of the house, a shiver runs down my spine. I may be able to handle myself, but that doesn't mean I want to be alone.

I try to shake off the unease as I make myself at home, exploring every nook and cranny of the house. But no matter how hard I try, I can't seem to settle and it's only for one reason that has nothing to do with Ivan.

Mike's face flickers in my mind, his smile taunting me from the depths of my memories.

I try to distract myself with mundane tasks, losing myself in the comfort of routine. But no matter how many times I scrub the countertops or rearrange the furniture, his presence lingers like a shadow, refusing to be ignored.

"Let's go for a swim and make use of this beautiful day," I say to Diesel as I walk into my room and change into my bathing suit.

"You know what Diesel? There's no one around and Damon's house is so private and set back from the road, who needs tan lines?" I remove my bathing suit and walk through the house naked, my bikini in my hand just in case. I dive in the pool to cool off, then immediately get out to let the sun dry me off.

I close my eyes and relish the warmth of the sun on my naked body. There's nothing more freeing than being in your birthday suit and enjoying nature.

Mike's face flits into my mind. Thoughts of his head buried between my thighs and how it felt for his tongue and fingers to touch my most sensitive spots.

Damn it, why can't I get him out of my head?

I'm wet now and not from the pool water.

I close my eyes, my hands travel down, my fingers circling my nipples as I remember what it felt like to have Mike's tongue there.

I bite my lip, trying to stifle the moan that wants to escape as my fingers trace the sensitive skin around my nipples. The sensation is heightened by the warmth of the sun and the scent of the pool water.

My mind drifts back to Saturday night, the way he looked at me as he pleasured me, his eyes filled with hunger and devotion. I can almost feel his hands on my body, his lips exploring every inch of my skin. My breathing becomes heavier, my pulse quickening as I lose myself in the memory.

My fingers go down, making a trail to my warm, soaking-wet center. Finding my pleasure spot and smiling.

I start to rub gently, my mind consumed by the sensations and memories. I can feel the warmth radiating from the sun, but it's his touch that I long for. The thoughts of him pleasuring me make my desire escalate, and I plead silently for fulfillment.

With a surge of arousal, I let out a soft moan that's barely audible, but my hand picks up its rhythm. My breath catches in my throat as I crave the taste of him, the sound of his moans, the warmth of his body against mine.

My mind floods with images, sights, and sounds from that unforgettable night. The way he tasted, the way his lips felt against mine, the feel of his body pressed against mine—all of it feels so tantalizingly close. The memories are intoxicating, and I find myself slipping deeper into a world of pure sensuality and desire.

As I continue to stroke myself, each movement bringing me closer to the edge, I can't help but think of how good it would have been if he were here with me now. There's a part of me that longs for that connection, the way his touch can send me into a frenzy of pleasure.

My arousal grows stronger, and the sun's rays now seem to be a part of my pleasure, caressing my skin with every stroke of my hand. I close my eyes and imagine his hands on me, exploring every curve and flaw, as if he's worshiping my body.

"Mike," I moan.

Fuck, why didn't I get this man's phone number?

I hear someone clear their throat and my eyes fly open. I'm staring right back into Mike's gorgeous green eyes.

Fuck, is he real? Where did he come from?

His eyes are glued to mine, hungry and filled with such raw emotion that it turns me on. I bite my bottom lip as his eyes travel downward, taking in my naked body and the way that I'm pleasuring myself.

"Can't a girl have some privacy?"

"You called out my name?"

"Are you like a genie that appears out of nowhere?"

"No, I was about to jump in *my* pool when I heard you say my name more than once. I walked over to check on you and..."

His eyes lock onto my center where my fingers are still playing with my swollen bud. I lick my lips. The idea of him catching me in the act is a turn-on that I didn't expect.

"*Your* pool?"

"I live next door."

"You're my brother's next-door neighbor?"

He nods, his eyes locking onto mine. I can already see the bulge in his swim trunks. Knowing that he's hard right now only makes this better.

Teasing him is fun.

"Yes. Should you be out here alone and naked?"

"*You* don't seem to mind it right now."

"No one would mind walking up to see you playing with yourself while also moaning their name at the same time."

"Busted," I giggle breathily. "This is much better than *that.*"

My eyes focus on the bulge in his pants. It's an absolute lie. I want nothing more than for him to drop to his knees and bury his face between my thighs to get rid of the ache there.

I want him to pick me up, carry me into the pool, and fuck me from behind.

I want that big cock to fill me up right now, but I'm not about to tell him any of those thoughts.

"Is that so?" he asks huskily as he clears his throat again.

"Very much."

I close my eyes and smile as I continue rubbing my pussy and using my other hand to tease my nipple. I can feel his eyes burning into me. I can feel the heat of his stare caressing me like the sun.

I'm not ready to orgasm yet, I don't want to give him that power. He won't ever be privy to getting to see that ever again now that I know who he is.

Yes, the sex was phenomenal, and the orgasm he gave me was mind-blowing but... a tremor of pleasure rocks through my body and I realize that I have to do something else if I want to remain in control.

I stop touching myself and gracefully stand up. I walk to the edge of the pool, letting my full hips sway and giving him the perfect view of my toned butt. I glance back and see that he looks like a wolf ready to eat the lamb.

I dive in the pool, staying underwater a little longer than necessary just so that I can calm my body down.

What would it hurt if we had sex again?

I can shut off my emotions, I've done it before. It's just sex, nothing else.

Yup, I can do this.

My brother is gone, so he'll never know it happened.

I just scratch the itch and it'll get him and that beautiful cock out of my head for good.

I deserve to feel that good again.

I deserve to have a mind-blowing orgasm more than once in my life.

Let's see if that was a fluke on his part.

I come up from the water, not making eye contact with him. I do the sexy shake of my head and slick my hair back as I come out of the water. I climb up the concrete steps certain that I look like all the supermodels when they do it.

There's a loud noise from the front of the house and Diesel immediately starts growling and barking, another dog nearby joins in. Diesel darts toward the front of the house and I trip up the steps.

Great, I'm going to have to fight Ivan off while naked.

I mean, not a bad way for him to die I guess.

Mike takes off toward the front of the house at a dead sprint. I roll my eyes and continue getting out of the pool.

I ring out my hair and try to fight off the nerves. I inhale and exhale, shaking my head, and put myself in fight mode.

Mike comes back around the corner.

"It was just a cat in some garbage cans."

Diesel is at his feet. Mike's eyes are laser-focused on mine.

"Thanks for saving me from the deadly cat. I'm sure its tiny claws of death would..."

He walks straight to me, picks me up, and throws me over his shoulder.

"What the fuck do you think you're doing?" I yell as I try to wiggle free of him.

Diesel barks. He looks at the situation and then lays down.

Some guard dog. Traitor.

"Stop flailing or you're going to make me drop you."

"I want you to drop me, asshole. What are you a fucking caveman? Who does this?"

"I'm not going to let you be over there alone, naked when..."

"I do not need to be saved by you. Get the fuck over yourself!"

I try to knee him, but my body is completely betraying me as I realize how turned on I am right now.

I went from horny, to fight mode, and then right back to horny on steroids.

Could he grab my ass and rub it for a minute? Maybe that'll help.

Damn him.

Also, why is he so hot?

6

Mike

When I heard her call my name more than once, the way she said it, I instantly went over to check on her. I felt like a creep watching her play with herself, but she clearly wanted me. She was definitely thinking about me.

This woman is going to be the death of me. She didn't even miss a beat while I watched her.

That was the hottest thing I've ever seen in my life.

When I heard that loud noise, the thought of her getting hurt crowded all logic out of my brain. I reacted.

Throwing her over my shoulder probably wasn't the best idea. I can smell the sweet scent of her arousal between her legs and her taut nipples are pressing against my skin.

I take her into the house and set her down in the kitchen. Her naked body slides down my bare chest.

Fuck. I can't hold back.

The second her feet are on the ground; my hand goes up to the back of her head and I pull her into a hot kiss. She whimpers against me.

I lean her back against the kitchen counter, pressing the bulge in my pants against her. It's desperate to break free of my swim trunks and find her.

Breaking the kiss, she looks into my eyes and whispers, "This is the only time this will ever happen again."

"We'll see about that," I chuckle.

I can see the lust in her eyes, mirroring my own. She reaches down and fumbles with the buttons on my swim trunks, finally freeing the beast that has been waiting for this moment. My erection springs forth, hard and eager, ready to claim her.

She wraps her fingers around my length and begins to stroke me, moaning softly as an overwhelming wave of desire takes over her body. I watch her eyes roll back in pleasure, her face flushing with arousal as she works me with fierce determination.

With one hand, I grip the back of her head and pull her closer, our lips colliding in a passionate kiss that leaves us both breathless. My other hand slides down her body, tracing the curve of her hips, the smooth planes of her stomach, and finally finding her waiting entrance.

I push two fingers inside her, feeling the tightness of her pussy surrounding me, and

she gasps, her breathing ragged.

"More," she whispers, her eyes glazing over with desire.

I oblige, sliding a third finger inside her, feeling her muscles clench and release as I stretch her open for me. She moans softly, arching her back against my hand, her fingers still wrapped around my shaft.

I pull my fingers from her wetness and move them to her mouth, guiding her to taste herself on my fingers. She opens her lips eagerly, licking and sucking them clean with a hungry intensity.

My heart beats wildly in my chest, the thrill of this taboo encounter giving me a high like nothing I've ever experienced before. She looks up at me, her eyes pleading, and I know what she wants.

"You want me, don't you?" I whisper, my voice barely above a whisper.

“No,” she replies as she drops to her knees in front of me.

Her eyes are locked onto mine as she looks up at me while also sliding my cock into her mouth.

I suck in a breath.

She’s so damn sexy. Her confidence is so hot.

Her lips wrap around me, the warmth and wetness enveloping and swallowing me whole. She takes me deeper into her mouth, her throat expanding to accommodate my length. It feels like a tight vice, her tongue swirling around my shaft as I struggle to maintain control. Her eyes never leave mine, a fire burning in her gaze that mirrors the desire coursing through my veins.

With a low groan, I reach down, my fingers threading through her hair, guiding her rhythm and pace. She responds eagerly, her mouth moving up and down, her tongue flicking and teasing my sensitive spot. I feel my orgasm building, the desire to cum overwhelming me with each stroke of her mouth.

But I can't let it happen yet. Not here. Not like this.

With a deep breath, I pull back, leaving her gasping and panting, a mixture of frustration and need shining in her gorgeous blue eyes.

Without hesitation, I lift her onto the kitchen counter, her legs spreading wide for me. She moans softly, licking her lips as I bend down to taste her.

“You’re so wet for me,” I breathe when I pull away.

I grip my shaft and guide it toward her wet center.

She gasps as she feels the head of my cock touching her entrance, her eyes wide with anticipation.

"Yes," she whispers, reaching down to guide me in.

With one swift motion, I push myself inside her, sinking deep into her tight warmth. Her walls tremble around me, gripping me tightly, and she lets out a cry of pleasure and pain.

"Fuck, you're so tight," I groan, struggling to maintain control.

Her eyes flutter shut as she takes a moment to adjust to the sensation of being filled by me, her body trembling with every thrust.

"Take me," she begs, her eyes filling with desire.

And so I do, slowly at first, relishing the feel of her body around me, but soon building momentum, driving myself deep into her with each hard thrust.

Her moans grow louder, more desperate, and she reaches down to touch herself. I move her hand away and remove her from the counter, while still inside her. I carry her into the living room, and I kiss her hungrily. Her hands are in my hair, tugging as she desperately tries to deepen the kiss. She grinds down on me.

When we're in the living room, I lift her and remove my rock-hard shaft from her. She whimpers as I set her down. She reaches for my cock, her eyes locked onto it hungrily. I turn her around and move her hands to the back of the couch. She instinctively wiggles her tight ass backward toward me.

I grip her hips and guide myself into her again.

"You feel so good, baby," I breathe in her ear.

I can feel her shiver as she glances back at me. She grinds back on my cock.

"Don't stop," she breathes, pushing back against me.

I continue to fuck her, my hips moving in a steady rhythm as her moans fill the room. She's so wet, her pussy hugging me like a vice, and I can feel her muscles clenching and releasing around my cock with every thrust.

As I pound into her, I reach around, and one hand grips a tit while the other begins to play with her clit. She gasps and arches her back, pushing herself back against me even harder. Her breathing quickens, her moans turning into wordless cries of pleasure.

"Fuck, please don't stop any of what you're doing. I don't want to cum yet. I want you to keep going."

My tongue darts out and flicks her ear and she whimpers.

"God, yessss, fuck Mike. Fuck me harder."

She writhes against me. I thrust into her harder, gripping her tit and focusing on playing with her swollen pleasure spot.

She's in a haze of pure ecstasy, her body trembling and convulsing with each thrust. Her moans grow louder and more desperate, a testament to how close she's come to the edge. I can feel her nearing her climax, the frantic squeezing of her pussy around me, and I know it won't be long before she cries out in pleasure.

"Cum for me, baby," I breathe.

With one hand, I grip her hips and pull her back against me, deepening my thrusts as my other hand continues to play with her clit. Her moans turn to screams as she bucks against me, the intensity of her orgasm slamming through her.

Her body shudders under me, her muscles clenching and releasing in waves, and I can feel her pussy pulsating around my cock as she cries out my name. It's the most beautiful sound I've ever heard, and I know I'm close to my own release.

"Fuck, I'm going to cum," I groan, my heart pounding in my chest as I thrust harder and faster into her, each movement driving me closer to the edge.

She looks back at me, my eyes meet hers, and I can see the same wild passion in her gaze. She grips the back of the couch, her knuckles turning white as she braces herself for the impact of my release.

With one final thrust, I bury myself deep inside her, my cock pulsing as I spill my seed into her waiting pussy. She cries out, her orgasm still reverberating through her body, and together we collapse onto the couch, our bodies entwined and our hearts pounding in sync.

We lay there, catching our breath, our bodies still shaking with the aftershocks of our intense passion. I run my fingers through her hair, feeling the cool strands against my skin, and she nuzzles her face into my chest, our breath mingling as we bask in the afterglow.

"That was insane," she whispers, her voice barely above a whisper.

"I know," I reply, my voice just as soft. "But we're not done yet."

She raises her head to look at me, her eyes filled with lust. "What do you have in mind?"

A wicked grin spreads across my face. "I'm thinking we should take this to the bedroom."

She nods eagerly, and we get up, our bodies still shaky from the intensity of the encounter. As we walk to the bedroom, I smack her on the ass. She giggles and rolls her eyes at me.

In the bedroom, I grab her in a kiss, push her onto the bed, and climb on top of her, my heart pounding with excitement.

Without breaking the kiss, I reach down and guide my engorged cock toward her entrance, eager to feel her walls tighten around me once more. Her legs wrap around me, pulling me closer, and I thrust deep inside her. The feeling is indescribable as if every nerve ending in my body is on fire.

Her moans are music to my ears, and I can't get enough of them. I thrust harder and deeper, my pace increasing with each thrust. Her body arches off the bed, her nails digging into my back as she cries out my name.

I pull out, leaving her panting and breathless, and with a lustful grin, I flip her over onto all fours. I position myself behind her and enter her from behind, feeling her body shake as she adjusts to the new position.

"Oh, yes," she moans, pushing back against me.

I begin to thrust, my hips moving in a steady rhythm as her moans fill the room once again. She's so wet, her pussy fits me like a glove.

As I pound into her, I reach around and grip both of her tits, feeling her nipples harden between my fingers. She gasps and arches her back, pushing her ass back against me even harder. Her breathing quickens, her moans turning into wordless cries of pleasure.

"Fuck, Mike, you feel so good inside me," she breathes.

She's nearing her climax, her body trembling with each thrust. I know she's about to cum, and I am too.

Her body convulses, her pussy clenching around my cock as she screams out my name. I can't hold back any longer, and I thrust deep inside her one last time, releasing into her, our bodies shaking with the intensity of the moment.

"Holy shit," she breathes. "Twice right in a row."

"I could probably go again. Walking outside and hearing you breathe my name while you were playing with yourself was the hottest thing I've ever seen."

"I liked it when you watched me," she purrs as she reaches up and kisses me.

She rolls over and climbs out of the bed.

"Where are you going?"

"Oh this isn't one of those things where we stay in bed all day snuggling and fucking," she laughs. "I got mine, I got off. I got stuff to do and that doesn't include you."

She saunters out of my bedroom and out the back door.

What the fuck?

That was the best sex of my life and she just walked out like I was nothing?

Women are usually begging me for a relationship after sex and this woman just walks away?

I need to step up my game.

7

Eve

How is that brut of a man so damn good in bed?

Why did I fall back into bed with him? This is bad. This is so bad.

With Ivan threatening me, it's not fair for me to get entangled with anyone, especially because Ivan will use it against me if it comes down to it.

I don't do relationships.

I especially won't do a relationship with an overprotective, egotistical, judgmental jerk like Mike Hunter.

"Why would you let someone talk to you like that? Why would you be out here naked?" I mimic him as I walk naked across the small space between his yard and Damon's.

Oh shit, is the other neighbor outside?

Nope, just a shadow.

I blow out a breath and shake my head. I open the gate and cross back over to my brother's yard.

"You're a lousy guard dog," I say to Diesel as I see him lying next to a gorgeous Blue Heeler with a pink collar. "Aww, who are you?"

Both dogs run over to me wagging their tails and looking for love and attention. I pet them and play with them both a bit.

"Piper Hunter?" I ask as I read the tag on the dog's collar. "Of course, Diesel would make friends with Mike's dog. You're a traitor Diesel, such a traitor."

I walk the rest of the way into the house. Piper goes back to her yard and Diesel whines as he follows me.

"I'm dickmatized by that bear of a man and you're pussy whipped by his dog. This is perfect. We're a pair, aren't we?"

Diesel barks a reply and I laugh. I go inside the house and get him some food, then I go to shower. I need to wash the smell of that gorgeous man off me or I will never be able to get him out of my head.

I stand under the icy cascade of water, the chill seeping into my bones as I try to wash away the memories that cling to me like a stubborn stain. But no matter how hard I scrub, I can't seem to rid myself of the scent and feel of Mike.

Damn him.

I step out of the shower, frustration bubbling up inside me. How can one person have such a hold over me? It's maddening, the way his face haunts my every waking moment.

I towel off and get dressed, the familiar routine of lacing up my running shoes a welcome distraction. Maybe a run will help clear my mind, and push Mike to the back of my thoughts where he belongs.

I leash up Diesel, his excited whines echoing through the house as he paces back and forth, his tail wagging furiously. It's almost as if he senses my turmoil, his own eagerness mirroring my need to escape.

He's being super pathetic anyway as he keeps staring out the window at Mike's house longingly while he whines.

"Try playing hard to get Diesel, she won't respect you if she sees you whimpering in the window. I guess I'm doing better than you because I'm not pining away for him in the window like a psycho."

Together, we step out into the crisp air, the cobblestone streets of Legacy stretching out before us. It's a picturesque town, the kind of place where time seems to stand still. I had forgotten how much I loved this place. When my parents died the town came together for Damon and me in so many different ways. They did a meal train for us for almost three months. Neighbors and friends of our parents would check on us often to make sure we had what we needed. Damon's football coach made sure he knew how to pay the utilities and balance the checkbook.

The funeral director and pastor told us they'd never seen the amount of people at a funeral in Legacy before. Not much consolation to us, but it spoke volumes to who my parents were.

We were always the house that hosted Saturday morning pancake breakfasts for the football team. Damon's friends were always in and out of the house as if they owned it.

My parents were the best, it was a hard loss for us. It was almost like the entire town was grieving with us. Maybe that's why I felt the need to enlist and get out of here as soon as I was able.

As we start our run, Diesel sets a brisk pace, his enthusiasm infectious. We weave through the narrow streets, past rows of quaint homes and bustling cafes. It's a small-town feel, the sense of community palpable in the air as everyone waves or says hello when I pass them. My childhood home still stands with a new family living there making their own memories. I run by, stopping at the sidewalk to take a look at the house. Tears bite at my eyes and I push them back, no time for emotions.

"Eve Carlisle? Is that you?" A voice asks behind me.

I turn around to see Mrs. White standing in her yard with weeds in her hand. I can't believe she recognized me and still lives next door.

"Hey, Mrs. White, how are you?"

She drops the weeds from her hands and gives me a hug.

"Thank you."

"Are you here for long?"

"Just visiting Damon right now," I smile.

"Well, we miss you around here and hope you'll stay for good."

"I didn't realize how much I missed it until I came back."

"It has a way of doing that."

"I should get back on my run."

"I'll see you around, dear."

I smile as Diesel and I take off on our run again. But try as I might, I can't seem to shake the memories that cling to me like a stubborn shadow. Mike's face flickers in my mind, his smile haunting me at every turn. I try to push him away, to focus on the rhythmic pounding of my feet against the pavement, but it's no use.

I slow to a stop, hands on my knees as I catch my breath, Diesel panting at my side. I haven't thought about this man in years and now suddenly I'm obsessed with him. There is no way.

He hated me growing up and he never made it a secret that he did. I had a crush on him when I turned thirteen, then I heard him tell someone that I was Damon's annoying little sister and things changed.

He was constantly correcting me and basically telling me that everything I did was wrong. By the time I was sixteen and he left for college while Damon joined the Marine Corps, I felt relieved to not have to deal with him anymore.

He would come home a lot and always thought he needed to check on me or correct me and what I was doing.

Good to see his audacity hasn't changed.

I glance up at Diesel, his brown eyes watching me with unwavering loyalty. "We're both pathetic, aren't we?" I murmur, a wry smile tugging at the corners of my lips.

He cocks his head to the side as if to say, "Who, me?"

I laugh, the sound echoing through the empty streets. "Come on, let's finish this run."

Together, we pick up the pace, the rhythmic pounding of our footsteps echoing through the quiet morning air. It's a small victory, but it's enough for now.

As we make our way back to Damon's house, the sun begins to peek over the horizon, it's a gorgeous site and I smile widely.

This is perfect.

I stop at the base of my brother's driveway. I tap in the code to open the front gate, stretching my arms in front of me and behind me as I do. When the gate closes behind me, I let go of Diesel's leash and let him run through the yard.

I fall into the grass closer to the opposite house from Mike's.

I don't want him to come out and talk to me.

I spread my legs out and stretch forward.

"Howdy neighbor!" a voice calls to my left.

I look up and see a dark-headed man grinning back at me from the wrought iron fence. His brown hair falls effortlessly across his forehead, framing a chiseled jawline that speaks of quiet strength. His eyes, a piercing shade of blue, seem to sparkle in the light, drawing me in despite my better judgment.

"How's it going?" he calls out, his voice smooth as silk.

"Hey," I reply, forcing a polite smile as I hurry past him, eager to escape his gaze.

But he's not so easily deterred. "You're Damon's new girlfriend, right?"

I pause and try to stifle a laugh. "No," I reply quickly, the words tumbling out before I can stop them. "I'm just visiting."

"Ah, gotcha. Well, if you ever need anything, don't hesitate to ask."

I nod curtly, already regretting the conversation. There's something about him that sets me on edge, a creeping sense of unease that prickles at the back of my mind.

"Thanks."

"I saw you sunbathing earlier. You looked… stunning."

I show no emotion on my face.

Then you probably also saw Mike throw me over his shoulder. Jerk.

I feel a shiver run down my spine, the hairs on the back of my neck standing on end. His words are innocent enough, but there's a predatory glint in his eyes that sends a chill through me. I'm grateful the wrought iron fence is in between us.

"I should get inside," I mutter, my voice barely above a whisper.

But he's not so easily dissuaded. "Come on, don't be like that. We could have some fun together."

I take a step back, my heart pounding in my chest. "I'm not interested."

"You're just playing hard to get. I like that."

"I assure you that I am hard to get and I'm not playing."

"Feisty, I like it."

"Conner, get lost," I hear Mike growl from behind me. "She's mine."*Mine?*

What did he just say?

And why did my whole body melt with those words?

"Yours?" Conner repeats with a roll of his eyes and a laugh. "Yeah, whatever."

"She told you she wasn't interested. Take the hint and go."

"I'll see you around, gorgeous," Conner says with a laugh.

He walks back to his house, and I glare at Mike. I shake my head in disgust before storming inside the house.

He follows right behind me. Diesel and Piper are close on our heels.

"You're welcome," he snaps. "That dude is no good."

I spin around and slap him across the face.

"What was that for?" he asks, as he barely registers the slap.

Jerk.

I feel a surge of fury rise within me, my hands trembling with suppressed rage. "That was for being a creep," I spit out, my voice laced with venom.

He raises an eyebrow, his smirk never faltering. "And what makes you think I'm a creep?"

"First, you were watching me masturbate and then you come out of nowhere like some stalker."

"You were masturbating for *me*."

"I'm not yours. I'm not anyone's. You need to stop saying stuff like that."

"I'm just trying to protect you."

His words are like a slap in the face, the condescension dripping from his voice like acid. "You're trying to control me, not protect me. Also, I don't need protection," I snap, my voice trembling with fury. "Especially not from you."

He tilts his head to the side, studying me with a curious expression. "Clearly you do," he says softly, his voice laced with something that sounds suspiciously like concern. "Otherwise, you wouldn't keep dropping yourself into situations where I need to swoop in and save you by pretending to be your man."

I feel a surge of indignation rise within me, my hands curling into fists at my sides. "Go fuck yourself," I growl, the words dripping with venom. "If you weren't such an egotistical asshole with a savior complex, you'd realize that I can protect myself from any man."

He raises an eyebrow, his expression unreadable. "Is that so?"

I nod, my chin jutting out defiantly. "Damn right, it is."

I want to slap him across the face again or kick him in the balls for being such a freaking asshole.

And kiss him, I definitely want to kiss him again.

How can I be so irritated with this man and only be thinking about kissing him?

That's toxic, right?

"You didn't seem to be handling the man on the phone. You didn't seem to be handling Conner either."

"If you would have minded your own business both times you would have realized that I don't need you. I don't need any man. I especially don't need a jealous, controlling one!"

"I'm not jealous," he says in a low voice as he takes a step toward me.

My entire body is on fire with need. I close my eyes and take a deep breath before blowing it out slowly.

"Can you just go back to your house and leave me alone? My brother isn't here for you to play with, and I don't want to be anywhere near you."

"You weren't saying that earlier," he snaps. He takes another step forward, closes his eyes, and drops his voice to mimic mine. "Oh, Mike please don't stop."

I slap him across the face again, scream in frustration, and then storm to my room. I slam the door and lock it.

Take the hint now, you big freaking jerk that I fucking want to kiss.

"Come on, Piper," I hear him say a minute later.

The front door opens and closes, and Diesel is at my door whining.

Maybe slapping him across the face was a little much, but he frustrates me the Hell out of me when he's trying to take control of me.

I'm not his. I don't belong to anyone. Especially not to him.

He cannot be attached to me in any way. He will die. Ivan will kill him if he finds me.

Tears fill my eyes.

"Fuck you, Mike Hunter," I say under my breath as I try to push away the emotions.

I spend the next hour trying to focus on anything and everything but Mike.

I could go across the yard and apologize for being psycho. I could tell him I'm sorry and that this won't work regardless of how much I want it to.

I could tell him everything about my life and why I'm here, but that would put him in danger, and I can't risk that.

I walk out of my room and realize that Mike didn't leave, instead he's sitting on the couch going through his phone.

"Why are you still here?"

"We were in the middle of a conversation when you stormed off. I figured we should finish it. I also don't trust Conner not to come over here to harass you more."

"There's an alarm system."

"That you didn't arm," he sighs.

Shit.

"I can handle myself."

"I'm sure that you can."

"Our conversation was over."

"No, it wasn't. You stormed off like you always do when you don't want to talk anymore."

"Then take the hint."

"I apologize if I seem overbearing or jealous. I'm not. It's not that I think you're not capable of taking care of yourself. I've always admired how smart and independent you are."

What?

"Then why do you act the way that you do?"

"Because I want to take care of you, even though you don't need me to."

I blow out a breath and shake my head.

"It can't happen."

"You keep saying that, but then you don't ever explain why that is."

"There's nothing to explain."

"Did you know who I was at the bar that night?"

"Obviously not," I sigh. "You gave me a fake name. Had I realized who you were I would have avoided you at all costs."

"Why?"

"Because you're off limits. You're my brother's best friend and you've always been a jerk to me."

"I don't think I've ever been a jerk to you."

I roll my eyes.

"Of course you don't. We've been through this."

"I also didn't give you a fake name."

"Yes, you did. I asked if you were Mark, the guy I was supposed to have a date with, and you told me yes."

"It was loud in there I thought you said Mike, I thought you heard Luca or one of the guys say my name."

"Did you know who I was?"

"No," he laughs. "I had no clue. It wouldn't have changed anything if I had though."

I freeze and look back at him in shock. He stands up and crosses over to me. He grabs me in a hungry kiss just as his phone starts vibrating incessantly.

"Shit, I need to go."

He walks out of the house without another word, Piper reluctantly following behind him. I stare at the door for a minute before I look down at Diesel."What did he mean by that?"

Diesel drops his head to the side and looks back at me with confused eyes.

I feel the same way.

I go to the kitchen and grab a bottle of water. I drink it quickly. Diesel is beside me nudging my fingers.

He starts whining to go outside. I grab a tennis ball and walk out the front door with him. We're in the meticulously cared for yard playing fetch when a bright blue sports car pulls up to the front gate of Mike's driveway just minutes after Mike left my house.

The driver punches in the code and steers toward the house when the gate opens. As the car pulls up next to his truck the horn honks and Mike comes outside with a giant grin on his face.

A gorgeous redhead who has poured herself into a too-tight dress and is wearing entirely too much makeup climbs out of the car.

"Mikey!" she calls out. Piper runs to her, and she bends down to pet her. "How's my favorite girl?"

Diesel barks and Mike's eyes lock onto mine.

Fuck, he sees me staring and most likely glaring.

The woman stands up and gives him a peck on the cheek before he engulfs her in a hug.

I will rip both of their faces off.

Damn it, why am I jealous? I'm no better than him.

How dare he fuck me when he's got a girlfriend.

He raced out of my house because this woman was coming over?

8

Mike

"Who's the hottie next door?" Kelsey, my public relations manager, asks as we walk into the house.

"Huh?"

She laughs, a twinkle of amusement in her eyes. "You know, the hot woman in Damon's yard playing with the dog. I could feel her eyes burning into my back. Is that Damon's new flavor of the week with a crush on you?"

I shake my head, a wry smile tugging at the corners of my lips. "Crush on me? No, she hates me. That's Damon's sister Eve."

Kelsey's eyes widen in surprise. "I didn't know Damon even had a sister."

I nod, leaning back against the couch. "Yeah, she's been traveling the world for the last ten years for her job. Just got back recently."

"Interesting. So, what's the deal with her? She seemed pretty upset to see a woman at your house."

"I assure you; she wasn't upset. She despises me."

“Mike, I love you, buddy, but you’re an idiot when it comes to women.”

“How would you know?”

She cocks an eyebrow and shakes her head. “How long have I been your PR gal? I’ve seen a thing or two.”

“She hates me. She slapped me across the face just an hour ago.”

“Oh damn, why?”

I sigh, running a hand through my hair. "Long story short, we have a complicated history."

Kelsey leans in. "Complicated how?"

“We had a one-night stand in Detroit.”

“You had a one-night stand with your best friend’s sister?”

“To be fair, I didn’t know who she was at the time. I thought she was a random hot woman in a bar that I clicked with.”

“You didn’t know who she was? Did she know who you were?”

“Maybe because we were in Detroit the thought didn’t cross my mind. Why would it? I haven’t seen her in ten years. She also did not look like that the last time I saw her. Her hair was a different color. When I saw her at the bar it was black and short. She’s really grown into her body. I don’t think she knew who I was because when I walked into Damon’s house the next day, she looked white as a ghost.”

“Does Damon know?"

I feel a knot form in my stomach, the guilt gnawing at me from within. "No, and you can't tell anyone, Kelsey."

She nods solemnly, her expression serious. "Got it. But why did she slap you?”

“I saw Conner talking to her.”

Kelsey closes her eyes and pinches the bridge of her nose. “Stop withholding information.”

“I’m not.”

“Okay, well, I’m going to fill in the blanks. Let me see...” She puts a red fingernail to her chin as she looks back at me thoughtfully. “You’re telling me about her which means you really like her and need advice. If you saw Conner talking to her and then she slapped you across the face I'm going to assume that you went Super Mike on her."

"Super Mike?"

"Yeah, you try to rescue, fix, protect."

"I do not."

"Yeah, you do. I get it. You lost your mom and little sister when you were young. I'm not saying it's a bad thing, but for someone who is probably extremely independent it's not easy to get used to."

"The two times we've slept together, she basically turns cold and just disappears after."

"Two times? You just told me about the one time in Detroit. When was the second?"

I look down at my watch and chuckle. "A few hours ago."

"Damn, okay," she laughs.

"I don't know what I'm doing wrong. Normally, women throw themselves at me."

"Well, maybe it's time to try a different approach. Take it slow, you know? And maybe try to take five seconds to breathe and think before acting when you're around her."

"Why do you say that?"

"Again, I'm assuming here. If she's been traveling for the last ten years, she's probably a very independent woman. If she turns cold and leaves immediately after the two of you sleep together, it's indicative of someone who is trying not to get hurt. It's clear to me that she likes you, but she probably doesn't enjoy you going Super Mike on her. Did you only do it with Conner? Which by the way, good job because he's a creep and a half."

"No, the day after we slept together, I was at Damon's house and overheard some guy threatening her over the phone. I may have told him I was her fiancé and that he needed to leave her alone."

"You told some guy that you were her fiancé? Who does that?"

"I panicked, maybe? I don't know. It just came out. I had this overwhelming urge to protect her."

"This is why I told you to take a pause and breathe around her," she giggles. "You're like the best guy in the world, Mikey, but you have to control your reactions."

"What do I do?"

"Let's start with pausing and breathing then we'll figure out the rest. Also, stop randomly hooking up with her."

"Why if we both want to?"

"It's really great when a man makes you feel sexy and wanted when he can't keep his hands off you, but at some point even the most confident woman is going to question if that's all the man wants."

"I've made it clear..."

She puts a hand up in the air. "Maybe you think you have in your neanderthal way, but most likely you haven't."

I inhale and exhale. I'm grateful for Kelsey, I really am, but sometimes she's annoying.

"Okay, I'll reevaluate my approaches."

"Who says you can't teach an old dog new tricks?"

"Why did you stop by again?" I ask her with a chuckle.

"Oh, there's a local podcast who wants to know if you'll do a show with them. They've sent me a list of questions and what they're looking for. It's nothing big and they don't have a huge following but I think it would be good for you."

"I hate podcasts and interviews."

"I'm aware. This is different. Take a look at the information and the podcast. Let me know what you think."

"You couldn't do that over the phone?"

"Um, no, because then I wouldn't be able to see Piper. I also worry about you. Normally, Damon keeps an eye on you but he's gone."

"Keeps an eye on me?"

"Why do you question when someone is doing nice things for you?" she asks quickly changing the subject.

"Because there's usually an ulterior motive."

"I'm hurt," she teases as she stands up. "I think the podcast will be good for you. I also think the hottie next door will be as well. Maybe I'll go introduce myself. Then again, her being jealous might serve you well."

"Please don't introduce yourself, then she'll know we were talking about her."

"I doubt that's what she'll think," she giggles. "When is Damon coming back?"

"You talk to him more than I do."

"Do I?"

I roll my eyes and shake my head. Damon and Kelsey have had an on-again off-again relationship for a while. They are great together, but neither of them will admit that they care for the other person because they're both scared of getting hurt.

"Did you think he replaced you?"

"No. I didn't know he had a sister though. It's weird he never mentioned her."

"They used to be pretty close but life took them in different directions. He's pretty surprised that she came to stay with him."

"I bet. I should get going."

Kelsey leaves and I fall onto my couch while looking at Piper.

"I think you're the only female I understand and you don't speak."

Piper barely picks her head up off the couch, unbothered by me.

Typical.

***

The next morning, the crisp morning air fills my lungs as I step onto the ice, the familiar sound of skates gliding across the surface echoing in my ears. Hockey practice is my sanctuary, a refuge from the chaos of everyday life—a chance to lose myself in the rhythm of the game and forget about everything else.

As I join Luca and the rest of my teammates on the ice, a sense of camaraderie washes over me, the bond of brotherhood forged through countless hours spent honing our craft. We glide effortlessly across the ice, the puck flying back and forth between us like a dance of shadows and light.

But amidst the laughter and banter, there's a nagging sense of unease gnawing at the edges of my consciousness. Eve's face flashes through my mind, her scared eyes haunting me like a specter in the darkness.

I try to push the unsettling thoughts to the back of my mind as we scrimmage against each other, the sound of sticks clashing and skates cutting through the ice filling the air.

Luca stands opposite me, his eyes alight with determination, a mischievous glint dancing in their depths. We've been teammates for years, but when we step onto the ice, all bets are off—we're rivals, competitors, each vying for the upper hand. Coach usually puts us on opposite teams during scrimmages because we push each other so hard.

I can feel the tension crackling in the air as Luca and I lock eyes, a silent challenge passing between us. With a nod, we both crouch into position, the puck resting between us like a silent arbiter of fate.

"Don't kill each other," Coach laughs as he blows his whistle.

In an instant, we're off—a whirlwind of motion and momentum as we battle for control of the puck. Luca darts to the left, his movements fluid and effortless, a testament to his skill and agility. But I'm not far behind, my strides long and powerful, my muscles tensed with anticipation.

As we circle each other, the puck weaving between us like a dancer in the spotlight, the banter begins—a playful exchange of taunts and jibes that fuels the fire burning within us.

"You call that a shot, Luca?" I jeer, my voice echoing in the silence of the rink. "I've seen toddlers with better aim."

His lips curl into a smirk, his eyes twinkling with mischief. "Funny, coming from a guy who couldn't hit the broad side of a barn."

I grit my teeth, the challenge igniting a spark of determination deep within me. With a burst of speed, I lunge for the puck, my stick connecting with a satisfying thud as I send it sailing towards the goal.

“Who scored three goals last game?”

“All luck.”

“We’ll see,” I laugh.

He is quick to intercept, his reflexes lightning-fast as he deflects the puck with a flick of his wrist. I curse under my breath, frustration bubbling to the surface as we continue to trade blows, each one more ferocious than the last.

With a flick of my stick, I send the puck sailing towards Luca, a feint designed to throw him off balance. But he's quick to react, honed from years of practice as he lunges to intercept the puck.

I watch as he deftly controls the puck, his movements fluid and precise. But I'm not about to let him have the upper hand. With a burst of speed, I close the distance between us, my heart pounding in my chest with adrenaline.

As he moves to pass the puck, I see my chance—a split-second window of opportunity that I know I have to seize. With lightning-fast reflexes, I fake left, the movement so quick it's almost imperceptible. Luca takes the bait, shifting his weight in anticipation of my next move.

But instead of going left, I veer right, my body moving with a grace and agility that belies my size. I can feel the ice beneath my skates, smooth and slippery as I execute the perfect deke—a move designed to throw Luca off balance and leave him in my wake.

And then, just when he least expects it, I spin—a whirlwind of motion and momentum as I pivot on my skates and launch myself towards the goal. Luca's eyes widen in surprise as he realizes what's happening, but it's too late—I've already gained the upper hand.

With a flick of my wrist, I send the puck sailing towards the goal, the sound of it hitting the back of the net echoing in the silence of the rink. I grin as I celebrate my victory, the taste of triumph sweet on my lips.

"I will never not be surprised when he does shit like that," Coach laughs. "The biggest guy on the team and he moves like the smallest."

"It's all in the hips," I chuckle.

"I cannot believe you got past me with that bullshit," Luca jokes.

"I love when people underestimate me."

"Me too," Coach interjects. "It usually results in us winning the game."

We skate off the ice, our practice ending for the day. It's all laughter and good-natured fun in the locker room before I head back home.

Halfway back to Legacy, my phone rings, the shrill sound cutting through the silence of the car. I glance at the caller ID and see Damon's name flash across the screen.

"Hey, Damon. What's up?" I answer, my voice tense with anticipation.

"I'm going to be gone a bit longer than expected. Can you still keep an eye on Eve, I'm a little worried."

"Why?"

"I've been seeing some weird things on the security cameras out front. It has me concerned."

Fuck, I forgot about his security cameras. Did he see me throw her over my shoulder?

"What kind of things?"

"There's been a black SUV driving slowly by late at night," Damon explains, his voice low and urgent. "And last night, there was a man looking through the garbage cans, lurking around the perimeter of the property."

“We heard him out there, I think. I heard a loud noise but when I went around to investigate there wasn’t anyone around.”

“Yeah, he knocked them over so that was what I saw.”

"Do you have security cameras around the back of the house?"

“Yes, but the one by the pool is blocked by a bird’s nest. I have to have my landscaper take care of that.”

“I’ll make her stay at my house.”

He chuckles on the other end. “Video that, because I’d love to see how that goes for you.”

“What do I do then?”

"I've reached out to an old Marine buddy of mine to stake out the house and see if he can find anything out. He’ll do some recon to see if he can track the SUV or find out who we’re dealing with. I’ll let you know what kind of car he’s driving in case you see him.”

“Okay. Let me know if there’s anything else I can do. When are you thinking you’ll be back?”

“Maybe the weekend. This kid is giving me grey hair,” he laughs. “All the talent in the world and no common sense.”

“That happens a lot,” I laugh.

We hang up the phone and I drive back to the house a little faster than before. If someone is snooping around the house that could mean that Eve is in danger by being there alone. And I can’t have that.

I can’t walk over there and be all overprotective without scaring her off. She’ll immediately push me away if I do that.

I think hard about what I can do to have a reason to go over there, but also get her to let me in the house and let down the walls she’s so carefully constructed around her.

Then I remember back to her being fourteen years old and getting her heart broken by Nick Watson, the same time Damon and I had both lost a huge football game. They took the three of us to Gadel's Diner to cheer us up. It's what they always did because according to Mrs. Carlisle, 'pancakes and milkshakes' was the best medicine. She was a doctor, they both were, and they would know, right?

After they passed away, we'd spent more than a few nights just the three of us at the diner. The days that Eve was having a hard time but had shut everyone out, I would get her pancakes and a milkshake and set it in front of her bedroom door and knock.

If she ever knew it was me doing it, she never said anything.

That's what I'll do, I'll grab her pancakes and a milkshake.

I step out of my car, the familiar sight of the local diner greeting me with its comforting glow. It's been a while since I've been here. Too long, maybe. But tonight, it feels necessary.

It's been years since we've shared a meal from this place, but I have a feeling she hasn't forgotten. I have a feeling she hasn't come here yet to get her favorite order either."

With that thought in mind, I push open the door to the diner, the bell above announcing my entrance. The scent of sizzling bacon and freshly brewed coffee envelops me, bringing back a flood of memories.

I approach the counter, where the waitress gives me a warm smile. "Hey there, Mike. Long time no see. What can I get for you?"

I glance at the menu briefly, but I already know what I want. "Two orders of pancakes, extra fluffy, and two chocolate milkshakes to go, please."

She nods, punching in the order on the register. "Got it. Coming right up."

This isn't just about food; it's about reaching out, making amends. Maybe even rebuilding a bridge that's been neglected for too long.

Finally, the waitress hands me the brown paper bags and the drink carrier, and I thank her before heading back to my car.

I drive home quickly, the anticipation building with each passing mile. Parking in the driveway, I grab the bags and the drink carrier, Piper rushes out the doggie door to greet me. Then she is bounding alongside me as we make our way next door.

I knock on the door, and a moment later, Eve answers, a surprised look on her face. Piper immediately darts past her, eager to reunite with her buddy Diesel.

"Hey, Eve," I greet her, offering a sheepish smile. "I know Damon is gone, but I hope you don't mind, I brought over some food from Gadel's. Thought you might enjoy it."

She eyes the bags and drink carrier curiously. "What did you get?"

"I remembered how much you loved their pancakes and milk-shakes."

Her hesitation is evident, but eventually, she gestures for me to come inside. We make our way to the kitchen, where I set the food and drinks on the island.

She takes a seat opposite me, and I start unpacking our meal. The aroma of freshly cooked pancakes fills the air, making my stomach growl in anticipation.

Her gasp of delight as she sees the pancakes is music to my ears. "Wow, these look amazing! I've missed this place."

I smile at her reaction. "I'm glad you like them. And I figured the milkshakes would be a nice touch too."

"How did you know?" she asks, a hint of curiosity in her voice. "I mean, it's been years since we've been here together."

I pause, unsure how to answer. "I just... remembered, I guess. Some things stick with you."

"Right. Well, thank you, Mike. This is really sweet of you."

I shrug, trying to play it off. "It's no big deal, really. Just thought it might be nice to catch up."

“Catch up on what?”

“Whatever.”

As we start to eat, Eve moans as she takes her first bite of the pancakes. She closes her eyes and relishes the memory through her tastebuds.

“How’d you get so lucky to get on a professional hockey team that’s an hour from our hometown?”

“I wouldn’t take anything else.”

“You’re that good that you had that kind of power?”

“Yup,” I chuckle.

“Nice. It allowed you and Damon both to stay here.”

“That it did. I don’t think Damon would have left regardless of where I would have ended up. His time in the Marine Corps only solidified that he wanted to live in Legacy.”

“He never told me that.”

“What about you? Do you think you’re back for good?”

“I’m not like Damon. My job isn’t like Damon’s. I can’t stay in one place for too long.”

“So it’s only a visit?”

“Maybe a little longer,” she shrugs as she continues eating. “What is it about hockey that you love so much, Mike?"

I take a moment to gather my thoughts, savoring the question as if it's the first time I've ever been asked. "It's hard to explain," I begin, a grin tugging at the corners of my lips. "But there's something about being out on the ice, with nothing but me, the puck, and the goal. It's like... everything else just fades away."

She nods, encouraging me to continue.

"Hockey's a game of speed, skill, and strategy. There's this incredible bond you form with your teammates, this unspoken understanding. You're all working toward the same goal, quite literally."

"But isn't it dangerous? I mean, you're constantly at risk of getting injured."

"Sure, there are risks. But that's part of what makes it so exhilarating. The adrenaline rush you get when you step onto the ice, the thrill of competition... there's nothing else like it."

"And what about the fans? The pressure to perform, to live up to their expectations?"

"Honestly, I try not to think about that too much. At the end of the day, I play for myself, for the love of the game. Of course, it's incredible to have fans cheering you on, but I can't let that dictate how I play."

“Do you have women just throw themselves at you because you’re an athlete?”

“I don’t pay attention to them,” I laugh. “We have puck bunnies that hang around the rink waiting for someone to take notice of them. That’s never been my thing though.”

“Puck bunnies?”

“That’s the nickname for women who are only there because they are highly attracted to hockey players.”

“That’s a thing?”

“So I’m told,” I laugh.

“Wild.”

“What about you? Do you love your job?”

“I do,” she smiles. “I didn’t realize how much I missed Damon and this town until I crossed back into the city limits. Out of sight, out of mind, I guess.”

“I felt that way after college.”

“I have so many good memories here, but the bad one I have is so big that it was hard to get past it for a while.”

“I understand that. It didn’t help that your parents were so prominent in the community, it was almost like you couldn’t go anywhere without being reminded of it.”

She nods slowly. “I guess it was kind of like that for you too, huh? With your mom and Stella?”

"Thanks for saying her name," I say softly. "A lot of people just refer to her as my little sister and don't say her name. That might sound weird, but..."

"I get it. She wasn't your little sister to me, she was my best friend until she moved away with your mom. We still talked, just not as much."

"I remember you two were inseparable."

"Sometimes I thought you hated me so much because she died."

I stop eating, fork suspended in the air, as I look back at her in shock.

"Why on Earth would that thought ever cross your mind?"

She shrugs. "It's the only reason I could explain why you acted the way you did toward me."

"How did I act?"

"Like an asshole."

"I never meant to be an asshole to you. Seriously. I never understood why you hid how smart you were, maybe that came off as me being an asshole."

"I never hid..."

"We'll agree to disagree."

She laughs and nods. "Tell me all the tea on the town of Legacy and the people we grew up with."

"I stay out of that stuff."

"You cannot be Damon's best friend and stay out of that stuff. My brother is the worst gossip known to man."

"That's an accurate statement."

She grabs her chocolate shake and takes a long drink from it, closing her eyes as she does.

"You put hot fudge and peanut butter in it too," she breathes. "That's amazing."

"I remembered," I laugh.

"How do you remember? Oh wait, you were probably with Damon when he ordered them all the time for me."

"Damon didn't order them for you, I did."

She narrows her eyes and looks at me questioningly.

"He would drop them in front of my bedroom door all the time."

"I did that."

"Why would you?"

"I knew what you were going through and I also knew how precious that memory of going to Gadel's was to you and Damon, to me too, and I felt like it was the only way I could help you."

"Why didn't you ever tell me that?"

I shrug. "I wasn't doing it for the recognition. Oh, remember the rumor that was going around about Jessa Kath dating the basketball coach?"

"Yeah."

"They're married with four kids."

"What?" she gasps. "How is he not in jail?"

"I don't know. He was at least fired from teaching kids though."

"I should hope so."

"Dalton James is the Chief of Police."

"The kid who stole Talon Falls mascot is now the Chief of Police? That's incredible," she roars with laughter.

"Yeah, I was shocked by it too."

"Do you remember when my parents took us all to the beach?"

"Yeah, that was the most fun I'd had in a while."

"I was so mad that they let you go but I couldn't bring a friend."

"Why couldn't you bring a friend?"

"They didn't like any of my friends," she laughs. "I can't blame them. I probably would have tried to bring a seventeen-year-old guy or something to make them mad."

"Yeah, you were good at trying to shock everyone."

"It's a gift," she shrugs as she smiles.

"I remember that hot pink bathing suit you wore that almost gave your dad and Damon a heart attack."

"I forgot about that," she giggles as her cheeks turn pink.

"I think about it often. You looked amazing."

She covers her face with her hands and shakes her head.

"I'm surprised my father had any hair left."

"Do you remember when you almost got expelled for exposing Tallie Lancôme and Jeanette Wright's bullying?"

"I was pretty proud of myself for that one. Playing the tape where the principal said that they were too pretty to be bullies and I was just jealous because I wanted to make myself ugly by choosing to dress and act the way I did, it was genius. Mom and Dad didn't think so."

"Au contraire," I chuckle. "I had a study hall pass to lift, but I had to check into the office before and after daily. When I walked in, your dad was in Mr. Latrie's office. Mr. Latrie was livid and yelling at your dad, telling him that he needed to control you. I'd never seen your dad so calm. He let him say his peace and then he stood up and told him that while some people thought you were weird or different, he was damn proud of you for not conforming to the societal bullshit standards that the world tried to put on women. He said he had never been more proud to know that his daughter not only stood up for herself and others, but she outed someone who was trying to keep her small. He then told the principal to go fuck himself and that he'd be contacting the school board about it."

"Mr. Latrie resigned a week later," she breathes. "I didn't know that Dad said that or that he was proud of me."

"You had to know they were both proud of you."

"I mean, I guess I always knew that they were proud of me, but I thought they were always so irritated with me for going against the grain."

"No, I even remember Damon saying that he wished he could be as ballsy and confident as you were. I felt the same."

"Thanks for telling me that," she murmurs.

"Of course."

She finishes up her pancakes before she takes another drink from her milkshake.

"Do you remember Kevin?"

"That douche you dated?'

"Yeah, that one," she laughs. "He messaged me a few months ago out of the blue. I think he was drunk and was talking all kinds of crazy stuff about how much he missed me, and I was the one that got away."

"Isn't he married?"

"Yes, according to social media to his soulmate and the light of his life," she says drily.

"Goes to show you that you can't believe what people post on social media."

"Truth," she smiles. "Thanks for this. It was really nice."

"You're welcome. This has been nice."

"It has. Piper and Diesel seem to have enjoyed it too."

The dogs lay in the corner of the kitchen snuggled up together.

I wish we were doing the same.

Eve stretches and stands up. Diesel is immediately at her side.

"I should probably get going," I say quickly. "I have an early flight in the morning for a game."

"You're leaving?"

"Yeah, I'll be back the following day though. You can call me or text me if you need something."

"Doubtful, but thanks," she giggles.

She cleans up our mess as Piper and I leave the house.

I want to grab her in a kiss and take her to the bedroom right now, but I also need her to know that I'm not just looking for sex from her so I'll go back to my house without trying anything.

9

Eve

THE FRUSTRATION BUBBLES INSIDE me like a pot on the verge of boiling over as I stare at my laptop screen, the dreaded loading icon mocking me from its stagnant position. It's been like this for days—sporadic internet connection, agonizingly slow speeds, and an endless parade of error messages. And as much as I've tried to troubleshoot the issue myself, it's become painfully clear that I'm in over my head.

With a resigned sigh, I reach for my phone and dial the number for the internet service provider, my fingers tapping impatiently against the screen as I wait for someone to pick up on the other end. Finally, after what feels like an eternity, a voice crackles through the line.

The customer service rep says they have a tech in the area and he'll be there within the next two hours. That's really great service.

Four hours later, as I lead the technician into the living room, I feel irritated.

"Afternoon, Miss, we got a complaint about your service," an older man drawls. "I'm Dave."

“Yes, I can barely get the laptop to connect to anything. I’ve reset the router a few times but nothing seems to be working.”

“Let me check a few things.”

I nod and he goes back outside the house, then returns a short time later.

"Wow, that's some slow internet you've got there."

I’m going to rip this man’s head off.

I resist the urge to roll my eyes, opting instead for a polite nod. "Yeah, tell me about it. We've been having problems for days now."

Dave nods sympathetically, his fingers flying across the keyboard as he runs a diagnostic test. But as the results start to trickle in, his expression grows increasingly perplexed—a furrow forming between his brows as he scratches his head in confusion.

"Huh, that's weird," he mutters, his voice muffled as he leans in closer to the screen. "I've never seen anything like this before."

I resist the urge to sigh in frustration, my patience wearing thin with each passing moment. "What's the problem? Can you fix it?"

He hesitates, his gaze flicking nervously between the laptop screen and me. "Well, it looks like your connection is fine, but the speed and security are definitely lacking. You're going to need an upgrade if you want to see any improvement."

I feel a surge of frustration bubbling inside me, my hands curling into fists at my sides. "How long is that going to take? I need the speed and security amped up ASAP."

He shrugs, his expression apologetic. "It could take a few days to get everything sorted out. We'll need to send someone out to install the necessary upgrades, and then it'll take some time for everything to sync up."

I grit my teeth, the urge to scream building inside me like a pressure cooker on the verge of exploding. But instead of giving in to my frustration, I take a deep breath and force myself to remain calm.

"Fine," I reply through clenched teeth, my voice strained with irritation. "Just get it done as soon as possible, okay?"

Dave nods, his expression contrite. "I'll do my best, ma'am. I understand how frustrating this must be for you."

With that, he packs up his tools and heads for the door, leaving me alone once again with my thoughts.

I have to get this project finished and sent today.

I'm going to have to bite the bullet and go next door.

“Diesel, do you want to go see your girlfriend?”

He whimpers, jumping up from the couch and wagging his entire body excitedly.

“Looks like we’re going next door,” I sigh. “I was hoping you’d growl or something.”

With Diesel's leash in hand, I make my way next door to Mike's house, using the gate by the pools to get across.

The prospect of asking for a favor from him fills me with a mix of anxiety and uncertainty, but with my brother's internet connection on the fritz, I don't have much of a choice.

I raise my hand and knock on Mike's door, my heart pounding in my chest as I wait for a response. The door swings open almost immediately, and Mike stands before me, a warm smile gracing his features.

He’s shirtless.

Damn it, why is he shirtless?

Piper darts out the front door and she and Diesel begin chasing each other.

"Hey there, Eve," he greets me, his voice friendly and inviting. "What brings you over?"

"Hey, Mike. I was wondering if I could borrow your internet for a bit. My brother's connection is down, and it's going to be a few days until we can get it back up and running. I've got a deadline today, and I need to get online."

Don't look at his eight-pack. There's nothing to see here, Eve. Keep your eyes up.

Mike's smile widens, his eyes crinkling at the corners with amusement. "Of course, Eve. You're welcome to use my Wi-Fi anytime."

"Thanks," I grin back at him. "Those two have become fast friends."

Avert your eyes, talk about the dogs.

Mike chuckles, his eyes sparkling with amusement. "Yeah, he and Piper hit it off right away."

As Diesel and Piper continue their game of chase, Mike gestures for me to come inside. "Why don't you come inside? You can use my office—it's quiet, and you'll have some privacy."

My eyes immediately go down to his athletic shorts that are leaving nothing to the imagination. I bite my bottom lip. I hear him chuckle lowly.

Damn it, did he notice?

"That's so nice of you. I've been procrastinating on this and it's definitely biting me in the ass."

"I'd like to bite your ass," he murmurs.

Did he just say what I think he did?

"What was that?"

"I said it usually does."

I nod, following him inside his massive home and closing the door behind me. He leads me down a hallway and into an office. The entire house is decorated with his hockey accolades, complete with a bookshelf filled with books on mindset and achievements.

The office is a large room with lots of windows, a desk and iMac with a cozy chair sitting in front of the desk. There's a black leather couch in the corner and a Himalayan salt lamp, plus sage on an end table.

My eyes flit to his quickly.

What a surprise find.

"Thanks, Mike," I say, turning to face him. "I really appreciate you letting me use your internet and giving me some space to work."

“Of course, I’ll keep an eye on the dogs so you can get some work done.”

With that, he leaves me to my work, the sound of Diesel's excited barks echoing in the hallway as I settle in for what promises to be a long day.

I blow out a breath and close my eyes.

Get him out of your head. You have shit to do.

***

Two hours later, just as I'm about to click the final send button, my phone buzzes on the desk, breaking the silence.

I glance at the screen to see an anonymous number flashing. It's most likely Ivan.

I don’t want to answer and I know that I shouldn’t, but I need to know what he’s up to and his whereabouts and I’ll only get that by speaking to him on the phone. He’s able to scramble his signal so I can’t trace the call, but it doesn’t mean I can’t get an idea of where he is by the background noise.

With a sigh, I answer, bracing myself for whatever venom he's about to spew.

"What do you want, Ivan?" I ask, my voice steady despite my fear.

“You, my love. Why must you play so hard to get?

I clench my jaw. “I’m not playing.”

He chuckles darkly. "You think you can stop me from finding you? You're just a little mouse in a maze, Eve. And I'm the cat."

“You’re definitely a pussy.”

“Keep laughing, I won’t stop at you. Diesel will be the first to go.”

I take a deep breath, forcing myself to stay calm. "What do you want, Ivan? Money? Power? Revenge?"

"Stop playing coy, bitch. You know exactly what I want."

"I'm not going to give in to you. I won't do anything you ask."

"Oh, but you will," he replies, his tone smug. "I know all about the skeletons hiding in your closets. And trust me, Eve, they're not pretty."

"I don't have skeletons."

"Did you get a new pup? She's awfully pretty."

My blood runs cold. I pause before replying.

"I don't know what you're talking about."

"Such a quaint little town you found. Learning about you as a child has been fun."

My stomach tightens. Before I can respond, he hangs up, leaving me staring at the phone in disbelief.

There's a knock on the door and I jump, clutching the phone for dear life.

"Sorry to bother you, I made dinner and thought maybe you were hungry."

"I'm not hungry."

"It's nothing fancy, just steak and potatoes."

"I'm not hungry," I hiss.

He sets the tray down on the desk and looks back at me in shock.

"What's wrong?"

"I'm not hungry," I repeat.

I can't be here. I put Mike in danger. I put Damon in danger.

Ivan is here, he saw Piper. He knows. He knows where I am.

I have to get out of here.

"I need to go."

"I wasn't trying to rush you. I didn't... I wasn't expecting us to eat together or anything," he says quickly.

He puts his hands up in the air and backs away slowly. I shake my head irritably as I stand up.

“I’m not some caged animal who will attack.”

I roll my eyes as I move past him.

“Why are you so touchy? Why can’t I ask what’s wrong?”

“It’s none of your business.”

“I wasn’t trying to infringe on you or anything. I literally thought you’d probably be hungry and wanted to do something nice for you. Why do you act so heartless all the time?”

“Heartless? I’m not acting like anything. This is who I am.”

“No, it’s not. I saw the look on your face when I opened the door. You can pretend to be pissed off at me, but you’re not.”

“I don’t know what you’re talking about.”

He glances down and sees that I’m still gripping my phone.

“Is it that guy? Did he call you again?”

“Mike, I do not need to be interrogated or protected. Mind your own fucking business.”

“You are my business,” he growls as he doesn’t let me past him.

“Fuck off.”

He pulls me into him and kisses me hungrily. My knees buckle and I fumble my phone and laptop trying to keep hold of them and not latch on to him.

My entire body is on fire with need. He begins to pry my laptop and phone out of my hand, setting them on the table nearby.

Nope. Can’t do this. I cannot do this. This isn’t safe for him.

I pull away, grab my things, and walk out of the room. Mike is calling after me, but I ignore him.

Diesel sees me and immediately falls into step at my heels. I storm out of the house, across the yard, and back to my brother’s house.

“Hey beautiful,” Conner hollers at me from over the fence. “Damn if you’re not looking sexy today.”

I would love it if Ivan fucked this guy up in his search for me.

“Fuck off, Conner,” I call out as I flip my middle finger up in the air.

"I love a feisty woman."

I roll my eyes and then into the house.

Creepy fucker.

I go to my room and pull out my secure phone, the phone given directly to me by my employer.

I should have done this in the beginning, the first time I was attacked I didn't want to engage the Coalition if I could handle it myself. That's no longer an option.

I dial Dirk's number. He and I served together in the Marine Corps. When he got out, he started a Coalition that fed Veterans jobs that closely match their skillsets. It pays amazingly, but it is also extremely dangerous because of the jobs we take on.

The phone rings once, twice, before Dirk's familiar voice fills my ear. "Eve? Is everything alright?"

"No, Sir. It's Ivan."

"He found you."

"Yes, Sir. He has followed me to my hometown," I admit the words tasting bitter on my tongue. "And I need your help getting rid of him."

"Are you sure he's there?"

"If he's not here, someone is. He knows things he shouldn't know."

Dirk curses under his breath, the sound sending a shiver down my spine. "Alright. We'll take care of this. I'll assemble a team and we'll find him, get rid of him once and for all."

"I hate having to call you."

"I'm aware," he laughs. "When I saw your number, I knew it must be big. I'll get Nat on the way to you as well."

"Thanks."

We say our goodbyes and hang up the phone, leaving me feeling a little better but still on edge. I know I have to be even more careful now, to watch my back at every turn. Nat, or Natalie, being on her way is a good thing. She's one of the most dangerous agents we have, but my brother won't question her being with me constantly.

I can stay around a little longer if Natalie is on her way and if Dirk is taking care of Ivan. Damon and Mike are safe, for now.

The front door opens and I immediately go into fight mode, Mike walks in.

"We weren't done with that conversation."

Shit, Eve, you were so flustered about Ivan and Mike that you didn't lock the doors or engage the security system.

What's wrong with me?

Mike is a distraction that's going to get me killed.

"What are you doing here?"

"We weren't finished with our conversation. I'm not some asshole who's going to let you run away from your problems."

"I'm not running away from anything."

"Bullshit. I can tell when you lie, Eve."

No, you can't. I'm a master at it because of my job.

"You have a lot of room to talk about lying."

"I've never lied to you."

"Quit deflecting."

"You have a lot of room to talk," he laughs. "Tell me what's going on so that I can help. I have plenty of financial resources to take care of anything."

"It's not about financial resources, Mike," I sigh. "I appreciate the gesture, but it can't..."

He takes a step forward and grabs me in a kiss.

What was I saying?

"At what point will you get the hint that I'm not going anywhere?"

Tears bite at my eyes but I push them back. I cannot get emotional or attached right now. I have to keep him at arm's length.

I can't get involved with him, it's a death sentence for him.

I would rather not have him and know he's alive and happy somewhere than lose him forever.

"I don't want a relationship with you, Mike Hunter," I lie. "I don't do relationships."

"Why not?"

"Because they're pointless when you live the life I do. I can get called out tomorrow to do a job and not see you for a year. Is that what you want?"

"No."

"Then back off and forget this. We can fuck, but you can't get attached to me."

He pulls back and eyes me carefully. He shakes his head.

"That's impossible to do."

"Not for me."

"You're lying to me."

"You can tell yourself a story, Mike. You can tell yourself that we're different, that I'll change because you're amazing and I'll feel something for you. It's just a story based on false information though. It's not you, it's me. You're a great guy but I can't be with you. I won't be with you."

"If that's your choice, then I'll respect it," he says before he walks out of the house.

Please don't respect it.

10

Mike

As I STROLL DOWN the cobblestone streets of Legacy, the familiar sights and sounds of my small hometown envelop me. It's a picture-perfect day, the sun shining brightly overhead, casting a golden glow on the quaint storefronts that line the main thoroughfare.

I step into the local bakery. I'm a stickler on what I eat during the season, but I allow myself a small cheat on an off day.

"Mikey, how are you," Patricia purrs as I walk inside.

"Hey, Patricia. I'm great as long as I get to come in here and smell all the amazingness you've created."

"I've set something off to the side for you."

"You didn't have to do that."

"I know," she chuckles. "But I know how much you love my apple pie and I wanted to make sure you got a slice."

"You're the best."

"Anything for one of my favorite customers."

She hands me the to-go container with the slice in it.

"I'll see you next week," I call over my shoulder as I head out the door.

I love my hometown and although I don't really flaunt my wealth or my accolades I make sure to pour back into the town of Legacy as much as I can. I donate to the local animal shelter, to the schools in town, and help out wherever I can. I always do it anonymously though, I don't need the recognition.

I drop the pie and a few books from the local bookstore in my car before I make my way to the local grocery store, the bell above the door chiming cheerfully as I step inside. The aisles are filled with the hustle and bustle of people going about their day, their voices mingling together in a symphony of small-town chatter.

I grab a cart and start making my way through the aisles, filling it with the essentials—bread, milk, eggs. As I reach for a box of cereal, I hear a familiar voice behind me.

"Hey, Mikey! How's it going?"

I turn to see Sarah, the only groomer in town, smiling brightly at me. "Hey, Sarah! I'm doing well, thanks. How about you?"

She shrugs, a playful glint in her eyes. "Oh, you know, same old, same old. How's our girl, Piper doing?"

"Crazy as ever."

"I can't wait to see her next week."

"I think it's her favorite time of the month," I chuckle.

We exchange pleasantries for a few more minutes before parting ways, each heading off to finish our respective errands. As I make my way through the store, I marvel at the sense of community that permeates every corner of Legacy.

I bump into Mrs. Jenkins next, the elderly widow who lives down the street from me. She's struggling to reach a can of soup on the top shelf, and I quickly step in to help.

"Thank you, dear," she says, smiling gratefully up at me. "You're such a gentleman."

I blush slightly at the compliment, feeling a swell of pride at being able to help out a neighbor in need. We chat for a few minutes about the latest gossip in town before I continue on with my shopping.

"Mikey, are you going to be at the fundraiser for the shelter next weekend?" Taylor asks.

"I will be away at a game, but I plan on stopping by this week. Some of my teammates gave me a few things for donations. Under the radar of course."

"Of course," she grins. "You're a Godsend, you really are. Those beds you helped us get have been great for the dogs."

"I'm glad. Piper loves hers so we wanted to share them. One of my teammates' wife made them, that helped too."

"Please tell her how much the dogs love them."

"I will."

I pay for my groceries and head back out into the sunshine, a smile tugging at the corners of my lips. I make my way to my car in the parking lot and begin loading things in the trunk.

"Mike, there you are!" I hear Eve call out.

I turn to see her and Diesel rushing toward me. She practically jumps into my arms before she grabs me into an X-rated kiss. My pants tighten in response as she molds herself to me.

She pulls away and makes a gesture behind her with her eyes.

"Hey babe," I say.

"I've missed you," she pouts. "I'm so ready to get home and..."

Conner comes out of nowhere, his eyes narrowed as he sees the two of us together. A black truck with tinted windows drives slowly behind Conner.

"Get in the car," I say loudly. "I'm ready to get you home."

She leans forward and grabs me in another kiss. Conner starts to walk away but the truck remains watching.

"Did Conner leave?"

"Yeah. Did you walk?"

"Diesel and I were on a run and Conner kept following me, trying to get me to talk to him I couldn't ditch him."

"Conner isn't your only problem."

"What?"

"Black truck, no plates, tinted windows. I can't see the driver. How long has that been behind you."

"What? It hasn't."

"I'm telling you that it is, right now. Get in the car."

"I'm not getting in the car with you. It's too dangerous for you right now."

"Damn it, Eve. I will throw you over my shoulder and put you in the damn car."

Her eyes flit to mine, her jaw clenching. "I don't need to be protected."

"I'm not saying you do, but I'm not going to allow something to happen to you while you're brother is gone. Not on my watch."

"It's not your watch."

"Stop fighting me and get in the damn car," I hiss.

She rolls her eyes and begins to turn. I drop the last of my grocery bags in the trunk and then grab her wrist lightly. I spin her back into me, close the trunk with my free hand and then use both hands to pick her up off the ground. Her legs wrap around me as I begin kissing her hungrily.

Distraction is the best option right now.

I carry her to the passenger seat of my car, still kissing her, and open the door. Diesel hops in and goes straight to the backseat. I slide her down, leaning her against the car door as I continue kissing her.

I pull away and she stares back at me breathlessly.

"I..."

"Get in the car."

She groans, glances behind her at the truck that has now pulled closer, and gets into the passenger seat of my car.

“I’m not happy about this,” she hisses as I climb into the driver’s seat.

“I don’t care.”

She pulls her phone out of the fanny pack at her waist and begins typing something in. When it doesn’t yield the results she wants then she discreetly begins taking selfies trying to get a picture of the truck.“I can’t get a good shot.”

“Do you know who it could be? Is it the guy from the phone?”

“The less questions you ask, the better off we’ll be.”

“That’s not an option.”

She rolls her eyes. I pull out of the parking lot and we steer toward home. There’s a vibrating sound, her glance flits to mine before she sighs and grabs another phone out of her fanny pack.

“Hello?” she says as her eyes stay trained on the side mirror, watching the truck that’s following us.

There’s a muffled male voice talking to her on the other end.

“Is it him?” I ask.

She shoots me a dirty look before she shakes her head.

“I can’t see the driver,” she says into the phone. “I needed to make sure it wasn’t you. I’ll get back to the house and wait for you.”

She hangs up the phone and then leans back into the seat. She closes her eyes, breathing in and out before she turns her head to look at me.

“Are you okay?” I ask.“I’m great. Pretend like you don’t realize we’re being followed please.”

“How do I do that?”

“I need you to be as nonchalant about this as possible. When we pull into the driveway it needs to be absolutely normal when we get out of the car. If the people in that truck think we’re on to them they will strike, and you absolutely can’t be around if that happens.”

“I have a concealed carry license and a firearms owner identification card. I have a gun under the seat.”

She laughs drily and shakes her head. "That doesn't matter. You're out of your league, Hunter. Do not get any ideas. None of this is like the cop dramas or whatever you watch on television, this is real life. The main character can and will die if shot."

"Are you going to tell me what's happening?"

"No."

"How is that okay? There's someone following us."

"They're following me. You took it upon yourself to get involved with no information, that's on you. As soon as we park, I will go back to my brother's house, and you will be removed and safe from the situation."

"I'm not letting you go to your brother's house alone."

"You don't have a choice. I'm not some weak woman who needs to be saved by the big burly man. Why is that so hard for you to understand? I am not that woman and will never be that woman."

"Just because I want to keep you safe doesn't mean that I think you're weak or that you are weak. You can be a total badass and still need help. It makes you more of a badass to ask for help."

She rolls her eyes and shakes her head in disgust.

"Can you pay attention to the road? They may be following at a distance but it doesn't mean someone isn't somewhere along the route home ready to attack. These bastards are good at slight of hand."

"I can multitask. Please don't tell me how to drive."

"You try to tell me how to live my life so when you stop doing that, I'll stop telling you how to drive."

"You're infuriating."

"Are you talking to yourself in the mirror?" she asks sweetly.

Infuriating. I want to stop the car and pull her into a kiss until she stops fighting me on everything.

Kissing can do that, right?

"Should I take a different route home?"

"What part of pretend like we're not being followed do you not understand?"

I bite down the words that I want to say and continue driving. Nothing I say will be right so there's no point in bickering with her any longer.

I punch the code in when we get to my driveway and the gates open, and we proceed to the house. The truck doesn't follow but drives around the block.

"You can stay at my house."

"I need to go to my brother's house. You cannot be involved in this."

"You told someone you'd wait for them. Do you have someone else coming to help you? Are you going to disappear again?"

"I've never disappeared."

"Damon has said numerous times that he's hoping you don't get spooked."

"He said that?"

There's a little emotion. That she quickly gets rid of, damn it.

"He did."

"It's not like that."

"Let me help."

"Mike," she sighs as she turns in her seat to look me directly in the eyes. "I appreciate that you want to help, that you want to protect me because of my brother but this is bigger than you can ever imagine. I'm not who you think I am and it's better that you stay in your house and forget about this and me. I am trying to protect Damon and you."

She grabs the door handle and gets out of the car quickly, but not before I see unshed tears. Diesel bounds out after her and she shuts the door. I immediately jump out and jog over to the passenger side before she can leave.

"I don't need to be protected either," I growl as I grab her arm and tug her into me.

I plant a hot kiss on her mouth, pinning her against the car. She instinctively wraps her arms around my neck and I hear her sigh against me.

There's a sound of a car nearby and she quickly pushes me away.

"I can't do this," she hisses as she brushes past me and jogs across the yard.

There's a loud boom from the street. Diesel barks and starts growling, he takes off toward the road.

11

Eve

"DIESEL, KOMM HER," I hiss as I check my surroundings.

Just a vehicle backfiring or something. I keep my head down and get back to my brother's yard before Diesel and I disappear inside. I peek out the window and see that Mike is looking around to see what the noise is.

I breathe a sigh of relief.

Tears prick at my eyes.

I was so terrified that he'd been shot.

Stop getting attached to this man. It cannot happen, Eve.

You have to shut the feelings off right now.

He cannot get hurt because of me. I have to stay away from him.

I go to my room and find the nine-millimeter that I have stashed. I load it, put it in my concealed holster and grab the knife from under my desk. It goes in a concealed holster as well.

I walk throughout the house making sure everything is secure. The alarm is on but that's not something that will keep men like Ivan and the members of the Tambov Gang out.

As I sit in the living room, a tumbler of whiskey on ice sits beside me on an end table. My legs are crossed as I patiently wait for the attack that's coming. My senses are heightened and Diesel is sitting at attention beside me on the floor. He's ready to attack if necessary.

I hear a noise at the front door. My muscles tense, adrenaline shooting through my body.

Is it Ivan? Is it finally him? Is this it?

My eyes flit around the room, taking in escape and entry points. I take into account anything that can be used as a weapon before the front door opens.

"Eve?"

Damon steps inside, his silhouette framed by the faint light filtering through the blinds. When he sees me sitting in the dark, he jumps for a second.

He looks at me, concern etched on his features. "Eve, what the hell's going on? Why is it so dark in here."

"Nothing. Just a long day."

His gaze pierces through my facade, and I know he sees more than I'm willing to reveal. "Bullshit, Eve. Mike told me you were followed."

I shake my head, my jaw clenching. "The less you know, the better. Trust me on this."

"I'm tired of your cryptic answers. I'm done enabling your bullshit."

"Fuck off."

"Damn it, Eve," he sighs. "You know damn well that I can protect myself. I don't know where you got this idea that you have to be the caped crusader for everyone in your life."

My phone vibrates. I snatch it up, relief flooding through me as I see Dirk's name on the screen.

Natalia has been held up. She'll be there as soon as she can. We have a line on Ivan. The team and I are following the lead. I'll keep you posted. Seems your brother reached out to someone to watch your house and protect if necessary. He's posted outside. I've done the checks, he's good. He'll be fine until Nat gets there.

My eyes flit to my brother before I glare at him.

"You hired someone to babysit me?"

"What are you talking about?"

"I can tell when you're lying."

"I saw some stuff on the camera of people driving by, parking out front and whatever. So yes, I hired a buddy to keep an eye on the house and run surveillance."

"Someone other than Mike?"

"I didn't hire Mike, he's just being himself."

"It's annoying. All of this is annoying. I can take care of my damn self."

"No one is questioning that. Get dressed, Mike's got a game tonight and you're coming."

"I hate hockey."

"I don't care, you're coming."

"Damon," I hiss.

My brother shakes his head and pulls out his phone. He opens it and starts going through screens before he shows me a picture.

"The entire world has seen pictures of you and Mike together, claiming that you're his fiancée. You shouldn't be here alone."

"Fuck. What?"

All of the articles he had screenshotted say that NHL star Mike Hunter has finally settled down with a mystery woman. I'm wearing sunglasses and a baseball cap in all the pictures of us making out in the grocery store parking lot, but it's still not good to have my face plastered everywhere.

If Ivan had been bluffing, it'll be easy for him and anyone else to know where I am now. I'm sure they have an alert set up on facial recognition software for my face. The Tambov Gang saw these photos before I did.

"Why do you look panicked?"

"Damon, I need to leave."

"You're not leaving. They'll expect that. We're going to go along with this fiancée thing. They're not going to attack in a public setting."

He's right.

Or am I only saying that because I want to believe he's right because I don't want to leave?

"Fine," I sigh. "But only because it makes you look good when your client looks good for dating a hot woman."

"Yeah, that's it," he chuckles.

***

The stadium looms before us, a colossal fortress of steel and concrete. I stand in awe, my eyes tracing the lines of the architecture, the vibrant banners fluttering in the breeze.

My first ever professional hockey game.

I don't want to admit that I'm a little excited to see Mike in uniform and in action.

"Ready for this, Eve?" he asks, his voice laced with anticipation. "Mike will be thrilled you're here."

"My fake fiancé better be," I roll my eyes and stick my tongue out at my brother.

We make our way through the throngs of fans, the air alive with energy and anticipation. The sea of blue and gold washes over me, jerseys adorned with names I don't recognize, faces painted with pride.

Damon nudges me with his elbow, a mischievous glint in his eye. "You're gonna love this, Eve. Trust me."

I roll my eyes, a smirk playing at the corners of my lips. "Oh yeah? And what if I don't? Are you gonna refund my ticket?"

"You didn't pay for your ticket. But don't worry, you'll be a die-hard fan by the end of the night."

"Doubtful. You've been telling me for twenty years that I'll be a fan of Mike and it still hasn't happened."

"That's because you're stubborn."

I look out on the ice and my eyes are immediately drawn to Mike. His helmet is on but I see his name stitched on the back of his jersey. He's a very tall, muscular man but his grace on the ice makes him look like a tiny ice skater. He's mesmerizing out there.

His head turns and he looks up into the stands and our eyes lock, he raises his head in acknowledgment before he skates with his team to their box.

The game is exciting from the start, but my eyes are only drawn to Mike's figure. Damon updates me on what's happening throughout the game and before I know it there's only a few minutes left.

On the ice below, Mike and Luca, the dynamic duo according to Damon, weave and dart with precision, passing the puck back and forth like a well-rehearsed dance.

Luca takes possession of the puck near the blue line, his movements fluid as he glides effortlessly across the ice. He scans the rink with hawk-like focus, searching for an opening amidst the sea of opposing players. His eyes lock onto Mike.

With a swift flick of his wrist, Luca sends the puck sailing through the air, a perfect pass aimed straight for Mike's waiting stick. Mike anticipates the move. He snags the puck out of the air with practiced ease.

The black and red uniforms of the opposing team close in, their sticks slashing at the air in a desperate attempt to thwart his advance.

But Mike is undeterred, as he maneuvers through the chaos with grace and finesse. He dodges a defenseman with a quick juke to the left, then another with a lightning-fast spin to the right.

With the goal looming before him, Mike shifts into high gear, his muscles coiled like a spring ready to unleash its energy. The goalie braces for impact as Mike winds up for the shot.

Mike unleashes a thunderous slap shot, the puck rocketing off his stick with explosive force. It sails through the air like a comet streaking across the sky.

And then, with a deafening crack, the puck finds its mark, burying itself in the back of the net with pinpoint accuracy. The stadium erupts into chaos, the roar of the crowd echoing off the rafters like a symphony of triumph. Mike raises his arms in victory, a triumphant grin spreading across his face as he removes his helmet and points towards the stands.

My heart skips a beat as I realize he's looking right at us, well, at me, our faces illuminated by the glow of the scoreboard above. I cheer with abandon, my voice lost in the cacophony of sound as I watch Mike's gaze linger on me for a moment longer.

"Shit," I hear Damon curse.

I look up and realize that we're on the jumbotron. They've pushed Damon out and it's just me with a heart circled around me as they cut from me to Mike and back to me.

"Fuck," I breathe.

"It's okay, you're wearing a baseball cap, they won't know it's you."

Yeah, that's not true.

"We have to get out of here."

Damon nods and the two of us quickly make a departure.

"I texted Mike and told him we'd see him back at the house."

"I don't want to see him."

"It'll be late before he gets back so you probably won't. I didn't want him to think we weren't grateful for the tickets."

I shake my head and roll my eyes.

***

By the time, we're home and settled my brother goes to his room for the night. I'm too shaken and amped up to sleep so I go outside to sit by the pool. The moonlight and sight of the water will calm me.

How could this have happened? I'm so careful about being incognito, about not being seen by people and now I'm plastered all over the place.

I don't just have to worry about Ivan, there will be more people coming for me now.

I hear a noise behind me. Diesel stands at attention, his noise pointed at Mike's house. Piper and Mike come out the back door, Mike's in his swim trunks. He glances up and our eyes lock.

Looks like we had the same idea.

"Hey," he grins as he walks over to me.

"We're not friends," I hiss as I turn my back on him.

"Who wants to be friends with a girl who has multiple personalities," he snaps back at me as he walks through the gate and over to my brother's property. "I guess it's true what they say, the crazier the woman the better the sex."

"Oh, fuck you. You think you're all high and mighty. Look at Mike Hunter smiling for the cameras, his face plastered all over the place with his hot new fiancée. Did you pay those people to take those pictures so you could play the big protector?"

"What? No. Why would I do that?"

"I don't know, Mike. Why else would people have taken pictures of us in a grocery store parking lot? Why would they put me on the jumbotron? How would they have picked me out of thousands of people if you didn't tell them?"

"I don't know. I didn't have anything to do with either of those things."

"I don't believe you. I'm not some piece of meat or eye candy that's going to be on your arm as the doting, loving, submissive girlfriend. You can go fuck yourself."

I stand up out of the lounge chair I had been sitting in. He takes a step toward me.

"Trust me, if that's what I wanted I wouldn't be interested in you."

"You can't be interested in me, Hunter!"

"Too late!"

We're inches apart, in each other's faces yelling at each other and all I can think about is kissing him. I take a step back. I need to make space between us before I do something stupid. I turn and dive into the pool. He follows me.

I come up for air and he's right in front of me his gorgeous eyes are full of fire and lust.

I can't do this. Get away from him. It's too dangerous.

"I don't do relationships. It only ends in you getting hurt and I'm not going to risk that."

He grabs me in his arms and kisses me stupid.

How does he make me forget what I was thinking every time?

12

Mike

The only way to get this woman to listen to me is to kiss her until she stops talking and overthinking everything. The second my mouth covers her she melts into me and audibly sighs. Her entire body relaxes.

Thatta girl.

I take a step forward and pin her back against the side of the pool. My hands find her breasts, she gasps and whimpers as she presses herself into me. My mouth goes down her neck, to the curve of her breasts as one hand reaches up and unties the tiny bikini she's wearing.

As soon as her boobs are free of the material, I use my mouth and hands to cover and suckle them. Her hands go down to my boxers as she pulls my hard length out. I glance up at her, a taut nipple in my mouth as I catch her hungry stare.

"Fuck me now," she demands, her voice barely above a whisper but filled with lust-induced desperation. I smile, my eyes never leaving hers. I slide her bikini bottoms down her thighs. She reaches down to grab them and puts them on the cement behind her, I do the same with my trunks.

I reach down into the water and cup her butt cheeks as I lift her up and guide my engorged cock inside of her. She gasps as I fill her.

"Yes, Mike, yes."

Her fingers dig into my back as I begin to thrust, each movement slow and deliberate at first. She arches her back, meeting my every thrust with her own, her hands wrapping around my neck. I lean down, our bodies melding together as I nibble on her lips, tasting the chlorine from the pool.

"Harder," she moans into my mouth, her breath hot and heavy. I oblige, picking up my pace, the water sloshing around us as we fuck in the deep end. Each thrust sends a tingly sensation through her body, a wave of pleasure washing over her as I continue to drive into her.

She bites her lip, her eyes locked on mine as I continue to thrust. She's not one to hold back; she meets each thrust with an equal force, her hips grinding against mine. Her nails dig into my skin, leaving small marks that will bear witness to this moment

"It is sexy as fuck when you take charge like this," she moans in my ear.

I slow down and move us both slightly so that I'm full hitting her G-spot.

"Oh yes, thank you."

As the pleasure builds within her, her legs tremble, and her moans become more pronounced. I grip her hips, feeling the tension in her body, knowing she's close. I lean in to kiss her, our breath mingling as I watch her, wanting to make this moment last as long as possible.

"Fuck me harder," she begs, her voice ragged. I pick up the pace again, feeling my own arousal building. With each thrust, I can feel her getting closer and closer to the edge.

I pull out of her, surprising her for a moment. She looks at me, confused, but then I spin her around and enter her from behind. Her body shakes as I push inside of her.

She braces herself against the cool tile of the pool, her hips rocking back and forth to meet my every thrust. I wrap my arms around her waist. Her moans echo through the quiet night, mixing with the sound of water splashing against the pool's edge.

Her body tightens around me. I grip her hips, feeling her muscles flex and release with each thrust. She cries out, her voice shaking with pleasure, and then she collapses against me, her body shuddering as the orgasm takes hold.

I feel myself swell inside of her, the pleasure building in me like a tidal wave. "Oh, fuck," I groan, and I thrust harder, the world around me fading away. My release floods her, and she gasps, a mixture of pain and pleasure on her face as I fill her with my hot seed.

My cock twitches inside her, milked by her tight muscles. We both pant heavily, our bodies still connected in the warm water of the pool. I pull out, my shaft dripping with our combined fluid. She slowly turns around, her eyes meeting mine.

"Wow," she whispers, a smile slowly spreading across her lips. "That was... intense."

I lean in and kiss her deeply.

“Stay with me tonight,” I say as I pull away from her breathlessly.

Her eyes instantly change, and she pushes me away before climbing out of the pool.

“Good sex changes nothing. Find someone else to fit your Barbie mold.”

She grabs her bathing suit off the cement, snaps at Diesel and the two disappear inside the house.

Fuck! I can’t chase her into her brother’s house.

***

The incessant ringing of my phone pierces the quiet morning, shattering the remnants of my dreams. With a groan, I fumble for the device, squinting at the bright screen as I answer.

"Hello?" My voice is gravelly with sleep.

"Mike," comes Kelsey's urgent voice on the other end. "You need to turn on the TV or check your social media right now."

I sit up, rubbing my eyes to clear the sleep-induced fog. "What's going on?"

"You and Eve are all over the place."

"Why?"

"Is this a real engagement and you failed to tell me or is this all stemming from you telling that guy she's your fiancée?"

"It's small-town gossip that's filtered into the real world."

"So things are good between the two of you?"

"No, Eve still despises me," I confess, the words heavy on my tongue. "She can't stand to be around me unless we're screwing."

There's a moment of silence on the other end before Kelsey bursts out laughing. "Well, that's a start."

"No, it's not. I don't know how to get through to her unless I'm kissing her."

"There are plenty of people who think that's an acceptable form of communication."

"Can't we do something to stop it? I hate all this attention."

"As your public relations manager, I have to say that good news is good press," Kelsey says, her voice tinged with sympathy. "We need to capitalize on this."

I sigh, running a hand through my hair in frustration. "Fine, do what you have to do."

After a brief exchange of goodbyes, I hang up the phone and bury my face in my hands. This wasn't how I envisioned my life turning out—embroiled in a fake engagement, surrounded by paparazzi and gossip. I hate public attention, but it seems like there's no escaping it now.

Piper jumps on the bed, whimpering and whining.

"I don't want to be up either," I tell her. "You have a doggie door for a reason. Why do you make me go with you all the time?"

She sniffs the air before she gets back down on the floor and starts walking in circles.

"Okay, okay, I'll go outside with you. You're the most spoiled dog on the planet."

She is eagerly waiting, tail wagging furiously as she dances around me.

The crisp morning air greets us as we step into the front yard, the grass dewy beneath my feet. It's not long before Diesel bounds over to join us, his tail wagging in greeting.

I furrow my brow, wondering if we left the gate open last night. As I glance around, my eyes land on Diesel in the midst of taking a giant crap in my yard. My heart sinks as I realize he's also dug under the fence, destroying my meticulously maintained lawn.

"Goddammit, Diesel!" I curse under my breath, feeling a surge of frustration rise within me.

With Piper and Diesel in tow, I make my way next door, my anger simmering beneath the surface. As I approach, I see Eve in the front yard, gracefully moving through a series of yoga poses.

Damn, she's beautiful.

I'm momentarily stopped in my tracks admiring the view.

"Hey," I call out, trying to keep my voice steady despite the irritation bubbling inside me.

"Hey, Mike."

She doesn't notice my intrusion; she keeps her eyes closed and continues doing her thing.

I take a deep breath, trying to rein in my frustration. "Your dog tore up my yard and then came over to crap in it."

Eve giggles, seemingly unbothered by the accusation, as she transitions into a downward dog position. My eyes involuntarily drift to her shapely behind, encased in those short shorts, and for a moment, I forget what I'm mad about.

"It's perfectly natural for dogs to poop, you know," she says, her voice light and airy. "And if you were to keep Piper on a leash when she's in heat, Diesel wouldn't have dug through the yard to get to her."

"In heat?" I repeat dumbly, turning to look at Piper. My eyes widen as I see Diesel mounting her, and I quickly yell, "No!"

Eve opens her eyes and starts laughing hysterically at the scene unfolding before her. "Looks like Diesel has a thing for Piper."

I grit my teeth, feeling a mix of embarrassment and frustration wash over me. "I was supposed to be breeding Piper."

Eve's laughter only intensifies at my confession. "Well, then you should have her on a leash so this doesn't happen."

I let out a sigh of relief, feeling some of the tension leave my body. "I promised a friend I'd breed her with her Blue Heeler."

"That's great," she rolls her eyes as she deepens her stretch. "As if there's not a million dogs on death row as it is."

"Do you really think you should be out here like this with Conner stalking you?"

"I can protect myself from Conner and any other pervert."

Her eyes flit back to mine as she catches me staring at her behind.

"You're giving him a free show."

She smiles at me, her eyes sparkling with amusement. "You know, a man like you shouldn't be such a prude when it comes to sex."

I feel the heat rising to my cheeks at her bold statement, my mind struggling to process her words. "I-I'm not a prude," I stammer, feeling utterly out of my depth.

Eve chuckles, a mischievous glint in her eyes. "Sure, sure. Whatever you say. Because it's totally normal for someone to freak out when their dog is having a good time."

This time I roll my eyes.

She's so damn frustrating.

“Can you keep him contained?”

“The responsible thing to do would be to spay Piper so she doesn't get cancer or any other number of problems later in life or keep her inside while she's in heat. You're lucky it's just Diesel in your yard right now. You keep her outside much longer and it's going to be a party of dogs fighting for her attention.”

“We've been outside for five minutes.”

“Be a responsible pet owner and learn things if you're going to breed.”

She stops what she's doing and picks her yoga mat off the ground. She calls for Diesel in German and he stops what he's doing and immediately comes to her. She doesn't even look back just walks into the house with her dog at her heels.

“Why don't you listen that well?” I ask Piper as she runs off to chase a squirrel.

“She's a feisty one, isn't she?” Conner asks from the other side of the fence.

“Have you been there the whole time?”

“When there's a show like that outside, where else would I be?”

“Stay the fuck away from her.”

“What will you do about it if I don't?”

I take a step toward the fence and Conner chuckles before walking off.

“You're out of your league with this one, Hunter!” He calls over his shoulder.

13

Eve

Two days later, I step into the arena, the cold air hitting my face as Damon leads the way to our seats near the ice. The excitement in the air is tense, the crowd buzzing with anticipation for the game ahead. As we settle into our seats, I notice a familiar face in the seat next to ours.

It's her.

The gorgeous redhead from Mike's house the other day. My heart sinks as I instantly feel a pang of jealousy. What is she doing here in these seats? Are she and Mike actually together and he's been cheating on her?

Damon catches my glance and introduces her, breaking through my thoughts. "Eve, this is Kelsey. She's Mike's PR rep."

So, not a girlfriend?

"It's a pleasure to meet you, Eve. I've heard a lot about you through Mike."

"You have?"

She laughs and nods her head. “Yeah, not sure why Damon never told me about you.”

My eyes flit to my brother as he shifts uncomfortably.

“Not sure why that’s a big deal.”

She shrugs her shoulders and lets out a long sigh.

“I’m going to run to the bathroom before the game starts. Do you want me to grab something from concessions for you?”

“No, thanks.” Kelsey and I say simultaneously.

My brother disappears quickly. I chuckle and look back at Kelsey.

"So... Kelsey, did you and Damon... ever date?"

“That obvious?” she giggles.

“A little. What’s his deal?”

"You'll have to ask him yourself. He’s amazing, we have so much fun together. He’ll be all about me, putting in effort and being sweet and then he just stops.”

“He’s clueless.”

We share a laugh, the tension between us dissipating. By the time Damon returns from the bathroom, Kelsey and I are chatting like old friends, the awkwardness of the situation long forgotten.

“Kelsey!” someone calls out from behind us.

She turns, waves, and then gets up to go talk to them

“Hey, you would tell me if something bad was going on with you, right?” Damon says quietly.“Why do you ask?”

"Mike thinks your life is in danger."

I scoff, trying to brush off his words. "Mike needs to mind his own business," I retort, my frustration bubbling to the surface.

Damon shakes his head, his brow furrowing in worry. "That's the weird thing, Eve. Mike normally minds his own business. It's really out of character that he's asking so many questions about you."

“I told you before, it’s nothing for you to worry about.”

"If you're in danger, sis, you're safe at my house," he says earnestly. "I want to make sure you know that I've made sure that the house is a fortress. Please don't leave."

I nod just as Kelsey comes back to join us.

I don't want to leave, bro, but I may not have any other choice.

The game begins finally. The players glide across the rink with precision and skill, each move calculated and executed flawlessly. And at the center of it all is Mike.

I watch in awe as Mike darts across the rink, his movements fluid and graceful. He weaves through the opposing team's defense with ease, his stick-handling skills mesmerizing to behold. With a swift flick of his wrist, he sends the puck sailing towards the net, narrowly missing a goal by inches.

The crowd erupts into cheers and applause, the excitement in the arena reaching a fever pitch. I can't help but get caught up in the energy, my heart pounding with every play. Watching Mike do what he loves is exhilarating, his passion for the game evident in every stride.

As the game wears on, Mike continues to dominate the ice, his presence commanding the attention of everyone in the arena. He executes a series of impressive passes, setting up his teammates for scoring opportunities that leave the opposing team scrambling to keep up.

And then, in a moment of brilliance, he takes control of the puck, deftly maneuvering past defenders as if they were mere obstacles in his path. With a powerful shot, he sends the puck soaring into the top corner of the net, the goalie left helpless to stop it.

The crowd erupts into cheers once again, the roar of the crowd echoing throughout the arena. I find myself on my feet, cheering alongside them, swept up in the excitement of the moment.

As the final buzzer sounds and the game comes to an end, Kelsey sits forward and giggles as she looks back at Damon.

“I think we made her into a fan.”

“I believe you’re right,” Damon laughs.

"Mike is so good out there, it's hard not to be. But don't tell him I said that."

"Why do you hate him so much?"

"He's annoying."

Damon chuckles and shakes his head. Kelsey gives me a quick hug.

"Here's my card. Text or call me sometime and we'll go to lunch. I'm certain you need a break from those two goons."

"Absolutely," I laugh.

Kelsey glances at my brother as if she wants to hug him too but walks away with a wave instead.

"Ready?"

"First of all, you're an idiot and should fix that. She's incredible. Second of all, yes, but I need to run to the bathroom."

"She's an off-limits subject."

"Says you."

Damon and I walk up the steps and he gets pulled away while I continue walking to the nearest bathroom.

I weave my way through the crowd, the excitement of the game still buzzing in the air. As I join the line, I can't shake the feeling of being watched. I glance around nervously, my senses on high alert.

And then I see him. A man, dressed in dark clothing with sunglasses and a hat pulled low over his face, ducking behind a pillar.

Fuck, is that Ivan?

The line inches forward, but I can't shake the feeling of unease. I keep glancing over my shoulder, expecting to see Ivan lurking in the shadows. When I catch sight of the man again, my suspicions aren't confirmed. I can't tell if it's him or not.

I try to calm myself as I enter the bathroom, splashing cold water on my face in an attempt to steady my nerves. But when I exit, Damon is nowhere to be found. Panic grips me as I realize he's not where I left him, and he's not answering his phone.

Finally, he emerges from the men's bathroom, and I breathe a sigh of relief. "Where were you?" I ask, my voice tinged with anxiety.

Damon furrows his brow, concern evident in his eyes. "Why do you look like you saw a ghost?" he asks, his voice laced with worry.

I shake my head, trying to brush off my fears. "It's nothing," I reply, though my words sound hollow even to my own ears.

As we make our way out of the arena, I hear someone calling our names. I turn to see Mike running after us, a grin on his face.

"Hey, Kelsey and I are grabbing dinner to celebrate me not screwing up the latest interview. You two are joining us."

"I'm beat," Damon says.

"No, you're not. You're avoiding Kelsey," Mike answers pointedly.

Oh shit, he called him out that's amazing.

"I think dinner would be lovely. I'd like to hang out with Kelsey more, she seems cool."

"Yeah?" Mike asks, not hiding his surprise as he falls back a bit.

"Yeah."

"Great, there's a restaurant we love, on the Hill. Your brother knows the address. I'll see you there."

"I wish you would have said no."

"We've got some time until we're out of the parking lot," I tease. "I'll fake sick if you give me a good excuse."

"I hate you," Damon sighs as he shakes his head.

"Now you know how I feel, brother."

"Kelsey is great, I just... I don't know what my hold-up is. It's the same thing every time though. We're so good together and we have a great time and then we sleep together and she gets weird."

My brother unlocks his car with the key fob and we climb in. He steers behind the line of cars and we make our way to the restaurant.

"Does she get weird or do *you* get weird?"

He's quiet for a minute before he shrugs his shoulders.

***

The ambiance of the restaurant on the Hill in St. Louis is warm and inviting, with soft lighting and the comforting hum of chatter filling the air. Kelsey, Damon, Mike, and I are seated at a cozy table, enjoying a night out together. The mood is light and jovial, laughter ringing out as we catch up on each other's lives.

As we delve into conversation, the topic naturally turns to Mike's game we attended earlier.

"Dude, that last-minute goal was incredible," Damon interjects, excitement evident in his voice. "It was like something out of a movie!"

"Yeah, you guys played really well tonight. It was a great game," Kelsey adds.

"It was definitely entertaining to watch," I chime in, eager to join the conversation.

“I think we brought her to the dark side, Mikey,” Kelsey laughs.

“Not quite yet,” I giggle.

Kelsey leans in, her eyes sparkling with curiosity. "So, tell me more about why you came back to Legacy, Eve. Are you glad to be back?”

I take a sip of my drink, gathering my thoughts. "Well, it's definitely different from city life," I begin, reflecting on my hometown. "Everyone knows everyone, and there's a real sense of community. It's quiet, peaceful... but sometimes a little too quiet. You don’t live there too?"

Avoid the why question and distract with something else.

“No,” she smiles. “Right here in the Lou. It’s a relaxing drive there though. I love the shops and the feel of the town. I could see myself settling there someday.”

Her eyes flit to my brothers before they go back down to her drink that she takes a long pull from.

“It’s good for that. I didn’t realize how much I missed it and Damon until I came back.”

"So, Eve, any eligible bachelors in Legacy catching your eye?" Kelsey teases.

I do not miss the subtle glance she throws at Mike.

What's that about?

"Not really looking for a relationship right now. It's not in my two-year plan."

"Two-year plan?" Mike asks.

"I have goals at work, with my career, financially and I'm not there yet."

"What is your career?" Kelsey queries.

"I work in tech."

"Ooh, that's so cool. I'm computer illiterate but I love that you're not. You're such a badass."

I shrug as I focus on the drink in front of me.

"Tell me more about your job," I say to Kelsey.

The conversation continues to flow effortlessly, laughter filling the air. We talk about our families, our careers, and our dreams for the future. Despite the occasional flirtatious comment from Mike, the evening is filled with warmth and friendship.

"Eve, I'm surprised you've been to two of my games already."

"Yeah, the first game where I saw that Luca guy made me want to come back. He is hot. Is he single?" I ask quickly.

Kelsey snickers and covers her face. Mike's face drops.

"Luca, really?"

"Oh, I don't need to know if he's single, I already slid into his DM's."

"You what?"

"He's a bit of a playboy," Kelsey interjects. "But he is really good at making you believe that you are the only woman in his world when the two of you are together."

"Good to know."

Mike clears his throat as he takes a long drink of his glass of whiskey. I can tell he's irritated by my admission.

I didn't message Luca and wouldn't. Contrary to what I want Mike to believe, I happen to enjoy the sex we're having, and I don't want that to end.

Teasing him is fun.

Even if it is putting his life in danger.

Damn it, I'm selfish. I really am going to have to end things with him and disappear.

My brother excuses himself to go to the bathroom and Kelsey is pulled away to go to another table to speak with someone she knows, leaving Mike and I alone at the table.

"Did you really message Luca?" he asks.

"What if I did?"

"It'll make it awkward at practice when I tell him to stay the Hell away from you."

"You can't control my life."

"You're right, but I can control my teammate choices."

"That's a dick move."

"It's a dick move to be fucking me regularly and then message one of my good friends. I didn't take you for that kind of woman."

I narrow my eyes at him. "I'm not that kind of woman and you're not going to accuse me of being anything just because you're jealous."

"Jealous?" he chuckles as he shakes his head. "Hardly."

"I know it's probably not normal for a woman not to throw herself at you at all times, Hunter, but some of us don't need to do that."

He nods slowly as Kelsey comes back to the table.

"Eve, got any good stories about your brother or Mike?"

"Plenty. I could show you pictures of the two of them that would make you cry from laughing so hard. They were the biggest dorks."

"This doesn't surprise me."

"We were not dorks, we were the kings of the high school."

I roll my eyes. "Self-proclaimed kings don't count."

"I was Homecoming King," Damon adds.

"That's not surprising," Kelsey laughs.

"It's like written somewhere that the captain of the football team has to be the homecoming king, the head cheerleader was the homecoming queen. It's so cliché."

"Was she your girlfriend too?"

"She was," Damon grins. "She was wild too."

"She was psycho, that's the term you were looking for."

"She wasn't," Damon laughs.

"Yes, she was," Mike adds. "She would show up everywhere we went and pretend it was a coincidence."

"Yeah, she did do that. She still texts me a lot."

"Not surprising."

"What was the stupidest thing they ever did?"

"Kaylie Dalton," I reply, my eyes flitting to Mike's.

"I never slept with Kaylie, that was all Mike."

"I don't understand," Kelsey interjects.

Mike waves at someone across the room before he stands up and crosses over to them."

"She was mine and his little sister's best friend at one time. She only liked boys that Stella and I did though."

"She gave the illusion of being a very sweet, cool girl," my brother says. "But she's anything but that. She was very jealous of Eve. She also made a fool of Mike. That was really shitty to bring her up, it still bothers him."

"She asked what stupid thing you guys did," I hiss. "How was I supposed to know it bothered him."

Maybe I was a little irritated and acted out.

I'd forgotten how angry it made me that he dated her and how pissed I was at her for what she did to him.

"Eve put Nair in her shampoo bottle in the locker room after she learned that Kaylie had cheated on Mike for the third time."

"I don't know what you're talking about."

"Wait, Mike stayed with a girl long enough for her to cheat three times?"

"To be fair, Mike was away at a state hockey tournament from like Thursday to Sunday and she slept with someone different every night. He didn't find out until he came home. He dumped her when he found out, but he learned who was and wasn't his friend that weekend."

"She's despicable."

"That makes me sad," Kelsey adds. "Mike's such a good dude."

"Is he really still upset over that?"

"Not because he misses her or ever cared about her, but Charlie was like a brother to us and he slept with her."

"I forgot about that."

"Charlie mysteriously had a snake in his locker on Monday. He pissed his pants and couldn't get away because whoever put the snake in his locker also put super glue on the handle."

"He was super glued to his locker with a snake in it?" Kelsey asks, her eyes flitting to mine.

"Yeah, he changed schools after that too. There's no coming back from pissing your pants your junior year of high school."

"Did Mike put the snake in the locker?"

"I'm pretty sure it was Eve."

"I hate snakes," I lie.

Well, it's not a complete lie. I do hate snakes, but I did pay someone to put it in there while I superglued the door handle.

I will never admit to the revenge things I did to the people that hurt Damon or Mike. It wasn't a lot, but I'll still never admit that I did them.

My brother rolls his eyes and makes a face at Kelsey just as Mike comes back to the table.

The conversation changes to current things and we continue laughing and talking. I didn't expect to have this much fun on what could be perceived as a double date, but here I am enjoying my time and wishing that Mike Hunter is coming home with me tonight.

I blow out a breath and try to focus on the table and the conversation, but my eyes keep falling on Mike and the way that he's trying to look at everything but me.

Maybe if I put my hand on his leg and... nope that's too noticeable.

I bump his leg gently, his eyes dart up to mine, and I smile slowly at him. He grins cockily back at me before grabbing his phone and typing something.

> I'd rather be eating you for dessert right now.
> Maybe we should wrap this up quickly.

I don't reply, just chuckle to myself as I put the phone down on the table again.

"We should get headed back to Legacy, bro. I'm exhausted."

"Me too," Damon laughs. "It's a long drive."

Who knows what will happen when we get home, but I know right now, I can't think of anything other than Mike's face in between my legs and that's a whole lot of trouble.

14

Mike

I STEP OUT OF the restaurant, the cool evening air hitting me as I join Damon, Kelsey, and Eve on the sidewalk. We're all laughing and joking. It's been a great night, filled with good food and even better company.

"I'll see you back in town," Damon says to me before he gives Kelsey a quick hug.

He and Eve walk to their car while I walk Kelsey to her car.

"You know Eve was lying about Luca, right?"

"I asked her about it and she deflected the question. Why would she lie about something like that?" I ask, trying to make sense of her words.

"Who knows? Maybe she was just trying to feel you out, or maybe she enjoys the reactions you give her."

I shake my head, still trying to wrap my mind around it. "But why?" I press, feeling a knot form in my stomach.

Kelsey laughs and grins at me. "As I already told you, I think she really likes you. But if you want to pursue something with her, maybe it's time to start keeping your dick in your pants. You know, so you can build something meaningful. You sent her a cringe text at the table, didn't you?”

Her words hit me like a punch to the gut, the truth of them sinking in. Maybe she's right. Maybe I've been too focused on the physical aspect of things, when what I really want is something more. Something real.

“It wasn't cringe. It was flirty.”

“No, it wasn't. You can't be sexting and expect her to think you want more than sex. How many times do I have to tell you this?”

I nod, a sense of determination settling over me. "Thanks, Kelsey," I say, my voice sincere. "I'll keep that in mind.”

“I really like her.”

“Maybe you should take your own advice in how you approach Damon.”

She sighs and nods.

“I love him so much and it's so easy to talk myself out of that boundary with him. I didn't today. I didn't offer, didn't ask... I just... didn't. If he wants something with me then he'll pursue me. In the meantime, I'll work on me and keep my options open.”

“He really likes you too.”

“He has a shit way of showing it,” she says as she climbs into her car.

She's not wrong.

I walk to my car in the parking lot and start my trek back home to Legacy.

The game was amazing, but it was even better to look up in the stands and see Eve going crazy with excitement as she watched me play.

I text her.

I'll be home in twenty. Meet me by the pool.

We're home already. Change of plans, I'm beat. Raincheck?

Damn it, this woman is so hard to figure out.

***

Piper is standing on top of me in my bed, her nose buried in my face as she tries to get me awake.

"You literally have a doggy door for this reason, why do I need to go outside with you? What's gotten into you?" I groan.

I gently redirect her so that I can get out of bed.

"It's six in the morning, Piper. I had a game last night. You're lucky you're cute."

She chuffs and spins in circles at my feet as she waits for me to follow her outside. I walk out the back door with her. I don't want anyone in town to get the idea that I'm a morning person, it's best to be in the backyard.

I overhear a muffled conversation coming from somewhere close by.

Who else could be up at this ridiculous hour?

Curiosity getting the better of me, I inch closer, trying to make out the words. I see a glint next door at Damon's pool and realize that Eve is on the phone with someone, pacing incessantly.

She sounds worried, her tone tense and urgent. My heart skips a beat as I listen in, my ears straining to catch every word.

"Where's Nat?" she asks, her voice tinged with concern. "I need to know where Nat is."

I pause, my breath catching in my throat. What's going on? Why is she so worried about Nat? Who is Nat?

"I saw Ivan yesterday at the game."

Ivan?

Who is the guy threatening her, Nat or Ivan?

Why was Ivan at the game? How did he know where she'd be?

Shit, this isn't good.

I inch closer trying to hear more while also being inconspicuous.

I pull out my phone and text Damon, urgency driving my fingers to type out a message. We need to take different precautions if this guy was at the game.

As I wait for Damon's reply, I continue to listen in on Eve's conversation. She's asking the man on the other end of the line when they'll be here, her voice trembling with fear.

"There was a note in my bedroom when we got home last night," she says, her voice barely above a whisper. "Ivan was there."

What?

Damon told me that no one could get in the house without the alarm being triggered. We need to figure something else out and fast.

Shit.

"Dirk, I need to know where you guys are or when you're going to be here. This is different. I can't be responsible for my brother or Mike getting killed because of Ivan or whoever else has found me."

Killed?

How many people are looking for her?

And why?

Piper is at my feet gazing up at me adoringly and I realize she wants to go back inside. Eve makes a noise, groaning as she shuts her phone.

"Fuck, fuckity fuck, fuck, fuck," Eve hisses.

I walk next door and see that there are tears streaming down her face.

Whoa.

"Are you okay?"

"No, I'm not. What the fuck? Are you spying on me?"

"No, I was outside with Piper and heard you cussing so I came over to check on you."

"I'm fine."

"Are you though?"

"It's none of your business."

"I feel like it kind of is. I heard you say my name."

"I don't know what you heard but it wasn't your name."

She raises her chin defiantly as she crosses her arms in front of her chest. She starts to turn away and I grab her wrist and pull her backward.

"You don't have to fight me so hard, okay? I want to help. I want to be here for you."

She shakes her head profusely. "That's not an option."

"Why not?"

"Because I said it's not. You're a great guy, Mike, but I'm not looking for a relationship of any sort. It's not who I am. How many times do I have to tell you that?"

Her phone rings and she jumps. I grab it out of her hand, shut it off, and set it down on the table.

She glares at me and tries to grab the phone again. I pull her into a hug and despite her fighting me, I don't let go.

"Stop," she hisses as I continue to hold on.

She's trying to punch and pull away, but I don't let go. She stops and buries her face in my chest. She doesn't look at me, but it's clear that she's crying, and I don't say anything.

I'll hold her for the next twelve hours if that's what I need to do to prove to her that I just want to be here for her. Her arms snake around my waist and she lets me hold her like that for some time before Diesel barks at something.

She pulls away, not looking me in the eye as she turns to go inside.

"Thank you," she says softly before she and Diesel disappear into the house.

Piper yips and I look down at her.

"Something tells me that was a pretty big deal."

She's unbothered and scurries back to our yard before darting into the house.

I need to figure something out if Eve is in danger. I'm not going to let her leave without a fight and I'm not going to let her safety be at risk.

***

Later that afternoon, I had put in a few phone calls to some security contacts I had, but am awaiting return phone calls. I'm hopeful someone will come through with information on Eve and then names she said in her phone call.

I'm lounging on the couch, flipping through the channels on the TV, when there's a knock at the door. The door opens and I glance up to see Damon standing there, a grin on his face.

"Hey, man," he says, stepping inside. "I figured we could watch some ESPN highlights here instead of my house."

"Sounds good to me," I reply, gesturing for him to take a seat.

As we settle in to watch the highlights, Damon leans over to me, a mischievous glint in his eyes. "So, Eve's been kind of annoying today," he says, his voice low. "I needed a break."

"Did you get my text earlier?"

"Shit, yeah," he chuckles. "I forgot to reply."

"I overheard Eve on the phone this morning."

"And?"

"She said someone was in her room, that when you guys got back from the game she'd found a note there."

"That's not possible. The alarm never went off."

"Maybe they knew how to trip it?" I shrug.

"Why wouldn't she tell me that?"

"She specifically told whoever she was talking to on the phone that she wouldn't be responsible for you or I getting killed."

He sits back and blows out a breath.

"Shit. This is serious."

I nod slowly. “She seemed really scared. I realize I don’t know her that well, but she doesn’t show a lot of emotion easily.“

"Yeah, if she’s showing any sign of fear that’s a big deal. She’s emotionally attached to being home, that’s got to be it. She’s been so good about shutting emotions off after she joined the Marine Corps. I think that’s why she hasn’t been home in so long.”

“Maybe. I need the information for your Marine buddy," I say, my voice firm. "I want to hire him to be Eve's private security."

Damon's eyes widen in surprise, but he doesn't protest. Instead, he nods slowly, understanding dawning in his gaze. "My sister will hate you for it, you know," he says quietly.

I meet his gaze, unwavering. "I don't care," I reply firmly. "It's a risk I'm willing to take to keep her safe."

Damon pulls out his phone and sends me the contact card for his friend.

“I’ll text him and let him know you’re going to reach out. I think it’s a good precaution to take. She knows I hired someone for surveillance, but she doesn’t know what he looks like.”

“Good, maybe he can blend in and she won’t know he’s there.”

“I don’t see that happening if he’s following her close. If she’s already on to someone following her she’ll be on high alert.”

“She mentioned a guy named Ivan, do you know who that is?”

“No clue.”

“She ended her call by saying that it was Ivan or anyone else who could be after her. What does she do for a living?”

“We’ve talked about this. I don’t know all of the details.”

“How do we get them?”

“Listen, if she’s working on military contracts then we will never get all the details.”

I nod and let out a long sigh. Damon and I talk about random things for the rest of the night as we watch ESPN and whatever games we can find on TV.

The Marine friend texts me back and lets me know what his fee will be and that he'll start immediately. I feel better knowing that I can protect her in this way.

***

I make my way next door with a box of pizza. Damon isn't home but I'm going to pretend like I don't know that because it will give me the opportunity to check on Eve and spend more time with her.

When I walk through the back door, I'm met with a surprising sight. Eve is there, alone in the kitchen with Diesel, the whiskey bottle in hand. She's barely dressed in a sports bra and shorts as she moves fluidly around the kitchen, dancing to the music playing on her phone.

"Hey, Mike," she says, flashing me a warm smile as I enter. "Damon had to head out of town again. He didn't tell you?"

I shake my head, playing along with her charade. "Nope, didn't hear a thing," I reply casually, though inside, my heart sinks at the confirmation of Damon's absence.

Eve gestures towards the couch, inviting me to join her. "Well, since you're here with food, you might as well stay," she says with a shrug.

I grin, feeling a sense of relief wash over me. "Sounds good to me," I reply, making myself comfortable on the couch beside her.

"I thought you two were attached at the hip, I'm surprised he didn't tell you."

"We're not attached at the hip."

"You've been having the same Sunday night dinners for at least twelve years."

"Creatures of habit. And it hasn't been religiously."

"Sure, sure," she giggles as she grabs the television remote and flips through the television.

She takes a long pull from her glass of whiskey as I open the pizza box and hand her a slice.

We dig in eagerly, savoring the taste of greasy cheese and tomato sauce. Eve watches me with amusement, a playful glint in her eyes.

"You really love your pizza, don't you?" she teases, reaching for another slice.

I grin, wiping my mouth with a napkin. "What can I say? Pizza is my weakness," I reply, taking a sip of my drink. "I give myself one cheat day during the season, today happens to be it."

Eve and I eat and flirt as she puts on an episode of 'Suits' and starts watching it. She puts her plate down on the coffee table and stretches out on the couch. She puts her feet in my lap and I absentmindedly begin massaging them.

"Oh, shit," she breathes. "I wasn't expecting that. Your hands are amazing."

I wasn't expecting my body to react that way to her breathy moan as I knead the balls of her feet.

"Gripping a hockey stick has its perks I guess."

"I guess," she murmurs.

Her eyes are closed as she lets out little moans of appreciation as I continue to rub her feet. I'm not sure how long I alternate feet until I feel her staring at me.

"I heard you and Kelsey went to dinner the other night."

"Is that really what you want to talk about right now?" she smiles back at me.

"What do you want to talk about?"

"I want to know what your hands feel like on my legs. On my back. On my butt. On my shoulders."

"That can be arranged," I grin as I make my way up her ankles and to her calf muscles.

"Oh, yesss."

I work my magic on her legs, kneading and massaging every inch with precision and care. She emits soft moans and sighs, her body arching ever so slightly beneath my touch. My fingers trace delicate patterns on her skin, and I can feel warmth spreading beneath my hands.

I continue my ascent, enjoying the sight of her eyes fluttering closed, her lips parted slightly in anticipation. I reach her waist, and I pause for a moment, giving her a chance to say something or to stop me if she's uncomfortable. She simply lets out a low whimper, wriggling her hips just the slightest bit, inviting me closer.

I hesitantly move upwards, feeling the heat between her legs as I trace my fingers over the sensitive skin of her thighs. She exhales sharply, a mix of pleasure and nervousness dancing across her face. I can tell she's waiting for more.

I need more too.

15

He's massaging my entire body. I've never felt anything this amazing before in my life. I want him to... oh, there it is.

Mike's hands go to the outside of my pants, slowly rubbing between my thighs. My hips buck, needing to feel him inside me as soon as possible. He applies a little more pressure and I moan loudly.

I put my thumbs in the waist band of my shorts and shimmy them off quickly.

I need him to have full access.

He grins cockily back at me. Normally I'd want to knock that smug grin off his face but right now I don't care. All I can think about is him buried inside me.

Mike's grin widens as he reaches out to help me undress further. His fingers graze the sensitive skin of my stomach, sending shivers down my spine. I close my eyes and savor the feeling of his touch, unable to contain the desire that is building within me.

He moves down, his eyes trained on me as his fingers go to my wet core. He slides his finger alongside my clit.

A soft moan escapes my lips, the sensation sending shivers throughout my entire body. My hands grip the couch cushions tightly, my knuckles turning white. Each touch, each caress, brings me closer to the edge.

Mike smiles, knowing exactly what he's doing to me. He presses his fingers against me, slowly sliding in and out, his eyes never leaving mine. The intensity of the gaze, the look of passion in his eyes, only adds to the pleasure coursing through me.

He increases the pace, his fingers moving faster and harder. My breath hitches as I feel the first wave of pleasure building. "Please," I beg, my voice barely above a whisper.

Mike, sensing my need, leans forward and buries his face in between my thighs. I gasp and moan at the same time.

He's so damn good at this.

I arch my back, my head thrown back in pure ecstasy. The sensation of his tongue circling my sensitive flesh, his fingers thrusting in and out of me is almost too much to bear.

I reach down and tangle my fingers in Mike's hair, pulling him closer to me. He responds by increasing his pace, his tongue dancing in harmony with his fingers. My moans grow louder and more desperate.

The moment comes, sudden and intense. I convulse beneath him, a wave of pleasure crashing over me as I cry out his name. My body shakes, my muscles tightening and releasing in a powerful wave of bliss.

As the intensity subsides, I collapse back onto the couch, breathless and reeling from the experience. Mike pulls away, his face flushed and his eyes gleaming with satisfaction.

He looks at me, a knowing smile on his lips. "That was amazing, wasn't it?" he asks, still out of breath.

I can only nod, my throat still too raw from my screams to speak. I reach for his hand, pulling him closer to me. "I think I might need another round," I whisper, my voice barely audible.

Mike's eyes light up with excitement. "With pleasure," he says, a playful grin spreading across his face.

He stands up and pulls me to my feet, his hands gripping my hips. He leans forward and captures my mouth with his.

Our lips collide passionately, tongues entwining as Mike's hands roam my body, caressing every inch of my skin. I tangle my fingers in his hair, deepening the kiss, feeling his desire as it matches my own.

I wrap my arms around his neck, and he lifts me up, carrying me towards the bedroom. My heart races as I anticipate what's to come. The anticipation is almost as intense as the pleasure itself.

He lays me down on the bed, his eyes locked with mine as he undresses. I watch, entranced, as he peels off his clothes, revealing every inch of his toned body. He is a sight to behold.

He straddles me, his arms on either side of my head, his breath hot on my face.

I reach down and grip his erection, stroking him gently. He moans and thrusts into my hand, his body trembling with desire.

I smile up at him, my eyes locked onto his. "Are you ready for me?" I ask, my voice low and sultry.

He nods, his eyes dark and hungry. "I've been ready for you from the moment I saw you," he whispers, his breath warm on my lips.

He lowers himself onto me, our bodies joining as one. I gasp, arching my back in pleasure as he enters me deeply, the sensation overwhelming me.

I wrap my legs around his waist, pulling him closer, wanting him as deep inside me as possible.

Mike sets a slow, steady rhythm, his eyes locked onto mine. It's both agonizingly slow and excruciatingly fast.

I reach up and grip his shoulders, pulling him closer to me. He groans, his lips finding mine in a deep, passionate kiss.

"Mike, yes."

"You feel so fucking good."

It's clear that he's trying really hard to move slowly and feel everything but I want him to not be gentle.

"Harder, please."

He picks up the pace, his hips moving faster and harder, his body slamming into mine. A moan escapes my lips.

My hips meet his with equal fervor, our bodies forming a perfect rhythm as we move together.

I feel him tighten his grip on my waist, his muscles bulging as he thrusts deeper and harder into me.

He leans forward, his breath hot on my neck as he whispers, "I'm going to come soon."

My heart skips a beat as I reply, "I want to feel you come inside me."

His eyes flash with hunger as he increases the tempo once more, driving into me.

"Oh fuck, Mike, I'm so close," I gasp, my voice a hoarse whisper.

He groans, his hips thrusting harder and faster. "Me too, baby. I'm going to come inside you."

I arch my back, lifting my hips to meet him, wanting to feel every inch of him as he explodes within me.

Suddenly, I feel him stiffen, his eyes widening as he loses control. With a final grunt, he thrusts into me one last time, his body shuddering as he releases deep within me.

I cry out in delight, my own orgasm building rapidly as he continues to move within me. My body trembles uncontrollably, my muscles clenching around him, as I reach my peak.

He collapses on top of me, our bodies still moving together in the aftermath of our passion. We lay there, panting heavily, our hearts racing in sync, our bodies sticky with sweat.

Slowly, he pulls out of me, his eyes never leaving mine. He rolls onto his side, pulling me towards him, wrapping his arms around me.

I rest my head on his chest, listening to the steady beat of his heart. I run my fingers through his sweaty hair, feeling his breath warm on my skin.

Our bodies slowly regain normalcy, our hearts calming down and returning to their regular rhythms.

"That was..." I begin, my voice still slightly hoarse.

"Incredible," Mike finishes for me, his voice soft and content.

"Unbelievable," I correct him, a small smile playing on my lips.

He chuckles, his chest vibrating against my cheek. "I guess we both have our own way of describing it."

Shit, I can't leave.

This has always happened before where I can leave and not get attached.

I can't stay here drawing circles on his skin or snuggling with him.

I clear my throat and stand up to go to the bathroom. I stand at the sink and stare at myself in the mirror.

You cannot get attached, Eve. You can't put his life in danger like this. You cannot be in a relationship. Go out there and tell him that he's just sex and that he can't get attached.

I blow out a breath and walk out of the bathroom and back into my bedroom. Mike is standing up, putting his clothes back on. Once he's fully dressed he walks over, kisses me on the cheek and then leaves without another word.

Is that how it feels when I do this to him?

Damn it, I don't like how this feels.

I fall onto the bed and stare off into space.

I told myself not to get attached and yet here I am, most definitely attached.

***

“I’m glad you enjoy hitting these games with me,” Damon grins as we step into the bustling arena, the familiar scent of sweat and anticipation filling my senses.

The crowd roars around me, a symphony of excitement and energy. My heart races with every beat of the music blaring from the speakers, matching the anticipation building inside me. Tonight is another hockey night, another chance to watch Mike, glide across the ice with effortless grace and power.

“Me too, it’s a nice bonding experience.”

"I can't wait to see Mike in action again.”

I nod in agreement, a smile tugging at the corners of my lips. There's something electrifying about watching Mike play, something that never fails to captivate me. He moves on the ice like a force of nature, his movements fluid and precise, his determination palpable in every stride.

We make our way to our seats, the crowd buzzing around us. The ice glistens under the bright lights, a pristine canvas waiting to be painted with the skill and finesse of the players. As the teams take the ice, the crowd erupts into cheers, each fan eagerly anticipating the showdown that is about to unfold.

The game is intense from the start, with both teams battling fiercely for control of the puck. Damon and I watch with bated breath as the players race up and down the ice, their skates cutting through the frozen surface with ease.

And then, like a bolt of lightning, Mike steals the puck from an opposing player and takes off down the ice. His movements are a blur of speed and agility, his focus unwavering as he dodges defenders with ease. I hold my breath as he approaches the goal, the tension in the arena reaching a fever pitch.

With a flick of his wrist, Mike sends the puck sailing past the goalie and into the net, the crowd exploding into cheers. I can't help but smile as I watch him celebrate with his teammates, his joy infectious as it spreads throughout the arena.

But my moment of elation is short-lived as I see another player bearing down on Mike with alarming speed. My heart lurches in my chest as I watch him brace himself for the impact, his determination shining through despite the imminent danger.

I reach out and grab Damon's arm, my fingers digging into his flesh as I watch in horror. But just as it seems inevitable that Mike will collide with the other player, he somehow manages to sidestep at the last possible moment, narrowly avoiding disaster.

Relief floods through me as I watch him skate away unscathed, his focus never wavering as he continues to battle on the ice. Damon squeezes my hand in reassurance, his eyes never leaving the action unfolding before us.

"What was that about?" he teases.

"He's your best friend," I reply quickly.

Showing Damon that I'm worried about his friend is a little too much for me. I excuse myself to go to the bathroom. I need a second to myself to collect my emotions.

I weave my way through the crowd. Out of the corner of my eye, I notice someone following me. I glance over my shoulder and make eye contact; he doesn't flinch or look away.

Ballsy bastard.

My heart quickens its pace as I resist the urge to break into a sprint. Instead, I continue walking, my steps measured and deliberate. I need to find a way to confront my pursuer without drawing attention to myself and without putting myself in danger.

I wait until we're away from the throngs of people, the hallway empty save for the two of us. With a quick glance around to ensure no one else is watching, I spin around, my body tense and ready for action.

The man following me staggers to a halt, surprise flickering across his face before it's replaced by a cold, calculating expression. But it's too late for him. I'm already moving, my training kicking in as I launch myself at him with all the force I can muster.

My fist connects with his jaw, the impact reverberating through my arm as he stumbles backward, caught off guard by my sudden assault. Before he can recover, I press my advantage, pinning him against the wall with a fierce determination.

"Whoa!" he yells. "I'm a friendly."

"Who sent you?" I demand, my voice low and menacing as I lock eyes with him, searching for any hint of deception.

The man's eyes dart around the hallway, his breath coming in ragged gasps as he struggles beneath my grip. "Mike hired me."

I tighten my hold on him, my anger simmering just beneath the surface.

"Mike?"

"He hired me to protect you," he explains, his voice trembling as he meets my gaze. "He is worried about your safety."

I release my grip on the man, the anger draining from me like water from a sinking ship. "Thank you," I say. "But I don't need protection. Especially from someone who clearly doesn't know what he's doing."

He starts to protest, and I ignore him. I continue to the bathroom.

How dare he hire someone to protect me? As if I'm some weak woman who can't protect herself. He's got a lot of nerve doing it without asking me.

16

Mike

I PULL INTO THE driveway, exhaustion weighing heavily on my shoulders after the intense game tonight. The sound of the engine cutting off is drowned out by the pounding of my heart, the adrenaline still coursing through my veins. But before I can even open the car door, I see her.

Eve.

She's walking across the yard, her expression a mixture of frustration and determination. As I step out of the car, she's already in front of me, pressing a finger against my chest with more force than I anticipated.

"What in the Hell, Mike?" she demands, her voice laced with disbelief. "Why did you hire a bodyguard for me? Do you have any idea how ridiculous and psycho that is?"

I blink, taken aback by her sudden onslaught of anger. "Eve, I—" I start, but she cuts me off before I can explain.

"Don't 'Eve, I' me," she snaps, her eyes blazing with intensity. "I don't need you to play the hero, Mike. I can take care of myself."

I swallow hard, trying to find the right words to convey my concerns without sounding patronizing. "I know you're strong, Eve. But with everything that's been happening lately..."

"I told you that I had it handled."

I run a hand through my hair, feeling the weight of her frustration bearing down on me. "I just want you to be safe, Eve. Is that so wrong?"

She takes a step back, her expression softening slightly. "No, it's not wrong," she admits, her voice quieter now. "But I need you to understand that I want you to stay out of my business."

Her words hit me like a punch to the gut, the realization sinking in that maybe I've overstepped my bounds. "I'm sorry, Eve," I say softly, meeting her gaze with sincerity. "I just... I worry about you. I always have."

"I don't need anyone worrying about me."

"I can't change the way I am."

"I'm not asking you to," she says softly.

I reach out and take her hand in mine. Surprisingly, she lets me. I lace our fingers together and tug her into me.

She looks up at me. I can see the turmoil within her, the battle between wanting to push me away and desperately needing someone to hold onto. I pull her closer, wrapping my arms around her in a tight embrace. For a moment, she stiffens against me, but then slowly relaxes into my embrace.

I kiss the top of her hair.

"I apologize if I overstepped. I don't want anything to happen to you."

"I've survived this long on my own, Hunter. I'll be fine."

"You don't have to survive on your own anymore though. You have me."

"I don't have you," she murmurs into my chest.

I pull away, reach down and tip her chin up so she's looking at me.

"Yes, you do. Whether you want me or not."

She chuckles and rolls her eyes.

"I don't like when you go neanderthal on me. Hiring a security guard for me is dangerous for the security guard. I almost killed him."

"Something tells me you're not exaggerating about that."

"I'm not. I thought he was following me to hurt me."

I blow out a breath and pull her into me again.

"I'll talk to you before I do something like that again. But he's still going to watch after you."

"Mike."

"No. You know he's there. What will it hurt?"

"I don't need anyone to protect me. I can take care of myself."

"It's not for you, it's for my peace of mind."

She pulls away and rolls her eyes.

"You're infuriating."

"As are you."

"This can't happen, Mike. I can't..."

"Stop being so scared of what could go wrong and think about how great it'll be when everything goes right. I'm not going anywhere and we don't have to go fast. Come in with me for some ice cream."

"You have ice cream?"

"Yes, I let myself have a treat after we win a game."

"What kind of ice cream?"

"Chocolate."

"I'm sold," she sighs as she pulls away from me.

I tug her back into me and kiss her hungrily.

She responds with equal fervor, melting into the kiss. The tension that once hung between us dissolves as we lose ourselves in each other. Our embrace is a mixture of passion and comfort, a silent promise of support and understanding. When we finally pull away, a smile tugs at the corners of her lips.

"Okay, ice cream," she says, her eyes sparkling with a newfound lightness. I take her hand and lead her towards the kitchen, grateful for this fleeting moment of peace amidst the chaos of our lives.

"Tell me more about you figuring out that Corey was someone I hired."

"You don't want to hear about that."

"I'll ask him then," I tease.

She rolls her eyes.

"You had a really good game tonight. You're such a graceful skater."

"I hear that a lot."

"Oh, I bet all the girls tell you that."

"Is that a pickup line or something?"

"No," she giggles. "It's the truth."

"I'll take the compliment," I say with a smirk, leading her into the kitchen where I grab two bowls and scoop generous servings of chocolate ice cream for us. As we settle at the table, she takes a small bite and lets out a contented sigh.

"Mmm, this is good," she murmurs.

"Was Damon asleep already?"

"Yeah, why?"

"Just curious."

"Is this where you kill me and stuff me in your freezer?"

"Don't be silly, I have a dungeon downstairs in my basement for that."

"Ohhh, I like being tied up and tortured."

"That can be arranged."

"I do like a dominant man."

"Noted."

"Did I tell you I saw Mrs. White the other day?"

"How did we go from that to Mrs. White, is there something I don't know?"

"No," she giggles. "I have ADHD and my brain jumps around a lot."

"I see her quite often."

"She's still alive and kicking. Out in her garden when she stopped me."

"Yup, she has prize-winning roses."

"I noticed."

"I saw Miss Elton about a month ago."

"She's still around? Man, she was my favorite teacher."

"She asked me about you. Well, she asked if Damon and I were still friends and then asked if I'd seen you recently. She said she was always fond of you and knew you'd do extraordinary things."

"And I can't even tell her what I do."

"How does that feel?"

"It's the life I chose."

"Do you know that on the trip to the beach your parents took us on, I was going to kiss you on the beach?"

"What?"

"Remember the first two nights we were there we hung out on the beach because we couldn't sleep?"

"Yeah."

"I was going to kiss you, but I chickened out. The next day you met that surfer dude, Zeke?"

"Pretty sure that wasn't his real name," she giggles. "I didn't know you were going to kiss me. I thought you were just being nice to me because of Damon or because you were bored."

"I was being nice to you because I liked you."

"You have a funny way of showing it."

"I was young and dumb," I laugh.

"I guess we were both young and dumb," she chuckles, a hint of nostalgia in her eyes. "But hey, look where we are now."

"Yeah, here we are."

"Did Damon know?"

"No. I never told him. He told me when you came home that he always thought you had a crush on me."

"He said that?"

"Yup, is it true?"

She takes a bite of her ice cream and then starts stirring around the last remnants of the frozen treat before she gazes back at me.

"I can neither confirm nor deny."

I laugh and grin back at her."Noted."

"I wish you had kissed me," she says suddenly.

"I can kiss you now."

"Nah, I should get back to the house before Diesel wakes Damon up."

She stands up and I chuckle. I stand up too and pull her to me in a passionate kiss.

She melts into the kiss, her hands finding their way around my neck. Our lips move together in a sweet, tender dance that speaks of unspoken feelings and desires. When we finally pull away, she rests her forehead against mine, her breath warm against my skin.

"I do need to go."

"Okay," I say as I slide my hand to hers and walk her outside.

She waves bye and I watch as she scoots through the gate and quickly into Damon's house.

That was nice. It's nice to see her letting her walls down around me finally.

17

Eve

It's a gorgeous morning and Damon's heated pool is calling my name. There's snow on the ground, but it won't stop me from jumping in. I've been up for the last few hours busting through some work and seeing if I can find Ivan myself.

He's a ghost. I'm one of the best trackers out there and I'm having trouble finding him.

I need to stop thinking about finding Ivan.

Truth be told, I need to stop thinking about Mike's gorgeous face too.

The pool water will help wash the men out of my brain, right?

I change into my bikini and step outside. Diesel immediately runs off to use the bathroom and I dive into the pool.

When I come up from the water and wipe my face Conner is standing on the edge of the pool with a towel staring at me. He's looking around as if he's on edge.

He's acting cagey as if he's on meth or something.

"What the fuck are you doing over here?"

"You need to get out of the pool."

"Diesel?" I call out.

I turn to look and see him growling and snapping at something on the other side of the fence. He's ready to rip someone's face off.

My stomach tightens as I glance back at Conner. He's on edge, his eyes trained right where Diesel is at.

"What's happening?"

"Get out of the pool now."

His eyes flit to the other end of the pool where I watch a cottonmouth snake slip into the water.

What the fuck? It should be dormant somewhere because of the cold. What's happening?

"Is that a...?"

"Get out of the water, now," he hisses.

Luckily, I had swam toward the steps anyway. I quickly pull myself out of the water. Diesel is still trying to get at something while Conner takes the pool net and scoops the snake up. He drops the net down on the ground where it's trapped and then proceeds to use a nearby shovel to chop it's head off in one fell swoop.

"What the fuck is happening?"

"I just saved your life," Conner says cockily as he winks at me.

"Did you do that?"

"If I did it, would I have come over to tell you and risk your dog eating my balls?"

"You don't seem too bright."

"I was out for a morning jog and saw someone messing around back here."

"Who was it? What did they look like?"

"I didn't get a good look," he shrugs.

"Diesel, sitz!" I call.

He gives one last growl and bolts for me. Conner walks back to his yard without another word, pool net in hand.

Thank God he's disposing that thing for me. I hate snakes.

"Hey!"

He doesn't reply, just continues walking. I scurry inside and put on some clothes. I strap on my weapons before I hurry back outside to walk the perimeter.

Around the spot where Diesel was growling it's obvious that the freshly fallen snow has been disturbed, but I can't see any shoe prints.

Ivan?

How the Hell did Conner know something was wrong?

I go back inside and try to tap into my brother's security cameras but I can't see anyone but Conner on them.

Did he do this just to throw me off track? To gain my trust because he's one of Ivan's men?

Diesel starts whining and when I look up I see that Piper is outside. I go out the back door again and walk over to Mike's house. He's not outside so I walk in the back door.

He's standing in the kitchen already dressed in a tee shirt and sweat pants.

Damn the luck.

"Hey," I greet him.

"Holy shit, Eve," he jumps as he whips around.

I giggle, realizing that this giant man is a little jumpy.

"Sorry, didn't mean to scare you."

"You're like a ninja. How do you move that quietly?"

"Practice," I shrug. "Hey, do you have security cameras?"

"Yeah, why?"

"Any chance I can take a look at the footage."

"Yeah, why?" he repeats.

"Don't worry your pretty little head about it," I answer nonchalantly. "Where's the feed?"

"Don't worry your pretty little head about it," he mimics as he crosses his arms in front of his expansive chest and then leans back against the granite counter.

I narrow my eyes and blow out a breath.

"I went out to swim earlier and Diesel was growling and barking at something. I want to see if your cameras picked something up."

"Do you think someone was out there?"

"Yes."

He picks his phone up and starts swiping through it before he hands it to me. The screen is already pulled up on the feed. I hit the three dots at the top right of the video and send it to myself. I watch it quickly though, noting that there's a tall man in all black that briefly comes into view.

Not enough for me to know who it is.

"Thanks."

I turn on my heel and start to walk back out the way I came.

"Wait! Do you want some coffee?"

I stop and slowly turn back around.

"I've got coffee brewing next door."

"Then I'll come next door and drink some coffee with you."

"Damon is home."

"We have coffee in the morning all the time. He's probably up by now making breakfast for me."

"You two have a very strange dynamic. Are you sure you're not dating?"

"What if we are?" he teases.

"Well, you're a piece of shit if you're cheating on my brother with his sister," I shrug before I walk back out of his house.

He laughs as he follows me. I glance back and realize he's barefoot walking across the snow and it's not even phasing him.

He's tougher than I thought.

"Don't you need shoes?"

"No, I haven't grounded yet this morning."

"Grounded?"

"Walk barefoot outside. It rids your body of toxins and energizes you. I do it every morning."

"Never had you pinned as a hippie."

"There's a lot you don't know about me," he laughs.

I shake my head as he follows me inside the house. Sure enough, Damon is up making breakfast.

"What's this about?"

"I needed to check his security footage. Yours isn't working."

"I moved that nest myself yesterday."

"Well, something is blocking it again," I shrug.

Damon shakes his head. "Why did you need to check his cameras?"

"Diesel was going crazy this morning and I needed to see if it was something to be worried about."

"It was probably a squirrel," Mike interjects.

"Diesel doesn't pay attention to squirrels or anything else. He was trying to rip someone's face off."

"Did you see anyone?"

I shake my head so that I don't verbalize the lie. It's better that way.

"A package came for you," Damon interrupts my thoughts.

I narrow my eyes. I'm not expecting anything.

I go into the living room and inspect the box without touching it. It's a very large, very heavy box and there's nothing to describe what's inside. I walk into my room, grab a pair of latex gloves that I have stashed and walk back out with a lighter.

"What are you doing?"

I pick up the package and walk out the front door and all the way down to the foot of my brother's driveway. I light the package on fire and walk away.

"What are you doing?" Mike asks. "Why would you set a package on fire?"

"I didn't order it, nothing good is inside."

I walk back in the house and shut the door, going directly back into the kitchen.

"Well this is an exciting morning," Damon laughs.

"Are you coming to my game tonight?" Mike asks.

"Hadn't planned on it. Especially not going to leave the house with this morning's events."

"Eve, you're more at risk by staying in this house than you are in an ice rink with fifty thousand people. Security is all over that place, it's too public for someone to attack," Damon tells me. "Go to the game."

I blow out a breath. He's right, I know he is. Ivan won't attack in such a public place.

"What time are we leaving for this game?"

"In a few hours."

"I'll be ready. Will Kelsey be there?"

"I don't know," he says as he quickly looks away.

"Yes, you do."

"Yes, she'll be there."

"You should ask her out. I really like her."

"I need to get a workout in."

"Go do that," I giggle as he disappears into the basement.

"What was in the box?" Mike asks quietly.

"I don't know."

"Are you going to go look?"

"Nope."

He shakes his head and exhales a sigh. I can tell that he wants to go look out the front window and see what was in the box, but he's not going to because I'm not.

He's predictable. I kind of like that.

"I like it when you come to my games. I like looking up into the stands and seeing you there."

"Yeah?" I smile.

He stands up and walks over to me. He pulls me into his arms.

“Yeah.”

He leans down and kisses me hungrily. When he pulls away he gazes into my eyes.

“I like when you do that.”

“There will be more of that after my game tonight. Wait up for me?”

I nod and he walks out the back door and back over to his house.

Damn it, I’ve got it bad.

I go toward the front door, open it and start outside to see what the contents of the box were.

It’s gone.

The box is completely gone. There’s no trace of charred remnants or anything. It’s as if it was never there.

***

As Damon and I drive towards Mike's game, the anticipation in the air is palpable. I’m excited to get to watch Mike play again.

The rhythmic hum of the car engine fills the silence between us, but my mind is buzzing with thoughts, and I can tell Damon's lost in his own world too.

I glance over at him, his eyes focused on the road ahead, a furrow of concentration etched on his brow.

"Hey, weird question. How long has Conner lived next door?”

“He moved in not long after I did. Maybe a week or so. He said that it was his grandmother’s house, and she gave it to him in her will. He’s a nice guy, just a little weird sometimes. Why?”

“I don’t know. Just wondered.”

Conner lived in the house next-door before I developed the security software. It would be weird to think that Ivan planted him there or anyone else that was out to get me. Maybe it’s a coincidence.

The atmosphere at Mike's hockey game is electric, buzzing with excitement and anticipation. The stands are packed with cheering fans, their voices blending together in a cacophony of excitement. The smell of popcorn and hotdogs wafts through the air, adding to the sense of anticipation that hangs heavy in the arena.

As Damon and I find our seats, I feel a surge of excitement. There's something exhilarating about being surrounded by the energy of a live sports event, the sense of camaraderie and shared passion palpable in the air.

The announcer's voice echoes through the arena, signaling the start of the game. I watch with bated breath as the players take to the ice, their skates cutting through the ice with precision and grace. And then, in a flurry of movement, the puck drops, signaling the beginning of the match.

My heart pounds in my chest as I watch the action unfold before me, the players darting across the ice with lightning speed. And then, in a moment that seems to happen in the blink of an eye, Mike gains possession of the puck, his movements fluid and confident.

I hold my breath as he maneuvers through the opposing team's defense, his focus unwavering as he zeroes in on the goal. And then, with a swift flick of his wrist, he sends the puck sailing past the goalie and into the net, the crowd erupting into cheers as the stadium lights up with excitement.

Pride fills me as I watch Mike celebrate his goal, his helmet lifted high as he points to me in the stands. My stomach flips at the sudden attention, the idea of my face being broadcast on the jumbotron making me feel both exhilarated and unnerved.

This is absolutely not what I need right now.

Before I can dwell on it too long, Kelsey arrives, slipping into the seat beside me with a bright smile. "Hey, sorry I'm late," she says, her voice breathless with excitement.

I smile back, the tension in my chest easing at her presence. "No worries, you didn't miss much."

As the game continues, Kelsey leans in, her voice low as she tells me about her latest client—a baseball player with a high-profile endorsement deal. I can sense Damon listening intently, a hint of concern flickering in his eyes.

"And how's that going?" I ask, trying to keep the conversation light.

Kelsey shrugs, a thoughtful expression crossing her face. "It's been a bit hectic, to be honest. But it's a great opportunity, so I can't complain."

"Hey, Kelsey, I was thinking... maybe we could grab dinner after the game? Catch up a bit?"

I glance at my brother, surprised by the sudden invitation.

"I can't stay out too late, I have an early meeting tomorrow."

He nods, a hint of disappointment flickering in his eyes. "Of course, I understand. How about tomorrow then? I'll take you out to dinner, my treat."

I can't help but suppress a laugh at his eagerness, the sound bubbling up from deep within me.

"Sure, Damon. I'll let you know," Kelsey says.

His flustered expression only serves to make me laugh harder, and I can't help but feel a sense of amusement at his expense. As the game continues, I find myself lost in the excitement of the moment, the thrill of the game washing over me like a tidal wave. And as Mike scores yet another goal, the roar of the crowd echoing in my ears, I'm glad that my brother roped me into coming to these games with him.

“Hey, I'm going to run to the bathroom,” I tell Damon.

“Okay.”

I make my way up the steps and to the nearest bathroom. I'm lost in my thoughts, smiling at how different my life has become since I returned to Legacy.

I like this life. Things are going so great.

The bathroom is mostly empty and I go directly into a stall. I'm sitting there doing my business when all of a sudden the bathroom stall door shakes violently, rattling against its flimsy hinges. My heart pounds, echoing in the small space of the restroom.

What now?

It's clearly locked.

"Someone is in here," I call out.

They continue trying to rip the door off its hinges.

"Listen, lady, it's occupied!"

There's a deep, throaty chuckle on the other end. I look down and see a pair of men's shoes on the other side of the partition.

Fuck.

Panic rises within me, quickening my breaths as I press my back against the cold tile wall. I climb up on the toilet seat and prepare for an attack.

The door jolts with such force that the lock snaps, rendering it useless. Ivan's menacing silhouette appears before me. His eyes gleam with a mixture of malice and amusement, sending a chill down my spine.

Ivan's laughter echoes in the cramped space, mocking and cruel. "You think you can hide from me, Eve? You think you can escape? The snake didn't do it's job, but I will."

Fear twists my gut, but I refuse to let it paralyze me. With a primal scream, I launch myself at Ivan, catching him off guard. We crash to the ground in a tangle of limbs, the impact knocking the breath from my lungs.

For a brief moment, I feel a surge of adrenaline coursing through me as I rain blows upon Ivan's stunned form. But he's stronger, more experienced in combat. With a swift motion, he reaches for something—a heavy object discarded on the tile floor.

Pain explodes across my skull as the object connects with devastating force, stars dancing before my eyes. Darkness encroaches on the edges of my vision, swallowing me whole as everything fades to black.

18

Mike

THE ROAR OF THE crowd still echoes in my ears as I navigate the maze of corridors beneath the arena. Adrenaline is still lingering, a reminder of the game we just played. It's been a tough season, but tonight, we emerged victorious once again. As I make my way towards the press area, I can't shake the sense of satisfaction that washes over me.

A reporter awaits me, her pen poised over a notepad, ready to capture every word. I offer her a weary smile, the exhaustion of the game evident in the lines etched across my face.

"Mike, congratulations on the win tonight," she begins, her voice laced with genuine admiration. "What do you attribute the team's success to, especially considering the recent winning streak you've been on?"

I take a moment to collect my thoughts, the weight of her question sinking in. The truth is, it's been a team effort, with every player giving their all on the ice night after night. But there's something more, something intangible that's propelled us forward.

"It's been a combination of hard work, dedication, and a never-say-die attitude," I reply, my voice steady despite the fatigue that threatens to pull me under. "But more than that, it's the bond we share as a team. We're more than just players; we're brothers. And that fuels us, driving us to push past our limits and achieve greatness."

The reporter nods, scribbling furiously as she absorbs my words. But before she can ask another question, the familiar buzz of my phone interrupts the silence. When I don't answer the caller continues incessantly. I shoot her an apologetic look before fishing it out of my pocket, glancing at the caller ID.

I look around and realize Damon isn't in the room as he normally is. I can see him standing just outside the double doors of the press room talking to police.

Police?

"Sorry, just a moment," I murmur, thumbing the answer button before lifting the phone to my ear. "Hello?"

"Eve's been abducted," Corey, the security guard I'd hired, says gruffly.

"What?"

"She made me, and then went into the bathroom and some guy grabbed her in there. He was helping her out in a wheelchair. I went after them and was attacked."

"What?"

"Eve has been kidnapped."

I grip the phone tightly, I'm surprised it doesn't shatter. I look around the room, not sure if I'm hearing him correctly or not.

Eve is missing. She's been kidnapped.

I specifically hired Corey so this didn't happen and it did.

"How could you let this happen?"

"I was attacked by two men when I went after her. They came from behind. I didn't have a chance to defend myself."

I slam the phone off and look around.

"Is everything okay?" the reporter asks.

I shake my head and stand up. I stomp over to Damon.

"What happened?"

"Eve is missing. Corey saw her in a wheelchair being pushed out by some man, she looked unconscious."

My hands clench and unclench at my sides as I pace the linoleum floor, each step a staccato rhythm of pent-up frustration. Damon is speaking calmly to the officers, giving them a very brief rundown on Eve's job and what could possibly have happened. He doesn't know much though, so he can't say much.

How can he be so calm right now?

Why isn't he demanding they rush to the parking lot to find the kidnapper now?

"Why aren't we out in the parking lot?" I snap.

"Security said a van pulled up and they loaded the woman into it. They didn't think anything of it."

"No one thought it was weird that the woman was unconscious."

"They didn't look that hard."

How can he be so composed when everything is falling apart around us?

My jaw tightens as I shoot him a glare, the intensity of my gaze a silent demand for answers.

But Damon ignores me, his focus unwavering as he continues to speak to the officers. Anger simmers beneath the surface, a volatile mix of emotions threatening to boil over at any moment. I want to scream, to lash out at anyone and everyone who stands in my way.

I start pacing, waiting for the cops to get enough information and leave to go find Eve. She could be hurt. She could be dead.

I rush to the nearest bathroom and vomit. The thought of her being murdered, of never seeing her again is too much.

What if she is dead? I never told her how I feel about her.

How do I feel about her?

Once I'm done retching in the toilet I go back out to where Damon is standing alone.

"Are they trying to find her? We need to go look for her."

"Mike, calm down," he says, his voice a soothing balm against the storm raging within me. "We just need to cooperate with the investigation. Let the police do their job."

I scoff, a bitter laugh bubbling up from the depths of my anger. "Their job? Their job is to keep us safe and look where that's gotten us! Eve is out there somewhere, and they're asking questions instead of looking for her. The security in this place is a fucking joke."

"We'll find her, Mike. But losing our heads won't help anyone. Let's just focus on what we can control."

With a frustrated growl, I turn on my heel and storm into the locker room. I change out of my clothes and hurry to the car. Damon is parked next to me.

"I'm going home, you should too. The officers said if she gets free the first place she'll run is home."

"Do you believe that?"

"No. I don't think she'll bring that to me. I may never know if she's dead or alive."

"What else can we do?"

"I don't know. There are some old Marine friends Eve and I share, I'll reach out to them. I think we should go back to Legacy and then we'll figure it out from there."

I nod and get into my car. I pull out of the rink parking lot, my mind is not on driving, that's for certain.

The drive home is a blur of twisted roads and tangled thoughts, each mile stretching out before me like an eternity. Irrational fears claw at the edges of my mind, whispering dark secrets and half-formed truths.

I reach out to the security contacts again. Of the three I reached out to, two returned my calls. Both offered to do some research and one pulled out, telling me that the names I had given him were people he didn't feel comfortable looking into.

The other contact, Sam, was familiar with the names and told me he would find out what he could. At this point I was just guessing.

I call Sam's number.

"Hey Mike, how goes it?" he asks in greeting.

"Eve has been kidnapped."

"Shit," he breathes. "Tell me everything you know."

I relay the story from Corey and what Damon had told the police.

"I don't know how they could have abducted her and walked through the entire rink without someone questioning them."

"They're good at what they do."

"Apparently, we need better security at the rink."

"I haven't been able to track Ivan to Legacy, he must be using fake identification and cards. He's hiding in plain sight."

I can hear him tapping away on a keyboard in the background.

"Eve mentioned on the phone that there could be more than one person tracking her."

"I'm aware. I put out feelers on the dark web. Any of the other entities looking for her aren't close to tracking her back to Legacy. The only one is Ivan."

"What does she do that you had to track this on the dark web? Should I be concerned?"

"She's not doing anything illegal," he chuckles in response. "She's just a very intelligent woman who created a security program for our military that's impenetrable. Ivan, the Tambov Gang, and any other despicable human being tracking her is doing it for their own financial or personal gain."

"They want to break into our military databases?"

"Yes and..."

"And what?"

“And sell secrets on the black market to other countries who are willing to pay top dollar for information like that.”

“Shit.”

“Yeah, from what I learned she designed it so that she’s the only one who can access the mainframe of it. The Tambov Gang needs her password as well as fingerprint, eye scan, and her voice to recite a verbal passphrase to get into the system. She covered all the bases.”

“Who is the Tambov Gang?”

“The Tambovskaya Bratva. Ivan is the head of it. Russian Mafia.”

“Russian Mafia? That’s a thing?”

“It is,” he chuckles. “It’s a very real thing. According to my research, they attacked her at her home not long ago and she went on the run.”

"Is that why she came back to Legacy?”

“Yes, all of her records show that she’s an only child who spent her life growing up in the foster system.”

“That’s not true.”

“Mike,” he laughs. “I’m aware. She goes by a different last name as well. It’s how she hides her reality from people like Ivan and the Tambov Gang, Vlad and the Kazar Gang, and others. She’s trying to protect her brother and anyone else close to her.”

“That sounds like her.”

“Her dossier is incredible. She’s a high-tech genius. Did you know that?”

“Yes,” I chuckle. “She’s always been that way, but she plays it down.”

“For good reason, I’m certain. You’d look at her and never realize she’s a nerd, that’s for sure.”

“She’s not a nerd.”

“No, you’re right. She’s a badass. She’s a black belt in Judo and Jiu Jitsu. Perfect Marksmanship among a dozen other awards in combat.”

“I didn’t know that. Makes sense why she always tells me she can take care of herself.”

"She certainly can. Okay, I may have some leads. I'll be in touch."

Before I can say anything else Sam has already hung up the phone.

Shit, I need to know that she's going to be okay.

What if Eve is gone forever?

What if we never find her?

As I finally pull into Legacy, my hands tremble on the steering wheel, the weight of uncertainty bearing down on me. I park in Damon's driveway without even realizing it, the familiar surroundings offering little comfort in the face of such overwhelming despair.

We need to get her back.

I step out of the car and slam the door shut, just as Damon pulls in. We both walk up to his house. He unlocks the door and lets me inside. Diesel doesn't make a sound.

That's odd.

My eyes focus on the dark room just as Damon flips on a light and unarms the security system.

A woman is sitting in the recliner in the living room. She is a vision in black, her jet-black hair cascading down her shoulders in waves of shadow. Her piercing light blue eyes seem to bore into my very soul as she looks us up and down with a slow, deliberate gaze.

Damon's voice breaks the silence, his tone laced with suspicion. "Who the hell are you?"

The woman's lips curl into a sardonic smile, a hint of amusement dancing in her eyes. "Names aren't important," she replies, her voice smooth as silk. "But let's just say I'm a friend of Eve's."

A chill runs down my spine at her words, a sense of unease settling over me like a heavy fog. Her accent feels off, as though she's forcing a southern drawl.

How does she know Eve?

And why does she seem so at ease in Damon's house?

Damon's brow furrows in confusion. "If you're a friend of Eve's, then why haven't I ever seen you before?"

The woman's smile widens, a knowing glint in her eyes. "Your security system is shit. Eve must be slacking that she didn't get that upgraded immediately."

"Eve isn't slacking," I snap.

Her cold eyes flit to mine before she laughs to herself.

"She does have a type," she smiles.

What does that mean?

"Who are you?"

"I told you that already. Let's not waste time on trivial things."

I exchange a wary glance with Damon.

Could this woman be the key to finding Eve? Or is she merely another player in this twisted game of deceit and betrayal?

She reminds me of Eve. They're a lot alike. The way they speak, the confidence.

Before I can voice my thoughts, the woman rises from her seat, Diesel at her feet as if he knows her well. She moves with a grace and poise that is almost otherworldly, her every movement a testament to her power and presence.

"We don't have much time," she says, her voice low and urgent. "But if you want to find Eve, you'll have to trust me."

Trust her?

"We don't even know who you are or why you're here," I snap.

Damon puts his hand out to me before he looks back at the woman.

"Hasło?"

The woman's eyes narrow slightly at Damon's words, a flicker of recognition crossing her features as he speaks in a language I don't recognize. She replies in the same language, her words fluid and confident, betraying a depth of knowledge that sends a shiver down my spine.

"Jestem twoją cienią."

"What was that? What did you say? What did she say?"

"Eve told me to ask in Polish for a passphrase if anyone ever came to me claiming to be her friend. If they reply with 'I am your shadow' then they can be trusted."

"Did she?"

Damon nods.

"But how do we know that she's not an enemy who knows the code."

The woman laughs and rolls her eyes.

"No one would know that phrase but a friend."

"My name is Natalia," she says, her tone as cold and unforgiving as the winter wind. "Eve and I served together. She's saved my life more times than I can count. And I was sent to protect her. But I've been on the run myself to get here."

Natalia? Nat? Is this who Eve was expecting?

That's a Russian name, right?

"What does that mean?" I demand, my voice rising with a note of desperation. "What are we dealing with here?"

But Natalia merely raises an eyebrow in response, her lips pressed into a thin line of frustration. "It means you're in over your heads," she says bluntly, her words a stark reminder of the dangers that lurk in the shadows.

Damon's brow furrows in concern. "What can we do?"

Her gaze pierces through us like a dagger, her words dripping with scorn. "Nothing," she says, her voice a whispered threat. "You sit back and do nothing. Because the people you're dealing with are deadly, and they won't hesitate to eliminate anyone who gets in their way."

"I'm not going to sit back and do nothing," Damon hisses. "She's my sister."

She shakes her head and laughs. "Let me do the dirty work, honey. It's what I'm trained for. I will tie you up if I have to."

"I served in the Corps too, I can help."

"You're adorable, Damon."

“How do you know my name?”

“I know everything about both of you,” she laughs. Her eyes flit to me. “You’re the cute neighbor who pretended to be her fiancé.”

“How do you know about that?”

“I know everything,” she repeats. “Give me the description of the man that kidnapped Eve.”

"According to some witnesses he was tall, with a menacing presence," Damon begins, his words measured as he recounts the chilling encounter. "His eyes were cold, like ice, and his voice sent shivers down their spine. There was a look of pure malice in his gaze. He was bald with ice blue eyes and a scar on his cheek.”

The woman's face pales, her features drawn tight. For a moment, there's a flicker of recognition in her eyes before she nods, a silent acknowledgment of the danger that lurks in the shadows.

"Ivan," she murmurs, her voice barely above a whisper. "It’s him."

"Ivan?" I repeat, my heart sinking at the mention of the name. "Who is he?"

The woman's lips curl into a grim smile, a hint of bitterness tingeing her words. "Ivan is a very bad man, CIA’s most wanted" she replies, her voice heavy with disdain. "And the fact that he abducted Eve himself isn't a good sign."

“What does that mean?”

“Ivan doesn’t do the dirty work. He’s the one who calls the shots. If he’s showing up in person it means he’s got personal beef with her.”

“Why does CIA’s most wanted have beef with Eve?”

“She holds the keys to the world for him and she won’t give it up.”

Why is this woman talking in riddles?

"We can't just sit back and do nothing," I insist, my voice firm despite the tremor of uncertainty that lingers beneath the surface. "We have to find Eve before it's too late."

"I understand your concern," she says, her tone gentle yet resolute. "But trust me when I say that Ivan is not someone to be trifled with. We need to proceed with caution if we have any hope of rescuing Eve."

I exchange a wary glance with Damon.

"Tell us what we need to do," I say, my voice steady despite the storm raging within me. "We'll do whatever it takes to bring Eve home."

"I already told you. I will handle it. My people are already in place. We'll bring Eve home safely."

How could we really trust this woman? What if she was sent to throw us off track?

"How do we know that though?" I ask.

She walks over to me with a sly smile on her face. She touches my cheek gently.

"You have to trust me. Eve doesn't allow anyone in her life that she doesn't trust completely. You have to have faith in her judgment."

"But Eve isn't the one telling us to trust you. Some woman we don't know is saying it."

"Both of you need to sit here and look pretty, nothing else."

She removes her hand and then sashays out of the house.

"How will we know if Eve is okay?"

"I left my card on the table. I'll be in touch," she calls over her shoulder.

She disappears into the night as though the second she stepped on the porch she became invisible.

"Did that just happen?" I ask as I follow her outside and realize she's nowhere to be found.

I turn around and look at Damon with wide eyes. He's shaking his head, but already dialing someone on the phone.

"I've never heard Eve mention that name."

"I have. She asked where Nat was when she was talking to whoever the other morning. I believe she knows her. Who are you calling?"

"My old commanding officer, who Eve served under a few years after me. He may know if Natalie is legit."

I nod as the man answers Damon's call. He puts him on speaker phone.

"Hey Cap."

"Carlisle, how's it going?"

"Not great, Eve was kidnapped today."

"Shit, what do you need from me?"

"Do you know a woman named Natalie, Natalia something? She showed up today telling us to stand down and that she and Eve served together."

"Natalia Prizrak?" he gasps.

"Maybe, she was forcing a southern accent. I caught flecks of a Russian or Polish."

"Her last name means ghost in Russian. She lives up to it."

"What do you mean by that?"

"It means that she served under me for about six months. She and Eve went on a mission and Natalia didn't return. She vanished into thin air. She was listed MIA, Missing in Action. Eve was destroyed because they were like sisters, about six months later I received a letter from someone stating that Natalia was alive and safe but that I needed to make it seem as though she wasn't. A week later, Eve was supposed to reenlist and changed her mind at the last second saying she got a better offer."

"The Coalition?"

"I believe so. It's more like an Urban Myth around here because I never hear from anyone who's supposedly been enlisted to them after it happens."

"Was Natalia set to reenlist too?"

"Yes."

"Are you certain she's in the Coalition with Eve?"

"I'm not certain of anything. I can reach out to some contacts and see though. Do you think that Natalia is responsible for Eve's kidnapping?"

"I don't know what to think," Damon answers with a sigh. "My gut tells me to listen to this woman, that she's trustworthy."

"Then go with that. Like I said, Eve and Natalia were like sisters when they served under me. They were forces to be reckoned with as well. Two intelligent, strong, confident women who didn't take shit from anyone. They were in my office a lot for beating the shit out of soldiers who didn't listen to the word no."

"Can you get some more information on Natalia or the Coalition?"

"I'll do my best. I'll be in touch."

"Thanks, Cap."

They hang up the phone and Damon looks back at me.

"Will Corey know anything about this Coalition?" I ask.

Damon shrugs. "I don't know. Possibly. For most of us, it was something we heard about but no one ever really believed that it existed."

"The guy I reached out to, Sam, he told me that Eve created some security system for the military and that's why these people are after her. He said it's the Russian Mafia, which makes me question if this Natalia woman is legit."

"Russian Mafia? Jesus."

"Yeah, that would explain what she said about us being in over our heads."

"Cap will get me the information we need. Your contact and Corey will be helpful too. I'm not going to sit back and trust this woman wholeheartedly with my sister's life. We're going to be doing whatever we can here, under the radar."

I grab the card Natalia left on the table and hold it up for Damon to see. He nods.

"I'll call Sam in the morning to see if he has any leads that we can follow."

"We can set up a command center at your house. I don't want it here in case Natalia shows back up."

"Did you go in Eve's room yet?"

"No, but if there was anything in there that woman would have already grabbed it, don't you think?"

"Yeah, but it doesn't hurt for us to look too."

The two of us walk into her room. If Natalia had already come in here, she left no trace of it.

Eve's clothes were spread out on her bed as if she were deciding what to wear to the game tonight. She had unpacked her suitcase and everything was neatly organized and separated in the closet and dresser drawers. Nothing looks out of place.

Damon drops to the ground and climbs under the bed.

"What are you doing?"

"Looking for hiding spots."

"Hiding spots?"

"Yes. Eve has always done that. She used to hide her diary from me. I found it once and from that moment on I never found it again."

"What makes you think you'll find a hiding spot now then?"

"I've gotten better at searching," he shrugs with a laugh.

Ten minutes of being under the bed he finally makes a noise.

"Did you find something?"

"Yup," he says as he shimmies out from under the bed. "She has a hidey hole under there."

He comes out holding a black bag. When he opens it, it's full of burner cell phones.

"Why would she need that many phones?"

"So she can't be traced."

"Do you think there's more than one hiding spot?"

"I'd be willing to bet there is."

Damon looks around the room and then walks to her dresser and starts feeling around in all the drawers. I walk to the closet and start doing the same thing.

"Holy shit," I breathe twenty minutes later when I find another hiding spot filled with cash.

Damon's eyes are wide as he glances at the money quickly.

"There's at least a hundred grand there. But maybe that's so there's not a credit card trail. I found credit cards with other people's names on them."

"Fraud?"

"No, other identities—I assume. My sister wouldn't be committing fraud or stealing."

I blow out a breath and nod. I hope he's right. The more we find, the more I realize that I don't know Eve Carlisle at all.

"Where the Hell did Kelsey go? She was sitting with you guys, right?"

"Shit. She left to talk to someone and then Corey came down to grab me and tell me someone took Eve. I didn't even tell her. I'll do that now."

"I'm sure she knows by now."

He nods and shakes his head. "I'm still going to tell her. I'm going crazy."

"Same here," I sigh.

19

Eve

My eyes flutter open to darkness, the heavy weight of sleep gradually lifting from my mind. As consciousness returns, I become aware of the stale, musty air that surrounds me, the cold touch of metal against my skin. Panic surges through me as I realize I'm bound to a chair, my limbs restrained by thick ropes that cut into my flesh.

My head is throbbing.

I strain against my bonds, the ropes biting into my wrists with each futile struggle. The room is dimly lit by flickering fluorescent lights, casting eerie shadows across the damp walls of what appears to be an old subway tunnel. A desk sits against one wall, a keyboard and two monitors sit on the desk and on the wall above it are more computer monitors.

My heart pounds in my chest as I take in my surroundings, a sense of dread settling over me like a shroud. I'm trapped, alone in the belly of this underground labyrinth with no hope of escape. And then, like a specter emerging from the shadows, he appears.

Ivan.

His presence fills the room like a suffocating fog, his eyes cold and calculating as they bore into mine. I recoil at the sight of him, the memory of his touch sending shivers down my spine. He approaches me with slow, deliberate steps, a smirk playing at the corners of his lips.

"You should have listened to me, Eve," he sneers, his voice dripping with malice. "You shouldn't have played so hard to get."

Anger surges within me, a wildfire burning bright against the darkness of my fear. "Go to hell," I spit, defiance lacing every word.

His expression darkens, a cruel smile twisting his features as he raises his hand in a swift, brutal motion. His palm connects with my cheek with a sharp crack, sending pain radiating through my skull.

I grit my teeth against the pain, refusing to give him the satisfaction of seeing me falter. But before I can summon the strength to respond, Ivan calls out to someone nearby, his voice echoing through the tunnel.

"Bring her over here," he commands, his tone laced with menace.

A pair of guards appear at his side, their faces obscured by shadows as they drag me across the room with rough, unyielding hands. I struggle against their grip, but it's futile. I'm at their mercy, a pawn in Ivan's twisted game of power and control.

Once we reach the desk, Ivan gestures to the computers with a mocking smile. "Log in," he orders, his voice low and dangerous. "And do what needs to be done with your precious prototype."

I shake my head defiantly, refusing to comply with his demands. "I'll never help you," I vow, my voice trembling with defiance.

His smile fades, replaced by a look of cold fury. "You will do as I say," he snarls, his eyes ablaze with rage. "Or you'll regret it."

I can't give in. I can't let him use me to further his twisted agenda. No matter what he does to me, no matter how much he tries to break me, I will never betray everything I believe in.

Ivan's cold command hangs in the air like a curse, sending a chill down my spine as he gestures to the guards beside him. With a mocking smile, he turns and walks away, leaving me alone with the two burly men who stand before me like silent sentinels of pain.

Fear fills me as they approach, their expressions masked by shadows as they circle me like hungry predators. I steel myself against the impending onslaught, my heart pounding in my chest like a drumbeat of defiance.

Without a word, one of the guards lunges forward, his massive hand wrapping around my throat with a vice-like grip. I gasp for breath as he squeezes, cutting off my air supply with ruthless efficiency. Panic claws at the edges of my mind as I struggle against his hold, fighting to draw in even the smallest breath.

But the guard shows no mercy, his fingers digging into my flesh with bruising force. Stars dance before my eyes as darkness encroaches on the edges of my vision, threatening to swallow me whole.

I muster every ounce of strength within me, summoning the courage to defy my captors even as they seek to break me. With a defiant roar, I kick out with all the force I can gather, striking the guard square in the chest.

He staggers back with a grunt of surprise, his grip loosening just enough for me to draw in a ragged breath. But before I can capitalize on the opening, the second guard moves in with terrifying speed.

His fist connects with my jaw with bone-crushing force, sending stars exploding across my vision as pain blossoms like wildfire in my skull. I taste blood on my lips as I struggle to remain conscious, fighting against the darkness that threatens to consume me.

"Big men hitting a woman when she's tied up, aren't ya?" I hiss. "Untie me and let's see how strong you are then."

"Mouthy bitch, someone needs to put you in your place."

"It sure as Hell won't be a pussy like you," I laugh wickedly.

He slaps me across the face, I barely register the pain.

"This is going to be fun," the other one says.

The guards continue their relentless assault, each blow driving me closer to the brink of oblivion. But with every strike, I summon the strength to endure, refusing to let them break me.

What feels like hours pass in a blur of agony and torment, the pain a constant companion as I cling to consciousness by the barest thread.

And then, just when I feel as though I can endure no more, the guards finally relent, leaving me battered and broken but still defiant. I hang limply in my restraints, gasping for breath as I struggle to make sense of the nightmare that surrounds me.

“Have you changed your mind yet?” Ivan asks as he comes back into the room.

“No,” I snap as I spit blood in his face.

“Why would you be so true to a country that doesn’t even value you or know you exist? They pay you scraps and you will die for it? Learn your worth.”

“I’m not selling my soul to a devil like you.”

“You already have,” he laughs. “Do the right thing and log in to the network for me. I have the scans I need, I just need you to log in. Give me what I want and this will all be over.”

"I won't do it," I hiss, my voice a defiant whisper in the darkness. "You can torture me all you want, but I'll never betray everything I believe in."

His laughter echoes through the room like a cruel taunt, the sound sending shivers down my spine. "We'll see about that, my love," he sneers, his voice dripping with malice.

With a swift motion, he reaches for a canvas bag nearby, its rough fabric coarse against my skin as he pulls it over my head. Panic surges within me as darkness descends, cutting me off from the world outside. I struggle against my restraints, fighting to draw in even the smallest breath as the bag tightens around my face.

And then, without warning, the water comes—a torrent of liquid that floods my senses with its icy touch. I gasp for breath as it fills my lungs, choking me with its suffocating embrace. Panic claws at the edges of my mind as I struggle against the relentless onslaught, fighting to keep my head away from the water.

But even as the darkness threatens to consume me, I refuse to surrender. I grit my teeth against the pain and the fear, mustering every ounce of strength within me to endure. I will not give Ivan the satisfaction of seeing me break. I will not beg for mercy.

Minutes stretch into hours as the water continues to pour, each moment an eternity of agony and torment. But I refuse to give him the satisfaction. I've been trained for this torture, Ivan isn't even scratching the surface of what I can endure. I may be battered and broken, but I am still standing—a testament to the strength that lies within me.

"You're a stubborn bitch, aren't you?" he snarls, his voice laced with frustration.

"I'll never do what you want," I vow, my voice trembling with defiance.

"Suit yourself," he growls in my ear.

He starts his onslaught with the water again.

The Coalition will be here to rescue me. I will get out of here alive.

Does Mike know I'm missing?

I close my eyes and think of surviving this torture if only by thinking of Mike's gorgeous smile.

I have to get back to him.

I have to tell him everything, but mostly I have to tell him that I love him and want to be with him.

Once I get passed this with Ivan, once he's taken care of Mike and I can be together.

The water finally stops, leaving me gasping for breath. My senses reel as I try to collect myself, the sound of Ivan's voice cutting through the silence like a knife.

"You're a stubborn bitch or you're just that stupid," he snarls, his voice dripping with venom.

I flinch at his words, a surge of defiance rising within me even as the bag remains firmly in place over my head. I refuse to give him the satisfaction of seeing me break, no matter what he says or does.

But as the torment goes on, it becomes clear that Ivan has no intention of letting up. The room falls silent, the only sound the ragged rhythm of my breath as I struggle to remain calm in the face of my captor's cruelty.

I take a moment to collect myself, forcing my breathing to slow as I try to calm the frantic pounding of my heart. With a shaky exhale, I begin to take stock of my injuries, the pain a constant reminder of the ordeal I've endured.

There are definitely some broken bones, the sharp ache of them radiating through my body like a symphony of pain. But despite the agony that radiates through me, I know that I'll be fine. I've endured worse, and I refuse to let Ivan's cruelty break me.

Even as I focus on my own pain, I can't shake the image of Mike from my mind. His face swims before me, a beacon of hope in the darkness that surrounds me. I long to be with him, to feel his arms around me and know that I'm safe.

The thought of him fills me with a fierce determination, a driving force that propels me forward even in the darkest of moments. I will get through this, I vow silently to myself. I will survive, no matter what it takes.

***

I wake up sometime later. I have no way of knowing how long I've been trapped here, my senses dulled by exhaustion, thirst, and hunger.

Delusion creeps in at the edges of my consciousness, distorting reality into a twisted kaleidoscope of pain and despair.

I cling to consciousness by the thinnest of threads, each moment stretching out before me like an eternity. The silence is deafening, broken only by the ragged rhythm of my breath as I struggle to remain lucid in the face of my torment.

The bag is ripped off my head and Ivan's presence fills the room like a suffocating fog, his expression unreadable as he gazes down at me with cold detachment. I meet his gaze with a steely glare, refusing to cower before him despite the fear that churns in the pit of my stomach.

"I won't do it," I hiss, my voice a defiant whisper in the darkness. "No matter what you do to me, I'll never help you."

Ivan's expression remains impassive, a mask of calm that belies the rage simmering beneath the surface. "You're making a mistake, Eve," he says, his voice low and dangerous. "Think of what we could accomplish together."

I shake my head stubbornly, my resolve unwavering despite his attempts to sway me. "I'll never betray my values," I vow, my voice trembling with defiance.

But his facade cracks, his calm demeanor giving way to a storm of rage and frustration. With a snarl, he lashes out, his hand connecting with my cheek with a sharp crack. Pain explodes across my face as I reel from the blow, but even as darkness encroaches on the edges of my vision, I refuse to yield.

His rage boils over, his blows raining down on me with merciless force. Each strike sends shockwaves of pain radiating through my body, but I grit my teeth against the agony, refusing to give him the satisfaction of seeing me break.

And then, with a final, brutal kick to the stomach, everything goes dark.

20

Mike

I PACE BACK AND forth, I don't think I've stopped pacing since Eve was taken. I can't focus. I can't eat. I can't sleep.

I'm going crazy not knowing if Eve is alive, if she's okay. My phone sits on the coffee table, its screen illuminated with missed calls and unanswered messages.

With a heavy sigh, I reach for the phone, my fingers shaking from lack of food as I dial my coach's number. The line rings once, then twice, before he picks up, his voice filled with concern.

"Mike, is everything alright?" he asks, his tone laced with worry.

I swallow hard, the words sticking in my throat like shards of glass. "Coach, I... I need to take some time off," I say, my voice barely above a whisper. "There's been a death in the family, and... I need to be there."

There's a moment of silence on the other end of the line, the weight of my lie heavy in the air between us. But to my surprise, my coach's response is immediate—and unexpectedly empathetic.

"I'm so sorry to hear that, Mike," he says, his voice soft with sympathy. "Take as much time as you need. Family comes first."

Relief floods through me at his words, a weight lifting from my shoulders as I thank him profusely before ending the call. But even as I hang up the phone, the reality of the situation crashes down on me like a tidal wave. Eve is still out there, lost and alone in a world that grows darker by the minute.

I hate having to lie, it's not something I do and it makes me sick to my stomach.

I glance over at Damon, who sits slumped on the couch, his expression weary and defeated. We've been waiting for what feels like an eternity, but still, there's no word on whether Eve is okay. The uncertainty gnaws at me like a ravenous beast, chipping away at my resolve with each passing moment.

"We can't just sit here and do nothing," Damon says, his voice tinged with frustration. "We need to find her."

I nod in agreement, a surge of determination rising within me. "You're right," I say, my voice firm with resolve. "We can't wait any longer. We need to do something."

"Corey can help us put together a team of Veterans that used to do this sort of thing in the military. Retrieval missions. I can't wait on this Natalia woman."

"The lack of communication doesn't seem like a good sign."

"That's what I'm saying."

"Call Corey and get this started. I'll pay whatever we have to, so we find her. I can't lose her."

"Can't lose her?" Damon asks as he cocks an eyebrow at me.

"I'm in love with her. I can't... I'm in love with Eve, bro."

"How in the Hell did that happen?" he asks angrily. "Are you the reason she's in trouble? I asked you not to..."

He takes a swing at me, and I parry out of the way quickly.

"Damn it, Damon, we can't get into a fight right now. You can be pissed at me but just know that I'm going to do whatever it takes to get Eve home. We have to focus on her right now."

He lets out a frustrated groan before shaking his head in disgust. "This isn't over."

"Understood."

Damon paces back and forth, his frustration palpable with every step. I watch him, a knot of worry tightening in my chest as I wonder how much longer we can endure this uncertainty.

Piper and Diesel are pacing as well, whining and walking circles around the two of us. They don't understand what's going on, they just know something is wrong and that Eve hasn't been back to the house in a while.

Diesel stares out the window a lot and does not want to eat anything. We're quite the attached pair.

Finally, Damon reaches for his phone, his fingers flying over the screen as he dials a number. I hold my breath, anticipation coursing through me as I wait for him to speak.

"Hey, Corey? It's Damon," he says, his voice urgent. "We need to talk. It's about Eve."

I lean in closer as he hits the speaker button.

"Have they given you any updates?"

"Nothing."

"I've been doing a little recon on my end since she was kidnapped on my watch, but I'm hitting dead ends."

"We need your help," I interject. "We need to assemble a team to find her and bring her home."

There's a pause as Corey processes Damon's words, the silence stretching out between us like a yawning chasm.

"I've got a few guys we can use," he says. "We'll be at your place later tonight to give the information we have."

Relief floods through me at his words, a surge of hope rising within me as I realize that we're finally taking action. Eve may be out there somewhere, lost and alone, but we won't rest until we find her.

My phone begins ringing and I glance down to see Sam calling me.

"Tell me you found her."

"Not yet. I do have some leads as to where she could be though. I've tracked some of the Tambov Gang back to a place nearby."

"Give me the address."

"Not a chance in Hell, bud," he laughs. "This is for informational purposes only. I'm calling a mutual friend who is also looking for her, as soon as we hang up so that I can give him what I have and offer my assistance. We'll find her and bring her back to you."

"Sam."

"It's not up for discussion. You'll know when we find her."

He hangs up before I can protest anymore.

"What was that?" Damon asks.

"Sam has a lead on where she could be, but he won't give me any information about it."

"Probably for the best. You'll go in half-cocked."

"No I won't."

"We need to stay calm and focused. We can't afford to let our emotions get the better of us."

I bristle at his words, my frustration boiling over as I struggle to contain the torrent of emotions that threatens to consume me. "I am focused," I snap, my voice sharp with anger. "Focused on finding Eve and bringing her home, where she belongs."

His eyes narrow in response, his own frustration bubbling to the surface. "And what do you suggest we do, Mike?" he counters, his voice laced with bitterness. "We're doing everything we can to find her. We just need to be patient. We've contacted everyone we can to help us locate her. We can't do this on our own. The Russian Mafia is no one to mess with."

"Are you scared?"

"Scared of dying to save my sister? No. Scared of getting my sister killed because we go in like two cowboys trying to save the day and getting you killed too, yes. We're not doing it. We're doing everything we can from here, by reaching out to all of our combined contacts and putting the wheels in motion."

I open my mouth to respond, but it catches in my throat as the weight of his words sinks in. He's right. We can't let our emotions cloud our judgment, not when Eve's life hangs in the balance.

With a heavy sigh, I nod in agreement, the tension between us easing slightly as we come to a silent understanding. We may be at each other's throats, but our goal remains the same—to find Eve and bring her home, no matter what it takes.

***

A few hours later, Damon's front door slams open and a figure strides into the room with purpose. My heart leaps in my chest as I recognize her—Natalia. She's all business, her demeanor commanding as she fixes us with a steely gaze.

"Didn't I tell you to stand down?" she snaps, her voice sharp with reproach. "We have this handled."

I bristle at her words, the frustration bubbling up inside me like a boiling cauldron. "We haven't had any updates," I retort, my voice tinged with bitterness. "And the clock is ticking. We can't just sit around and wait."

Damon nods in agreement, his expression grim as he meets Natalia's gaze head-on. "We need to find Eve, now," he says, his voice firm with resolve.

But Natalia remains unmoved, her gaze unwavering as she levels a stern look at us both. "Hiring people to go in blind will only get your friends killed," she says, her voice low and dangerous. "You need to trust me on this."

How did she know that we hired someone else? Did they tap our phones?

"You can't just come in here with threats and riddles," I say, my voice trembling with anger. "We need to find her. She could be dead for all we know because you people took too long."

Natalia's lips curl into a sardonic smile, a hint of amusement dancing in her eyes. "Do you truly think we're not working on getting her back?" she asks, her voice dripping with sarcasm. "Stand down, or I'll have you both arrested."

I grit my teeth against the urge to lash out, the frustration boiling over as I struggle to contain my anger. "We can't just stand by and do nothing," I say, my voice hoarse with emotion.

"Trust me," she says, her voice softening slightly. "We're on the brink of rescuing her. Just give us a little more time."

Does that mean they know she's alive?

"Does that mean she's alive? Do you have confirmation of that?" Damon asks.

Natalia nods.

"What confirmation?"

"Just trust me."

"What have you done to prove to us that we can trust you?" I snap.

She glares at me before she rolls her eyes. "I have two men outside watching this place. If you leave, you'll be arrested. If anyone comes in, they'll be arrested with you. Do not go rogue on me or you'll get your sister killed."

"How do we know that you haven't already killed her?"

"You're being ridiculous," she laughs.

"Am I? The day she goes missing you just break into the house and tell us you're a friend. Seems awfully convenient, doesn't it?"

"You don't have to trust me, I guess," she shrugs nonchalantly. "Eve does and that's all that matters."

"We don't know that."

"I do," she snaps. She laughs and shakes her head. "You two probably think she's this weak female that needs to be rescued. Some damsel in distress, right, that can't fight her way out of a paper bag? You'd be wrong. She doesn't need either of you to swoop in and save her. I wouldn't be surprised if she hasn't already saved herself. She's the toughest bitch I know."

She gives us both disgusted glares before she leaves the house.

"How did she know we hired someone?"

"Did Corey tell her?" Damon asks out loud. "Is he working with all of these people and that's how they got to my sister? Did I put her in danger?"

"Maybe they tapped our phones," I offer. "She broke into your house before with no visible signs of a break-in. That time that I overheard Eve on the phone afterward she destroyed that phone she was on."

"Damn if Natalia is not hot," Damon laughs. "Any other time and place I'd be hitting on her hardcore."

"Focus," I chuckle.

"I am, I am."

The two of us start looking through Eve's things and the room again to see if we could find any more clues to her whereabouts or if we could really trust this Natalia woman. We don't find anything new, but I commit to memory some of the names her credit cards are registered to.

I'd venture to say that Natalia had cleaned out anything to lead back to the why of Eve being abducted to make sure no one learned the truth, but I'm speculating.

I need to know that she's okay soon or I'm going to lose my mind.

21

THE DARKNESS OF THE room envelops me like a suffocating shroud as I sit bound to the chair, my limbs heavy with exhaustion and hunger. Ivan's cruel laughter echoes in the air. He's been starving me, withholding food and water in an attempt to break my spirit.

I struggle to stay conscious, my mind swimming with delirium as I fight against the relentless onslaught of pain and despair. Ivan comes in regularly, his eyes cold and calculating as he demands that I log in to the computers and do his bidding. But I refuse, clinging to the last shreds of my defiance even as he threatens me with torture and death.

"No," I whisper hoarsely, my voice barely above a whisper.

Ivan's expression darkens, a cruel smile twisting his features as he reaches for the bag once more.

The water cascades over me, soaking me to the bone as Ivan pours yet another bucketful over my head. I clench my teeth, forcing myself to remain calm despite the panic rising within me.

As Ivan turns away to grab another bucket, I seize the opportunity to act. With a burst of adrenaline, I focus on controlling my breathing, willing myself to stay calm despite the suffocating darkness that surrounds me. The ropes binding my hands and feet feel like iron chains, but I refuse to let them hold me back any longer.

With a swift, deliberate motion, I wriggle my wrists, the rough fibers of the rope chafing against my skin as I work to loosen the knots. It's slow going, every movement agonizingly deliberate as I fight against the resistance of the bindings. But I refuse to give up, fueled by a fierce determination to escape this nightmare.

And then, finally, I feel the ropes begin to slacken, the knots loosening under the pressure of my relentless efforts. With one final tug, I wrench my hands free, the sensation of freedom flooding through me like a tidal wave. But there's no time to celebrate, no time to revel in my small victory.

As I hear Ivan turn back towards me, a fresh bucket of water in hand, I steel myself for what comes next. With a surge of adrenaline, I rip the bag off my head in one swift motion, launching myself at him with all the pent-up fury of a caged animal.

The element of surprise is on my side as I tackle him to the ground, his surprised grunt lost amidst the chaos of our struggle. We grapple with each other, locked in a deadly dance of fists and fury as we fight for control. But I refuse to back down, rejecting to let fear dictate my actions any longer.

I land blow after blow, each strike fueled by a fierce determination to survive. Ivan fights back with equal ferocity, his strength surprising me as we trade blows in a deadly game of cat and mouse. But I refuse to let him win, refusing to let him break me down any further.

With a sudden burst of strength, I land a solid punch to his jaw, the force of the blow sending him reeling backwards. I seize the opportunity to strike, raining blow after blow upon him with a relentless fury that takes even me by surprise. And then, finally, with one last, decisive blow, I send him crashing to the ground.

He growls and jumps up in one graceful movement. I get in a fight stance, broken and bruised and ready to take him out once and for all.

There's a loud book behind me and suddenly the room is filled with the sound of chaos as a team of people in all black storm the room.

Ivan leaps toward me, attempting to grab me to shield him from the bullets that are about to rain down on him. I parry out of his reach and land an uppercut to his abdomen, before I kick him away from me.

Diesel charges into the room, silent as his eyes are locked on my abductor. Ivan grabs a gun from behind him and goes to take aim. I lunge forward just as Diesel leaps through the air. A shot rings out just as I slam my broken body into Ivan's.

He yelps, growls, and yanks at my hair. I knock the gun out of his hand just as Diesel latches on to his balls.

Ivan screams out in agony as he starts punching Diesel in the skull. He's locked in tight and not letting go. There are more shots fired as members of the Tambov Gang pour through another door, trying to protect their leader.

I roll to take cover. Ivan is screaming in agony, ordering his people in Russian to shoot Diesel. No one is listening as they're all trying to keep themselves from getting killed.

A black figure crouches beside me, handing me the gun in their hands. They gesture for me to move forward.

Ivan isn't paying attention as Diesel has let go of his balls and has latched onto Ivan's thigh, his teeth are sunk in deep as he's pulling apart the meat.

Ivan and members of his Gang have been captured numerous times but they always, always, get out on some technicality. If I don't end this now, then I will always live in fear of him returning.

By the looks of it, he's going to have a lot of hate toward me and Diesel.

There's only one thing I can do.

I take the gun and stand up, putting myself in Ivan's view.

"You dumb bitch!" he screams as he tries to lunge for me.

Diesel isn't letting go of him anytime soon though.

"I may be a dumb bitch, but I've outsmarted you. And I'm the last thing you'll see before you go to Hell," I grin as I aim at the center of his forehead. I pull the trigger and feel as the bullet leaves the chamber.

His eyes widen in shock as the bullet makes contact. He flies backward and his body slumps to the ground in a heap.

I'm safe. They came for me.

They saved me.

Diesel lets go of Ivan, knowing that he's no longer a threat. He comes running directly to me. I slump to the ground, laughing as he licks my face excitedly.

"Boy did I miss you," I whisper as my injuries start to take their toll on me.

I struggle to keep my eyes open, my vision swimming with exhaustion and delirium. The figure pulls their mask up, revealing a familiar face that sends a surge of relief coursing through me.

"Natalia," I whisper, my voice barely above a hoarse whisper. "It's about time, bitch."

She laughs, the sound ringing out like music in the darkness. "You always did have a way with words, Eve," she says, her voice warm with amusement. "I told them bringing Diesel would be beneficial. Not only did he sniff out your scent when the other K-9's didn't, he disabled Ivan."

"He's the best dog in the world."

With Natalia's help, I manage to stand, my limbs trembling with exhaustion. She supports me, guiding me out of the room as the chaos swirls around us.

"Man, that brother of yours is hot."

"Really? This is what you say to me?" I tease.

"Well, they were both hot. That Mike has it bad for you. They also were the biggest pains in the ass during all of this. They tried to go rogue."

"They're both consistently a pain in the ass for me so that sounds about right."

A medic rushes to my side, checking me over for injuries as they load me onto the stretcher and then put me in the back of a waiting ambulance. Diesel is close by, whining and trying to get on the stretcher. Natalia corrals him.

"Their hearts were in the right place but they didn't know what they were getting into."

"Hopefully they still don't. Ivan is dead, right?"

"Yes, I checked myself. You're safe."

"We'll see about that," I sigh.

"How in the Hell did you walk over here?" the medic asks.

"Determination," I shrug.

Natalia laughs. "She's like the Energizer Bunny or a cockroach, not sure which."

"Funny."

"You're lucky to be alive, Eve. You know that right?"

"I do."

"Also, how does your brother and Mike have the contacts they do? Dirk almost fainted when a man reached out to him to give your location."

"Mike found my location?"

"No, he hired a former CIA agent/Marine who got a lot of information with very few names. The man is good at his job. How he got Dirk's number is still a mystery."

"Jesus," I breathe.

"That man could have died for you," she teases.

"Shut up," I sigh.

I close my eyes and inhale and exhale slowly. I am grateful that Mike and Damon did what they could to help find me but they truly could have gotten themselves killed or me killed.

I put them both in danger by coming back to Legacy. I put Kelsey in danger. I put the entire town of Legacy in danger by returning.

The threat of Ivan might be gone, but it doesn't mean there won't be someone else in the Tambov Gang coming for me, the Kazar Gang or any other criminal for that matter.

***

The sterile white walls of the private hospital surround me like a cocoon as I lie in the crisp white sheets of the bed, the steady beep of the monitor a comforting rhythm in the darkness.

The IV drip beside me hums softly as it delivers much-needed fluids into my veins, replenishing my parched body and bringing me back from the brink of exhaustion. I close my eyes, letting the cool liquid soothe me as I drift in and out of consciousness.

"You should call your brother or that hottie boyfriend of yours."

"He's not my boyfriend."

"Are you sure about that?" Natalia teases.

"Positive."

"Doc says you'll need to be here a few more days before we can get you home. They'll debrief you when he releases you."

"Looking forward to that."

"They're just looking for information. I think they want to see if he said anything of use."

"Nope, just threatening me if I didn't do what he asked."

"Call your brother," Natalia says again as she stands up and squeezes my hand.

She leaves the room and I stare off into space for a bit.

After what feels like an eternity, I finally muster the strength to reach for the burner phone Eve brought me, my fingers trembling as I dial Damon's number. The phone rings once, then twice, before he picks up, his voice filled with relief and concern.

"Eve? Is that you?" he asks, his voice tinged with urgency.

I swallow hard, the lump in my throat threatening to choke me as I struggle to find the words. "Damon," I whisper hoarsely, my voice barely above a whisper. "It's me. I'm okay."

There's a moment of stunned silence on the other end of the line before Damon's voice fills the air, his relief palpable even through the phone. "Thank god," he breathes, his voice trembling with emotion. "We've been so worried about you. Where are you? We'll come get you right now."

I smile weakly at his words, touched by his concern. "I'm at a private hospital," I say. "Natalia brought me here. But don't worry, I'll get a ride home."

There's a pause on the other end of the line before Mike's voice chimes in, his concern evident even through the phone. "Are you okay?" he asks, his voice tight with worry. "Will you be safe now?"

I nod, even though I know they can't see me. "I'm okay," I reassure them, my voice steady with determination. "And yes, I'll be safe now. Natalia and Diesel are here with me, and they won't let anything happen to me."

There's a sense of relief in their voices as they hear my words.

“Diesel? Natalia's people took your dog? I've been so consumed with worry that I didn't notice his absence.”

“I guess you’re not such a great uncle after all.”

“We’re coming to get you,” Mike growls. “Give us an address.”

“No. You can’t. When I’m released Natalia will bring me home. I promise.”

"Eve," Mike says gruffly. "You cannot tell me that you're okay and then tell me I can't come to you. I'm about to go crazy. I need to see you."

"You have to trust me. It's not... you can't be here."

"Eve, please."

"The doctor is on his way in the room. I'll call you guys later," I lie as I quickly hang up the phone.

That was a bad idea.

I want to get out of here as soon as possible and land in Mike's arms now.

***

The private hospital room feels strangely empty as I sit on the edge of the bed, my fingers tracing absent-minded patterns on the crisp white sheets.

The doctor enters the room, a clipboard in hand, his expression grave as he approaches. He checks my vitals, his brow furrowing in concern as he studies the readings.

"Well, Miss Eve, it seems you're recovering quite well," he says, his voice gentle but tinged with seriousness. "Your hydration levels are back to normal, and your injuries are healing nicely. I see no reason why you shouldn't be discharged today. Honestly, I don't know how you only have a broken arm and some ribs. With all that bruising, it's a miracle really."

Relief floods through me at his words as I realize that I'm finally free to leave this sterile prison behind.

"That's the best news I've heard all week," I laugh. "Thank you."

He leaves and a nurse comes in to finish the discharge. Natalia walks in a few minutes later.

"We get to go home, Diesel," I say as I rub the back of his head.

He snuggles in closer to me.

"I hear I'm springing you free," she teases.

"Thank goodness."

"Yeah, Damon and Mike have been blowing up the burner phone number I gave them. I'm ready to be rid of them."

"They're ridiculous."

"No, it's sweet. We don't get stuff like that in this life, Eve, relish it."

"You're right," I sigh.

Natalia's phone vibrates. She glances down at it and then looks over at me.

"Dirk wants you in his office before we leave."

"I didn't think I'd get out of here without seeing him," I shrug.

The private hospital is all part of the Coalition's compound. Dirk's office is on the other side of the building. Natalia and I make our way there.

The heavy oak door creaks as it swings open, revealing a dimly lit room bathed in shadows. Dirk's offices all over the country are the heart of the Coalition's operations—places where decisions are made and secrets are kept.

The room is spacious, with high ceilings and walls lined with bookshelves filled to the brim with dusty tomes and ancient artifacts. The air is heavy with the scent of old leather and musty paper, a tangible reminder of the history that surrounds us.

At the center of the room sits a massive oak desk, its polished surface gleaming in the dim light. Behind it sits Dirk, his imposing figure silhouetted against the backdrop of the room like a dark shadow. I always tell people that Dirk reminds me of Cyborg as he's all rippling muscles and a bald head, he looks as though he'll rip your head off until he smiles at you. Which he rarely does.

"You're looking much better, Eve," Dirk grins as we walk into the room.

I sink into a chair in front of him. To my left and right, three other high-ranking members of the Coalition sit in silence, their presence looming over me like a specter of doom. They're also very intimidating as none of them have missed gym day or ever smile much either.

"I'm feeling much better."

"You're a tough woman, that's for sure," Ronaldo says beside me. "Ivan's torture tactics have toppled our toughest men before."

I nod, unsure of what to reply.

"While the threat of Ivan has been removed, there are still two other entities gunning for you," Dirk interjects.

My blood runs cold at his words, a surge of fear coursing through me as I realize the gravity of the situation. "Two?" I whisper, my voice trembling with disbelief.

Dirk nods, his eyes glinting with a steely resolve. "Yes," he says. "And we need to be prepared for whatever may come."

I glance around the room, taking in the stern expressions of the other members of the Coalition. They sit in silence, their eyes fixed on me like hawks stalking their prey.

I feel a shiver run down my spine as the weight of their scrutiny bears down on me like a crushing weight. This is no ordinary meeting. This is a gathering of power, a gathering of minds united in the face of an unimaginable threat.

"Both entities have put a reward out for you on the dark web," Sam explains as he leans forward so I can see his face. "We're monitoring the situation closely, and we don't feel there's an immediate threat at this time."

"Same thing that Ivan wanted?"

"It seems that way. I think Ivan's interest in you put you on their radar. We'd done good covering you until then. None of these people should know who you are."

"Should I go into hiding? Change my identity?"

"These entities aren't key players, or anything we need to worry about right now," Ronaldo answers.

"We believe they're newbies trying to make a name for themselves. They're all about bluffing right now," Tank interjects.

"You're free to go back to your brother's. We'll do everything in our power to keep you safe."

"I'll go back to my home in California. I can't risk my brother's safety if there are others coming for me."

"I want you to remain in Legacy," Dirk says, his eyes flitting to Natalia who is sitting behind me now. "Your brother is a valuable resource and knowledgeable. I have a contact within the police department too."

"Who do you know in Legacy's police department?"

"Not important," Dirk laughs. "Your brother's next-door neighbor is one of our guys too."

"Mike?"

"No, the other neighbor."

"Conner, the creepy guy?"

"He's one of our top agents, he was being that guy so he could get intel. When you took on the job with us, he moved in next door to protect Damon and keep tabs on you if you ever ran from the Coalition."

"You mean kill me in my sleep?" I joke awkwardly.

I heard stories about what happened if you tried to get out of the Coalition and they weren't done with you yet. They can tell me he was placed as a protector of my brother, which is true, but he'd also be the one to kill us both.

"Conner contacted me prior to you calling me when you realized you were being followed on that run. He noticed the vehicle and pretended to be hitting on you so they'd leave you alone. He saved your life the morning you were abducted as Ivan had sent someone to break into the house and kill you and Damon in your sleep. The snake was a backup and Conner halted that too."

"What about the package I received?"

"Full of cottonmouth snakes and a remote detonated bomb as well. You set it on fire and walked away. He took care of it."

"But why would they try to kill me? I thought they needed me to do their dirty work?"

"According to my source, Ivan was getting desperate. He was in panic mode because we were closing in on him and you were harder to capture than he anticipated. He figured if he killed you the Kasav Gang couldn't have you either. Then he had the opportunity to kidnap you and took it."

"I never pegged Ivan for the jealous type," I giggle.

The Kasav Gang is a rival of the Tambov, run by Ivan's former best friend turned mortal enemy. Ivan will stop at nothing to make sure he outdoes Vlad in everything.

"The Kasav Gang will probably send you gifts for killing Ivan."

"Why didn't Conner show himself as a friendly ever?"

"You know that's not how we operate. He's one of our top agents in many ways. He wanted an easy job so he was tasked with Damon."

"He plays creepy very well."

"Maybe so, but you didn't make him. I think that's the first time that's happened."

"He's good in that area, I guess. I always make someone. Will he remain there?"

"Yes, he's been tasked with keeping your brother and you safe. If you leave or take on another mission, he'll remain to protect Damon still."

"Is remaining in Legacy a direct order?"

"No, I will never take your free will away from you, but I will tell you that as your friend, Legacy is where you should return to."

"Yes, Sir."

"Natalia will take you home. We'll be in touch."

I stand and leave the room, Natalia close behind me. We leave the compound and go to her black Ferrari that's waiting for us outside.

"Nothing like making sure people notice you," I tease.

"It's faster than they can notice me," she laughs.

I climb in the sleek car and Natalia steers us back to Legacy.

"Natalia," I say finally, breaking the silence that stretches between us like a yawning chasm. "I don't think I should go back to the house. I'm putting Damon and Mike in danger, and I can't do that."

Her expression softens with sympathy as she meets my gaze. "I understand your concern, Eve," she says, her voice gentle. "But Damon and Mike are resourceful. They'll know how to keep you safe."

"I can't risk it."

"Then what are you saying?"

"I need to leave."

"Are you saying that you need to leave because of their safety or because you're scared of getting too close to Mike?"

"Because of their safety. This has nothing to do with Mike, I don't even like being around him."

"Bullshit. You're really good at lying and most people wouldn't be able to tell, but you know that I can."

"You're seeing what you want to see."

"Okay. Well, if he's not yours that means he's on the market and fair game."

I clench my fists at my side, my stomach twisting with anger.

"Yup, have at him."

I can see her smile before she looks away.

Bitch. She better be playing with me.

I don't want to lose him. I don't want anyone else to have him, but I can't be in a relationship with him or anyone else. I chose this life knowing that it would be a lonely one and I've made peace with it.

When we finally arrive at Damon's, the house is empty. Natalia drops Diesel and me off and leaves. I look online and realize that Mike has a game tonight, that's probably where Damon is.

Good. That makes this easier.

I go to my room and pack my things. I go to the hidden compartment in my jewelry box and pull out one of my fake passports.

Allison Lachlan, that's my name now.

I sit down at the desk when everything is together and book a flight to Maui as well as an Airbnb and a rental car. Then I pen two letters, one to Damon and one to Mike.

"Let's go, Diesel."

He whimpers and whines a bit, knowing that we're leaving a place we've both come to think of as home.

"You know the drill, it's not safe and we can't put anyone else in danger because of my choices."

He chuffs and follows at my heels while I load my luggage and his travel crate into the car. I leave the letters for my brother and Mike on the kitchen table, lock the door behind me and leave.

Tears stream down my face as I pass the sign that says "You are now leaving Legacy, come back soon."

This is for the best, it really is.

22

Mike

"Have you heard anything from Natalia or Eve?" I ask Damon as we leave my game.

"Nothing."

"This is ridiculous. How do they expect us to just sit around and wait for some sort of word?"

"I'm happy to know that she's okay. I'm glad she called me. I really think she's going to leave and not come back."

"Why do you think that?"

"It's what she always does. She can't handle the thought of someone getting hurt or in trouble because of her. And Diesel is gone."

"I hope you're wrong."

"Me too."

"I'm going to propose to her when she gets back."

"What? Mike, I don't want to spook her."

"It's not going to spook her."

"Do you even know my sister?"

"Yes," I chuckle. "This whole thing has made me realize that she's the one."

"Well, I'm happy for you both but... my sister isn't... she told me a long time ago that she couldn't get involved with someone because of her career choice and she's made peace with that."

"Things change."

Damon doesn't protest, just nods his head in acceptance. Both of us climb into our separate cars and head back to Legacy.

***

I step out of my car, exhaustion clinging to my bones like a heavy cloak as I make my way up the driveway to my house. The game was brutal, but we managed to clinch the win in the final minutes. It should be a moment of celebration, but the worry that's been gnawing at the edges of my mind refuses to fade.

I open the front door to the house and Piper is immediately there waiting for me. She bounds out of the house, her tail wagging eagerly as she sniffs the air. I watch her for a moment, a faint smile tugging at the corners of my lips.

I hear a strange sound inside the house and slowly walk inside. There on Piper's dog bed are four tiny little things wriggling around.

"Piper!?! You had your puppies while I was gone?"

She comes bounding back in the house with a yip as she rushes over to the bed to display her proud accomplishment.

"Aw, I'm sorry I wasn't here, sweet girl," I say as I rub the top of her head.

Four perfect little pups, a perfect mix of Diesel and Piper whine on the bed, waiting for their mother to feed them.

I sigh and smile down at them.

Wait until Eve hears that Diesel is a daddy.

I feel my phone vibrate. I swipe to answer, my heart skipping a beat as I brace myself for whatever news Damon has to share.

"Damon, what's up?" I say, my voice tense with anticipation.

There's a moment of silence on the other end of the line before Damon speaks, his voice tight with emotion.

"Eve must have been here while we were at the game. She left us notes on the kitchen table."

"She left me a note?"

"Yeah. All of her stuff is gone from her room."

My heart sinks at his words, a surge of panic rising within me as I struggle to comprehend the gravity of the situation. "I'll be right over," I say, my voice barely above a whisper as I hang up the phone.

Piper whines at my side sensing the tension in the air.

"I'll be back," I say to her as I make my way next door to Damon's house. I push open the front door, my heart pounding in my chest as I step inside.

He is waiting for me in the living room, his expression grim as he meets my gaze. "All of her stuff is gone," he says, his voice heavy with sorrow. "I don't know where she went, or why. I expected this, but it still hurts. Why wouldn't she tell me?"

"Because you'd talk her out of it."

"Of course I would."

I run a hand through my hair, frustration bubbling to the surface as I struggle to make sense of the situation. "Did she say anything in the note?" I ask, my voice tinged with desperation.

He shakes his head, his expression pained. "Nothing except that it is better this way."

I swallow hard, the knot of worry tightening in my chest as I struggle to contain the flood of emotions that threatens to overwhelm me. "We need to find her," I say, my voice urgent. "Now."

"I'll reach out to Natalia; she might know something."

Damon hands me the letter addressed to me as he walks off with his phone to call Natalia.

I open the envelope and unfold the paper.

Mike,

I am so grateful for meeting you that night at the bar. I'm grateful that I got to know you differently than how I had always seen you my entire life.

You're a very special man.

A long time ago, I chose a career that wouldn't allow me to have personal relationships. In order to do what I love, what I was born to do, it was necessary. I've never regretted that choice until now, having to walk away from you. My life is too dangerous to allow anyone else into the fold, it would be reckless and selfish.

I wish you nothing but happiness.

Love,

Eve

"This is bullshit," I growl as Damon walks back into the room.

"What did she say?"

"That she can't be in a relationship because of her job, that her life is too dangerous. She can't just leave and not give me a choice."

"She thinks she's protecting you."

"Coming from the woman who doesn't want me to protect her that's bullshit. What did Natalia say?"

"She thought this would happen, but she doesn't know where Eve went."

"Can she find out?"

"She's looking into it."

"I need to go home," I mutter as I stalk out the front door.

As soon as I'm in the silence of my house I go to the basement to my home gym and start hitting the heavy bag suspended from the ceiling.

How dare she leave without telling us where she's going.

I take out all of my frustration and hurt on the bag before I go back upstairs to the shower. A million different emotions are raging through me right now, but the most prevalent is hurt.

I'm extremely hurt that she didn't bother to ask me how I felt or what I wanted.

***

The days drag on, each one feeling like an eternity as I search for any sign of Eve. I've hired a private investigator, poured over every lead, and scoured every corner of the country, but still, there's no trace of her. It's like she's vanished into thin air, leaving nothing behind but a void that threatens to consume me whole.

I sit at my desk, the weight of uncertainty pressing down on me like a leaden weight as I stare at the screen of my phone, willing it to light up with a message from her. But the screen remains stubbornly dark, devoid of any sign of life.

Damon's words echo in my mind, a constant reminder of the harsh reality that I'm struggling to accept. "Let it go, Mike," he had said, his voice tinged with sadness. "If she doesn't want to be found, we have to respect that."

But I can't let it go, not when the thought of her consumes every waking moment of my day. I refuse to accept that she's gone, that I'll never see her again. I'll do whatever it takes to find her, no matter the cost.

I reach for my phone and I compose yet another text message to her.

Eve, please, if you're out there, just let me know you're okay,

I type, my heart pounding in my chest as I hit send.

I push away from the desk, frustration bubbling to the surface as I struggle to contain the torrent of emotions that threatens to consume me. I've done everything in my power to find her, but still, she remains out of reach.

I pace back and forth, the walls of my house closing in on me as I try to make sense of the senseless. How could she just disappear like this, leaving no trace behind? It doesn't make sense, and yet, here I am, grappling with the harsh reality of her absence.

She's been gone for a month, and we've heard nothing from her. When I go to my mailbox that Saturday morning there's a cardboard priority envelope addressed to me with no return address and a postmark from California. Inside is a postcard, a scenic beach in Maui with an address scribbled on the opposite side.

"If you're looking for love, you'll find it here," it reads.

Is this from Eve? Is this where she's at?

Did Natalia do this?

I immediately go to Damon's house. He's walking outside as I come up.

"Hey Mike, how's it going?"

"I just got this in the mail."

I hand him the postcard. "Do you think that's where Eve is?"

"I do. I'm going to find out."

"What are you going to do?"

"I'm going to find her."

He nods.

"Are you sure about this?"

"I've never been more positive about anything in my life."

"Okay, then I'm here for it."

I get on my phone and make arrangements for a private plane to take me to Maui, pronto.

"If Eve won't come back to me, then I'll go to her."

"Are you taking Piper or do you want her and the pups to stay with me?"

"She hates flying and she shouldn't be away from her babies yet, if you want to keep her that would be great."

"Yeah, I kind of miss having a dog around," Damon laughs.

"Perfect."

Two hours later, I'm packed and boarding a plane for Hawaii. The engine of the plane roars to life as we prepare for takeoff, the sound drowning out the cacophony of doubts and fears that swirl within me. I've never been one to give up easily, and I won't start now.

As the plane ascends into the sky, I stare out the window, the world below shrinking to nothing more than a patchwork of green and blue. The familiar ache in my chest grows stronger with each passing moment, a constant reminder of the void that has consumed me since she left.

Hours pass in a blur of clouds and sky, until finally, the plane touches down on the tarmac of Maui's airport. I step off the plane and into the warm tropical air, the scent of salt and sea filling my senses as I make my way to the waiting car that will take me to the address on the postcard.

The drive through Maui is a blur of lush greenery and winding roads, the scent of flowers and saltwater mingling in the air as we wind our way through the island paradise. But despite the beauty that surrounds me, my thoughts are consumed by one thing and one thing only—finding Eve.

I pull up to the address on the postcard, a modest beachfront cottage nestled among the palm trees. My heart pounds in my chest as I step out of the car and make my way to the front door. I knock.

But there's no answer. And Diesel doesn't bark. I knock again, louder this time, but still, there's no response. Panic surges through me as I realize that Eve may not be here, that I may have come all this way for nothing.

I try the door, but it's locked tight, refusing to yield to my efforts. Desperation wells up within me as I reach for my phone, dialing Eve's number.

But there's no answer. I try again, and again, but still, there's nothing but silence on the other end of the line. My heart sinks as I realize that she's not going to pick up, that she doesn't want to be found.

I leave the cottage and go into the city to find a place to stay for the night. Once I find a nice resort to stay at and get settled into my room I dial Damon's number, the phone ringing once, then twice before he picks up.

“Did you find her?” he asks as he picks up.

"I went to the address on the postcard," I say, my words coming out in a rush. "But she wasn't there. I don't know where else to look."

“I had a feeling this wouldn't be easy. Maybe she just wasn't home. You'll find her.

“I will. I'm not going to give up until I do.”

***

The next day dawns bright and clear, the promise of a new day hanging in the air as I set out once more to search for Eve. I go to her house once more, but she doesn't answer and I don't hear Diesel barking in response to my knock.

I wander the streets of the city, my eyes scanning the crowds for any sign of her, but she remains elusive.

And then, as I turn a corner, I catch a glimpse of a figure in the distance, a flash of jet-black hair that sends a surge of hope coursing through me. Could it be her?

She was wearing a jet-black bob when we first met. Is it the same wig? Why is she wearing a wig?

I quicken my pace, my heart pounding in my chest as I follow the figure through the crowded streets. At some point, she ducks behind a group of people and I lose her just as quickly as I found her.

Was it really her or did I just think I saw her?

I continue looking for her with no luck. A few hours later, I return to stand outside the beachfront cottage once more, my heart pounding in my chest as I summon the courage to knock on the door. But once again, there's no answer.

Is she avoiding me?

Was the postcard a hoax to throw me off?

23

Eve

The plane descends gracefully, dipping below the clouds to reveal the breathtaking landscape of Maui spread out below us. I press my forehead against the window, my breath catching in my throat as I drink in the stunning sights unfolding before me. The vibrant green of the lush forest contrasts beautifully with the azure blue of the ocean, creating a mesmerizing tapestry of color that stretches as far as the eye can see.

Beside me, Diesel lets out an excited bark, his tail wagging eagerly as he takes in the sights with me. I reach down to scratch behind his ears, a small smile playing on my lips as I revel in the beauty of this new beginning.

As the plane touches down on the tarmac, a sense of excitement courses through me, mingled with a twinge of sadness. Leaving Legacy behind wasn't an easy decision, but I know it's the right one.

Diesel misses Piper and I miss Mike and Damon, but this will keep them all safe and that's what matters most.

Stepping off the plane, the warm tropical air envelops me like a comforting embrace, carrying with it the scent of salt and sea. I take a deep breath, filling my lungs with the sweet fragrance of exotic flowers and freshly cut grass, a sense of tranquility washing over me as I soak in the sights and sounds of this new paradise.

With Diesel trotting faithfully at my side, we make our way to the cottage that will be our home for the foreseeable future. Nestled on the edge of the ocean, it's a quaint little hideaway, surrounded by swaying palm trees and vibrant tropical flowers.

Inside, the cottage is cozy and inviting, with whitewashed walls and wooden furnishings that lend it a rustic charm. The sound of the ocean fills the air, a soothing melody that lulls me into a sense of peace and serenity.

As I unpack our belongings, I can't help but feel a pang of longing for Mike and for the familiar comforts of home that I've left behind. But I push the thought aside, reminding myself that this is what I need to do.

The days pass in a blissful blur as Diesel and I settle into our new routine, exploring the island and immersing ourselves in its beauty. We spend our mornings walking along the pristine beaches, the warm sand soft beneath our feet as we watch the sunrise over the horizon.

In the afternoons, we venture into the heart of the island, hiking through lush rainforests and cascading waterfalls that seem to spring forth from the very earth itself. Everywhere we go, there is a sense of magic and wonder, a feeling of being part of something greater than ourselves.

But amidst the beauty and wonder of Maui, there is a sense of restlessness that gnaws at me, a feeling that I can't quite shake. I miss the thrill of the chase, the adrenaline rush of a mission accomplished. I miss the feeling of purpose that comes with knowing that I'm making a difference in the world.

And so, one evening as the sun sets in a blaze of fiery hues, I pick up my phone and dial Dirk's number, the familiar ringtone echoing in the stillness of the night. He picks up on the second ring, his voice crisp and professional.

"Eve, to what do I owe the pleasure?" he says, his tone tinged with curiosity.

I take a deep breath, steeling myself for what comes next. "Dirk, I need another mission. Something to keep me busy."

There's a pause on the other end of the line, the silence stretching between us like a taut wire. And then, finally, Dirk speaks, his voice tinged with concern.

"Eve, you need to stand down and rest," he says firmly. "You've been through a lot, and burying yourself in work isn't going to solve anything."

I bristle at his words, frustration bubbling up within me. "But I need something to do, Dirk. I can't just sit around and do nothing."

He sighs, the sound heavy with resignation. "Fine. I'll see what I can do. But promise me you'll take it easy, Eve. Promise me you'll take care of yourself."

I hesitate for a moment, the weight of his words sinking in. And then, finally, I nod, knowing that he's right. Knowing that I need to take a step back and focus on healing, on finding peace amidst the chaos of my past.

"I promise," I reply softly. "Thank you, Dirk."

***

The sun rises over the horizon, casting a golden glow over the tranquil waters of Maui's coastline. I stand at the water's edge, the soft sand warm beneath my bare feet as I watch the waves roll in with a mesmerizing rhythm. Beside me, Diesel wags his tail eagerly, his excitement mirroring my own as we prepare for another day out on the waves.

Surfing has become my sanctuary in the weeks since we arrived in Maui, a source of solace and joy amidst the uncertainty that still lingers in the back of my mind. We're rarely at the cottage these days, constantly on the go as we explore every inch of this beautiful island paradise.

It just feels so lonely at the house. It makes me miss Mike more when I'm there so I force myself to find things to do to keep my mind busy.

As I strap on my surfboard and paddle out into the ocean, a sense of exhilaration courses through me, mingled with a hint of nervous anticipation. The waves loom before me like towering giants, their crests crashing against the shore with a thunderous roar.

But I refuse to let fear hold me back. With a deep breath, I push myself forward, propelling my board through the water with determined strokes. The salt spray stings my skin as I paddle out past the breakers, the thrill of the open ocean calling to me like a siren's song.

As I reach the lineup, I pause for a moment to catch my breath, the rhythmic rise and fall of the waves soothing my frayed nerves. And then, with a surge of adrenaline, I push myself to my feet, riding the crest of the first wave with practiced ease.

The rush of wind in my hair, the sensation of weightlessness as I glide effortlessly across the water—it's a feeling like no other, a moment of pure freedom that I cherish with every fiber of my being. For a brief moment, all thoughts of the past and the future fade away, leaving nothing but the present moment and the exhilarating rush of adrenaline.

As I carve through the waves, I can't help but feel a sense of peace settle over me, a feeling of being truly alive in a way that I haven't felt in far too long. And with each wave that I conquer, each moment of triumph and exhilaration, I feel myself growing stronger, more resilient in the face of whatever challenges lie ahead.

But amidst the beauty and serenity of the ocean, there are moments of doubt that linger in the back of my mind. There are times when I think I see Mike in town, his familiar silhouette disappearing around a corner before I can catch up to him.

I shake my head, chiding myself for my foolishness. There's no way he could have tracked me down here, no way he could have known where I've been hiding all this time. And yet, the nagging sense of unease persists, a constant reminder of the dangers that still lurk in the shadows.

"I must be losing my mind, Diesel."

He whines beside me, shaking his head as if he's saying no.

The burner phone in my pocket vibrates and I glance at it.

Natalia.

"So you left without telling me?" she asks in greeting.

"I didn't know where I was going."

"Bullshit."

"It's better this way."

"You're a chicken shit," she laughs. "Seriously. Why would you choose to go somewhere and isolate yourself from everyone? Don't you miss being around your brother and Mike?"

"Of course I miss them. It's just a matter of time before the other members of the Tambov Gang come looking for me."

"They'll look for you at Mike and Damon's houses. You left them exposed."

"No, I didn't. Dirk said they were safe. He said Legacy is safe."

"If you believed that, you would have stayed."

"I..."

"Exactly. Your leaving puts them in more danger."

This is why I didn't tell her where I was going, she would try to spew logic and reason at me.

"I can't risk them getting hurt because of me. The Tambov Gang or whoever else will realize that I left and that they don't know where I am and they'll leave them alone."

"You're wrong."

"The media is already saying that Mike is single and dating again. It's fine."

"He's not dating again," she laughs.

"How do you know that?"

"Because I have been keeping track of them both to make sure they're safe."

"Thank you," I sigh. "So, Mike isn't dating?"

"No, he's not. He's been driving himself crazy looking for you. He's not even close to being right with his leads though."

"No one knows where I am, he won't ever be able to find me."

"Keep telling yourself that."

"Natalia, what did you do?"

"I didn't do anything. I don't know where you're at. I'm sure you're not hard to find though. I can hear the beach in the background."

"It's a sleep track."

"Sure, it is," she laughs. "I don't understand why you would give up happiness for solitude, but it is what it is. Stay safe, love."

She hangs up the phone and I stare down at it for a few minutes.

I don't know why I gave up happiness for solitude either. I can't risk knowing I'm at fault for Damon or Mike losing their lives though.

***

The gentle rustle of palm leaves and the soothing crash of waves against the shore provide the backdrop to my morning routine. I'm sipping on a cup of freshly brewed coffee, Diesel lounging lazily beside me as I take in the breathtaking view from the lanai of our cottage. The sky is a canvas of vibrant hues, streaks of pink and orange painting the horizon as the sun begins its ascent into the sky.

My phone buzzes, interrupting the tranquility of the moment. With a curious glance, I pick it up to see Dirk's name flashing on the screen. My heart skips a beat as I answer the call, anticipation, and apprehension warring within me.

"Eve," Dirk's voice is as crisp and authoritative as ever. "I've got an update for you."

I hold my breath, waiting for him to continue.

"I don't have anything concrete yet, but it seems the threats against you have died down," he says, his tone measured. "You're free to leave Maui at your convenience."

I gasp, the words hitting me like a bolt of lightning. It's what I've been waiting for, what I've been longing for ever since we arrived on this island paradise. And yet, the news leaves me feeling strangely unsettled, a knot of anxiety coiling in the pit of my stomach.

"How... how did you know where I was?" I stammer, my mind racing with questions.

He chuckles, the sound echoing through the phone. "Let's just say you left a few breadcrumbs behind. Chartered a private plane with one of the fake identities I gave you, didn't you? It was an easy find."

I curse under my breath, cursing myself for my carelessness. Leave it to Dirk to always be one step ahead of me, to always know exactly where I am and what I'm up to.

"Thanks for the update, Dirk," I say, forcing a note of gratitude into my voice. "I'll be in touch."

As I hang up the phone, a sense of unease settles over me, mingled with a hint of relief. The threats may have died down for now, but I know they won't stay dormant forever. And as I gaze out at the endless expanse of ocean stretching out before me, I can't help but wonder if I've made any more mistakes that could lead trouble to my doorstep.

But for now, I push those thoughts aside, focusing instead on the beauty and tranquility of the moment. With Diesel by my side and the warm tropical breeze caressing my skin, I remind myself that I am safe, that I am free to leave this island paradise whenever I choose.

24

Mike

I CONTINUE MY SEARCH for Eve in Maui. It's been almost a week since I arrived on this island paradise, and still, there's no sign of her. But that hasn't stopped me from trying. I've become borderline obsessive, returning to the cottage at least three times a day in the hopes of catching a glimpse of her.

Each time I think I see her, my heart lurches in my chest, only to plummet back down when I realize it's just a trick of the light or a figment of my imagination. But still, I can't shake the feeling that she's out there somewhere, just beyond my reach.

I've tried calling her phone countless times, but it always goes straight to voicemail. It's like she's disappeared off the face of the earth, leaving no trace behind. And yet, I refuse to give up hope. I refuse to believe that she's truly gone.

With a heavy heart, I dial Damon's number, my fingers trembling slightly as I wait for him to pick up. He answers on the third ring.

"Mike," he says, his tone guarded. "Have you found anything?"

I sigh, running a hand through my hair in frustration. "No, nothing," I admit, my voice tinged with defeat. "If she's in the cottage, she's not answering."

"Maybe she's not there or maybe she's gone a lot."

There's a moment of silence on the other end of the line, the weight of Damon's concern hanging heavy between us.

"How's Piper and the puppies? The pictures you're sending are awesome."

"Piper and the puppies are doing great," he says, trying to change the subject. "I've grown accustomed to the runt of the litter. He's got quite the personality. I've named him Draco, like a dragon."

"A dragon?"

"Yeah. I know he'll live up to the name."

I force a small smile at the image of Damon with the puppies, grateful for the distraction. But the nagging ache in my chest remains, a constant reminder of the emptiness that comes from being separated from Eve.

"When are you coming back?" Damon asks, his voice gentle. "Or what happens if you find her and she doesn't want you?"

The question hangs in the air between us, heavy with unspoken fears and uncertainties. But I refuse to entertain the possibility that Eve doesn't want me. I refuse to believe that our love isn't enough to overcome any obstacle.

"That thought hasn't crossed my mind," I reply firmly, my voice laced with determination. "Because I know that we're meant to be together. She'll come back to Legacy with me, I'm sure of it."

There's a long pause on the other end of the line, the silence stretching between us like a taut wire. And then, finally, Damon speaks, his voice tinged with sadness.

"Sometimes love isn't enough, Mike," he says softly. "Sometimes you have to let go, even if it's the hardest thing you'll ever do."

I bristle at his words, my chest tightening with anger and frustration. How could he say such a thing? How could he suggest that I give up on the woman I love?

But deep down, I know he's right. I know that love alone isn't always enough to conquer the obstacles that life throws our way. And as I hang up the phone, the weight of his words hangs heavy in my heart.

I get stuck in my head for a while and realize that it's almost nine o'clock at night. I decide to go out to the cottage the next morning and see one last time if I can find Eve.

I'll sleep and start new in the morning.

***

I'm at the cottage early and when I knock there's no answer.

I decide to take a walk around the house, hoping for some sign of where she might be. As I round the corner, my breath catches in my throat as I spot a private beach stretching out before me, the azure waters of the ocean lapping gently at the shore.

And there, on the beach, I see them. A figure lounges on a chaise lounge, a dog by her side, basking in the warm glow of the sun. My heart skips a beat as I recognize Diesel, his tail wagging eagerly as he catches sight of me.

As I approach, the figure stirs, sitting up and peering over her oversized sunglasses to get a better look at me. And then, our eyes meet, and time seems to stand still.

It's Eve.

For a moment, I can't move, can't speak, can't do anything but stare in awe at the woman before me. She looks happy, and content, but as she realizes who I am, her expression shifts from surprise to shock to anger.

"What are you doing here?" she demands, her voice tinged with frustration.

"Just out for a leisurely stroll."

"How did you find me?"

"Piper can't stop thinking about Diesel, she was able to sniff him out."

She looks behind me, when she doesn't see Piper, she rolls her eyes and crosses her arms in front of her chest.

"You're unbelievable," she mutters, her tone tinged with exasperation. "Can't you take a hint?"

"I'm here to take you back to Legacy," I say, my voice firm. "I miss you, Eve. So does Damon. Come home with me."

She scoffs at my words, her expression incredulous. "You must be dense if you think I'm going back there," she says, her voice sharp with anger. "I told you it's not safe for you to be around me."

I take a step closer to her, determined to make her understand. "I don't care if it's safe for me or not," I say, my voice soft but resolute. "I love you, Eve. And I want to be with you."

She shakes her head, her eyes flashing with frustration. "You don't love me."

I reach out to her, cupping her face in my hands as I gaze into her eyes. "Woman, don't tell me how I feel," I say, my voice low and intense.

I lean forward and capture her mouth with mine. She immediately responds by wrapping her arms around my neck and forming herself to me.

"I've missed you so much," she says breathlessly when she pulls away.

"I've missed you too. We're grandparents by the way."

"Grandparents?"

"Diesel and Piper have four beautiful babies."

"What?"

"I was surprised too," I laugh.

"So much for you wanting Blue Heeler grandkids."

"That just goes to say love finds its way."

I pull her into another kiss, this time I cup her butt cheeks and pick her up. I start walking toward the cottage. I can't wait to make love to her. We're kissing the entire time until I'm finally inside and laying her down on a bed.

I gaze down at her luscious curves in a barely-there black bikini. She's breathtaking and I can't wait to taste her again.

As I lean in to kiss her neck, she lets out a soft moan, her fingers tangling in my hair.

I trail kisses down her collarbone, feeling her pulse quicken beneath my lips. She arches against me, her body a symphony of curves and softness. I reach for the strings of her bikini top, slowly pulling them loose as she looks up at me with desire-filled eyes.

With a flick of my wrist, the bikini top falls away, revealing her flawless skin and the swell of her breasts. I lower my head to kiss each one, savoring the salty taste of her skin against my lips. She gasps at the sensation, her hands skimming down my back as she pulls me closer.

I move lower, my knees moving her knees apart so that I can go in between her thighs and bury my face there.

"Mike," she moans as my tongue darts out along her slit.

I slip a finger inside her, feeling her walls clench around me. She lets out a soft cry, her hips bucking slightly against my face. I can feel her desire building, the heat of her passion rising, and it only fuels my own desire even more.

I pull back, my lips still tingling from the contact with her skin. She's breathing hard now, her eyes wide and her cheeks flushed. I trail kisses up her body, my fingers lightly grazing her sensitive skin as I go.

"Baby, I've been dreaming of this moment for so long," I whisper, my lips just a hair's breadth away from her mouth.

She gazes into my eyes, her own filled with a mixture of desire and love. “I’ve missed you too,” she says softly, her voice shaking with emotion.

I brush a lock of hair from her face, tucking it behind her ear. “I want to make love to you so badly right now,” I confess, my voice low and steady.

She nods, her eyes never leaving mine. “Then let’s do it.”

I slip off her bikini bottoms, revealing her proud and shy nest. She hesitates for a moment, her face a picture of vulnerability and anticipation.

I pull my pants and shirt off before I position myself between her legs.

Gently, I press myself against her, feeling her warmth and wetness. She lets out a soft sigh as I begin to move, my hips rocking slowly at first, then picking up pace. She meets my thrusts, her hips rising to meet mine with a primal rhythm.

Our breaths are ragged, our moans mingling in the heat of the moment. I lean down to kiss her, our tongues entwining in a dance of passion. She wraps her legs around my waist, pulling me closer, deepening the sensation.

I grip her hips, moving faster now, the intensity building between us. She cries out, her body trembling as she reaches her climax, her walls contracting around me. I'm not far behind, my own release surging through me as I bury myself inside her.

We collapse onto the bed, our bodies panting and shaking. She looks at me with a smile.

“I’m glad you’re here.”

“Me too. I’ve been looking for you for the last week.”

“You have?”

“Yes, you’re never home.”

“Staying here alone made me think of you and I couldn’t bear it. Diesel and I took a lot of hikes, I learned to surf.”

"You'll have to show me your moves."

"Mike," she sighs.

"Don't start that stuff again. Can you just trust me, please? Give it a shot."

"Okay."

***

The next morning she takes me for a hike in Maui.

The sun is just starting to peek over the horizon as she leads me through the lush forest, the morning dew glistening on the foliage. We walk in comfortable silence, the sound of our footsteps echoing through the trees.

She takes a detour and leads me to a secluded waterfall, the water cascading down into a crystal-clear pool below. She helps me climb down to the edge of the pool, where we sit on a rock and look out at the view.

"Do you want to swim? The water is ice cold, but refreshing."

I nod and wade into the water, feeling my body adjust to the temperature as she joins me. We hold hands as we swim around, taking in the serene beauty of the scene.

"This is incredible. I don't want to leave."

"But you have to," she giggles. "You have a job back home."

"Fair point."

We get out of the water and get dressed. We start to walk back toward the car. I pull her into me and kiss her just before we leave the trail.

I pull away, both of us breathless as I gaze down at her. She buries her face in my chest before I drop to one knee.

I reach into my pocket and pull out a small velvet box, her eyes widening in surprise as I open it to reveal a sparkling diamond ring.

The words I had been rehearsing for weeks suddenly escape me, so I simply speak from the heart. "Will you marry me?"

"Mike, what are you doing?"

"I'm proposing," I chuckle.

Her eyes are wet with unshed tears.

"But my brother."

"He knows and gives us his blessing."

"Mike, you don't know what you're getting yourself into. I..."

"I don't care, Eve. I love you and want to spend the rest of my life with you. We will figure out anything and everything as it comes our way. Marry me."

Her bottom lip trembles as she reaches out to touch the ring, her fingers grazing the smooth surface. She looks up at me, her expression a mix of joy and fear.

"Mike, I never thought... I never imagined..." Her voice falters.

I take her hands in mine, feeling her warmth seep into my skin. "Eve, we can face anything together. I believe in us. Do you?"

Her eyes search mine, searching for reassurance, for certainty. And then, with a smile, she nods.

"Yes, Mike. Yes, I will marry you."

Relief floods through me as I slip the ring onto her finger, sealing our promise to each other. In that moment, as we hold each other close, I know that whatever challenges lie ahead, we will overcome them together.

Epilogue

Eve

ONE YEAR LATER

As I stand at the threshold of the quaint beach cottage, the soft sound of waves crashing against the shore fills the air around me, a soothing melody that sets the stage for the momentous occasion about to unfold. The sun dips low on the horizon, casting hues of pink and orange across the sky, painting the scene in a breathtaking palette of colors.

I take a deep breath, the scent of salt and sea mingling in the air as I prepare to take the first steps down the aisle. The pathway is adorned with delicate flowers and flickering candles, creating a path that leads straight to the man of my dreams.

Man of my dreams. I never thought this moment would happen.

Damon stands beside me, his arm linked with mine as he guides me forward with a reassuring smile. "You look beautiful, Sis," he says, his voice filled with pride.

"Thanks," I grin. "What a twist of fate, right?"

"I think I always knew there was something special between the two of you."

"We just needed to join in that," I giggle.

"You're a stubborn one, that's for sure."

"I get it from my big brother."

"There is a really hot blonde in the front row sitting on your side, who is she?"

"Kelsey?"

"No silly, not Kelsey," he laughs. "Someone else."

"I didn't invite anyone else. Maybe she's the wife of one of the players?"

I'm certain the blonde is Natalia but her identity needs to remain hidden for now. There are too many people here, even if Mike does trust them all.

"Maybe. Kelsey looks happy."

"Yeah, she does."

Kelsey had recently met someone who seems to be perfect for her. Damon was hurt, but he couldn't blame himself when he couldn't decide if he wanted her or not for so long.

Piper and Diesel are both up at the altar along with Damon's dog, Draco. They're such a big part of Mike and me that we couldn't leave them out.

Mike chartered a private plane to make sure his teammates were all here, as well as Kelsey and their coaches.

It's a beautiful moment for us.

"Mom and Dad would be so proud and so happy right now."

"They always loved Mike like one of their own."

The music begins and we start down the aisle together.

As we reach the end of the aisle, I see Mike standing at the altar, a smile spreading across his face as he catches sight of me. My heart skips a beat at the sight of him, the love and adoration in his eyes sending a surge of warmth coursing through me.

Damon gives my arm a gentle squeeze before stepping aside, his eyes filled with emotion as he watches me take my place beside Mike. "Take care of her, Mike," he whispers, his voice choked with emotion.

Mike nods, a grin spreading across his face as he clasps my hand in his. "You got it, buddy," he says, his voice filled with confidence.

Damon shoots him a playful wink before taking his seat among the guests, a smile still lingering on his lips as he settles in for the ceremony.

As the music continues to play, Mike and I turn to face each other, our eyes locked in a silent exchange of promises and vows. The world falls away around us as we speak, our words a testament to the love and laughter that has brought us to this moment.

"I promise to always make you laugh, even when you're feeling down," Mike begins, his voice laced with humor. "And to never let you forget how much I love you, even when you're driving me crazy. I promise to protect you and keep you safe even when you're fighting me like a feral cat. I vow to never leave my socks lying around... unless it's for a sock puppet show to entertain you. I solemnly swear to share the last slice of pizza, even if it means I go hungry. And most importantly, I promise to be your partner in crime, your rock, and your biggest fan through all of life's adventures."

"And I promise to love you even though I show that by driving you crazy. I promise to always pretend your dad jokes are hilarious, even when they make me groan inside. I vow to never let the toilet seat debate divide us, though I reserve the right to grumble about it occasionally. I solemnly swear to share my desserts with you, but don't push your luck with the chocolate ice cream. And most importantly, I promise to be your partner in mischief, your confidante, and your forever teammate in this wild ride we call life."

I can't help but laugh at his words, the sound ringing out across the beach as we exchange vows that are equal parts heartfelt and humorous. This is us, I realize, two imperfect people coming together to create something beautiful in the chaos of life.

And as we seal our vows with a kiss, the cheers of our friends and family echoing in the air around us, I know the next chapter of our journey together will be more beautiful than I could have ever imagined.

***

The reception is in full swing, the air filled with laughter and music as friends and family gather to celebrate our union. The setting is intimate, with fairy lights twinkling overhead and the sound of waves crashing against the shore providing a soothing backdrop to the festivities.

I watch as Mike moves gracefully among the guests, his smile bright and infectious as he greets each person with warmth and charm. He's a natural at this, I think to myself, a born entertainer who thrives in the spotlight, even if he believes otherwise.

But as he catches my eye from across the room, a flicker of something passes between us—a shared secret that only we know. And in that moment, I'm reminded once again of the sacrifice he's made for me, the decision to marry a woman who can't give him the full details of her career, who also has an extremely dangerous job that could bleed over onto him.

Luca approaches us, a grin spreading across his face as he claps Mike on the back. "You're going to be missed on the ice, buddy," he says, his voice tinged with regret.

“What are you talking about?”

“I see you retiring soon.”

“Not happening quite yet,” Mike laughs.

I feel a surge of pride well up within me as I listen to him speak, the depth of his love for me shining through in every word.

"With a wife this hot, I wouldn't want to leave her," Luca flirts as he winks at me. "But seriously, I couldn't be happier for you."

He walks away and Natalia sidles up next to me, blonde wig and all.

"I wasn't prepared for your brother to look so hot in a tuxedo."

"Gross," I giggle. "Have you talked to him yet?"

"No."

"Why not?"

"Biding my time, maybe?" she smiles.

"Go talk to him. He hasn't stopped asking about you or taken his eyes off you."

She makes a face before smiling at me.

"I'm really happy for you. And if you can find happiness, I can too."

"You forced the happiness with that postcard you sent Mike," I tease. "But I'm grateful for it."

"I have no idea what you're talking about. I really didn't send any postcard."

"Sure," I laugh as she hugs me quickly and then walks away.

"I might have sent it," Conner laughs as he comes up behind me.

"Really, I hadn't pegged you for the romantic type."

"I'm not, I just couldn't stand seeing a grown man so pathetically moping around like a lost puppy dog. Didn't make our neighborhood look good."

I laugh out loud and shake my head.

"Thanks for protecting me when I was nothing but a bitch to you."

"It's part of the job. I had an inkling the Tambov Gang was in town that day, something told me to follow you and I'm glad I did."

"Me too."

"Dirk's over by the water, in case you didn't notice him."

I giggle and nod. Conner and I look toward the crashing waves and make eye contact with Dirk. He too is incognito. He nods, gives me a thumbs up and walks along the beach and away from the cottage.

"I still don't know why Conner was invited."

"He's harmless," I reply.

Mike pulls me into him and kisses the top of my head.

"Is it too soon for me to throw you over my shoulder and take you to bed?"

"I don't think so," I giggle.

He bends down and does just that. I'm laughing as he makes a peace sign and tells people we're out.

It couldn't be a more perfect ending to a perfect day.

THE END

***

A Note from the Author

Dear Reader,

If you enjoyed Mike and Eve's journey, you'll *love* 'Pucking My Silver Fox!

A Sneak Peek is just a few pages away...

Now, a quick favor: Will you please scan this QR code with your smartphone's camera app and write a review for this book? It doesn't need to be long—-a couple of sentences will suffice. The QR code will take you *directly* to the review section of the book's Amazon page, and your feedback can help others discover their next great read!"

Scan this QR code to leave a review

Thank you so much!

Let's continue our literary adventures, one page at a time.

Love,

Livvy

Pucking My Silver Fox
An Enemies to Lovers
Brother's Best Friend Romance

Wham, bam, no thank you, ma'am—

That was the end of a one-night stand with my brother's off-limits best friend. Or so I thought.

But now that we're in a fake relationship, all bets are off...

Ryder Lafferty is perfect— bronzed, primal and ripped beyond belief, with muscles and manhood that strain to be released.

I couldn't resist. And he did not disappoint.

He pleasured me like no man my age ever had before, awakening a fire long thought dead.

I wanted more.

But he disappeared.

Years later, I return to our small town and run into Ryder, now a billionaire hockey star and single daddy of the cutest little girl ever.

When a violent gang target her, Ryder and I pretend to be a couple for protection.

As we navigate lies and deceit, our desire intensifies to the nth degree. Skin against skin, we tumble, toss, and electrify the night.

And the way he treats his baby—and me—melts my heart.

Despite numerous warnings from friends and family that this will never work,

I can't stop myself.

Ryder's daughter is at risk. And so is my heart...

Scan this QR Code to get your copy of "Pucking My Silver Fox" now!

Pucking My Silver Fox

An Enemies to Lovers Brother's Best Friend Romance

Prologue

Gia

THE RHYTHMIC POUNDING OF MY FOOTSTEPS on the wooden slats of the boardwalk matches the beat of the Eminem song playing through my head. I'm lost in another world as I focus on the burn in my lungs and muscles.

There is nothing better than a morning run and watching the sunrise on the beach.

As the sky starts to lighten, I stop for a second and put my hands on the back of my head as I inhale and exhale taking in the beauty before me.

I close my eyes and breathe in and out slowly again before I start back on my run.

This is exactly what I need before I meet the half-brother and half- I didn't know existed until a few months ago.

I don't get anxious, but I'm a nervous wreck about it all. This run was necessary to get rid of all the jitters.

"Oof," I breathe.

I fall backward after hitting a solid wall of something.

That's what I get for not being aware of my surroundings.

Strong hands grab my elbows and steady me.

"Whoa. Shit. Are you okay?" a deep southern drawl asks quickly.

I look up into soft gray eyes and my stomach flips. They're attached to a man with a chiseled jaw and a flat top buzz cut.

"Yeah. I'm sorry. I wasn't paying attention to where I was going."

"Neither was I," he chuckles. "I was enjoying that sunrise."

"Same," I smile back at him.

He smiles too and my stomach somersaults this time.

Damn, that changed his entire face and made him even more gorgeous.

"Are you sure you're okay?"

"Yeah. I'm a tough girl."

"Are you from around here? I don't think I've ever seen you before and it's a pretty small town."

"I'm not. I'm visiting."

"I'm Ryder."

"I'm Gia."

"How long are you visiting for?"

"That's still up in the air."

His phone vibrates and he looks at it quickly.

"I need to get going. Hopefully, I'll see you around again."

I nod and smile before I take off at a jog again. Slowly making my way I run back to my hotel before I jump in the shower.

I should have asked for that man's phone number.

He lives here and you don't, what would be the point of that? A Marine is never in the same spot for long.

I blow out a breath. I signed my life over to the Marine Corps just over three years ago and that's where I'll remain. I want to travel the world, so getting ideas about a man with an amazing smile isn't what I need to be doing right now.

Focus on making a good impression today.

I eat breakfast and bury myself in a good romance novel. I can't focus on anything though as I keep staring at the clock.

I'm to meet my siblings for the first time ever at two. I feel like time is at a standstill.

I'm going to vomit.

***

Five hours later, I take a deep breath and look at myself in the mirror. The floral sundress I'm wearing makes my blue eyes pop. My long, blonde hair falls in waves down my back.

I rarely look like a girl. I'm almost always in uniform or in workout clothes.

"Okay, let's do this."

I blow out a breath, grab my things, and leave my room to go to my car. The small beach town of Ash Cove is quaint and adorable. It doesn't take long to get from one side of town to the other either.

I pull up to the gorgeous brick house in a cookie-cutter subdivision. My GPS announces that I've arrived at my destination.

"Why are there so many cars here?" I ask myself out loud.

I check the text messages in the group chat between my half-brother Josh, my half-sister Talia, and me. It definitely says today at this time.

Here goes nothing.

I get out of my car and walk up to the front door. Just as I'm about to knock it flies open and a tall, muscular man is backing out of the door, another man is right in front of him.

"We'll be right back, Sarah, I swear!" the other man yells.

I try to dart out of the way as the first man spins around and comes face to face with me.

It's him!

Damn it, is he my brother?

"Oh shit! Here I am about to run into you again!" he chuckles.

"Again? Gia?"

"I almost knocked her over on my morning run."

"Yes."

"I'm Josh," the other man says as he engulfs me in a hug. He leans back into the house. "Talia, get out here."

"Gia, as in your long-lost sister?" the man asks.

"The one and only," I reply with a mock curtsy.

Why am I such a dork?

"Gia, this is my best friend, Ryder. He failed to tell anyone that he was coming home from his deployment today and showed up to surprise us."

Best friend? Are they the same age? There's no way this Ryder guy is in his thirties.

"Deployment?"

"Afghanistan for a year."

"Gia is a Marine."

"Is that so? I'm a pilot in the Army."

"Wow, that's impressive."

He shrugs nonchalantly.

"Gia?!?" a dark-headed woman shrieks as she rushes out the door. "I'm Talia!"

She engulfs me in a hug.

"Hey Talia," I grin as I pull away. "It's so nice to finally meet you."

"This is my wife, Sarah," Josh says, pointing to a gorgeous blonde who is clearly pregnant.

"Hi Gia, I'm so happy you could make it today. Come in, come in. The boys were headed to get some more beer."

"We'll be right back," Josh interjects as he squeezes my arm.

He and Ryder take off while Talia grabs me by the arm and leads me inside.

"I guess if you're going to get introduced to the family it's only fitting you meet Ryder too," Sarah laughs. "He and Josh have been inseparable since childhood."

"They're both annoying. Two older brothers that I didn't ask for. I'm so excited to get a sister," Talia gushes.

"I was apprehensive about reaching out," I admit as Sarah gestures for me to sit down on the couch. "But I'm glad I did."

"Me too," Talia giggles. "When I saw that I had a sister I think I stared at the results on the app and your text for an hour not knowing what to do."

"Had I known how he left your mother, I probably wouldn't have."

"That wasn't your fault though. It was his choice to use and manipulate her and everyone in town for his benefit. You weren't even born yet."

"He never told you that he had other children?" Sarah asks.

I shake my head and inhale slowly. "Never. He constantly told me he didn't ever want kids but that he got stuck with me and didn't have a choice."

"That's lovely."

"It is what it is. I've made peace with it."

"You should write a book about it," Talia sighs. "The stories you told us about how you were stealing jewelry at the age of four or how he used you as a scapegoat for everything is so wild."

"Yeah, I've thought about it," I answer quietly.

"Did I hear Ryder say that the two of you ran into each other this morning?" Sarah interjects with a raised eyebrow.

"We did, literally smacked into each other."

"That's adorable. He's single and a really good guy," Talia teases. "Even if he's annoying."

I hold up my hands. "I'm not looking for anything right now. My life is the Marine Corps."

"I get that, he's quite a bit older than you too," she sighs. "I would just love for you to stick around Ash Cove longer and I'm blatantly ignoring how mismatched you two would be with a decade of age difference.."

"Do you drink, Gia?" Sarah asks.

"I do."

"I am dying for a virgin margarita, you in? You and Talia can have tequila in yours."

"Of course."

The three of us go into the kitchen and Sarah starts pulling out ingredients and placing them in front of the blender. We're talking nonstop, laughing as we get to know each other better.

This is nice. I've never had this before.

Before long, Josh and Ryder return. Ryder's eyes fall on me immediately.

There's that gorgeous smile again.

Talia nudges me and I can't help but giggle at her.

"I see y'all didn't wait for us to get back."

"I'm having FOMO. I can't wait until this baby boy is out of me so I can join in on Margarita nights again," Sarah smiles.

"How far along are you?" I ask.

"Thirty-six weeks. He'll be here before we know it."

"That's amazing."

"It doesn't feel amazing right now," Sarah laughs. "I'm miserable."

"But you're beautiful," Josh gushes as he wraps his arms around her and kisses her on the cheek.

Talia makes a gagging sound, and everyone laughs.

"Where are you stationed at, Gia?" Ryder asks.

"I was in Okinawa. I just got transferred to Quantico, that's why I was able to take this trip."

"You were stationed in Japan?" Sarah gushes as she slaps at Josh. "You didn't tell me that."

"Yeah," I laugh.

"That's amazing."

"It's pretty cool. It's not someplace I would have gone on my own and it's nice."

"What did you do that you were transferred to Quantico?" Ryder asks.

"If I told you, then I'd have to kill you," I tease with a wink.

He chuckles, his eyes locking on to mine.

"Virginia is so close," Talia interjects. "We can visit each other a lot. This makes my heart so happy."

"Don't you drill at Fort Eustis sometimes?" Sarah asks Ryder.

"I do, which isn't too far from Quantico."

"Small world."

"How long have you been in the Marine Corps?" Ryder interjects.

"Three years, how long have you been in the Army?"

"Fourteen."

Whoa, he's way older than I thought he was. He does not look like he's thirty-two. I guess being Josh's best friend it would make sense that they're the same age.

He's still hot though.

"You're thirty-two?"

"Yes, is that bad?"

"No," I giggle. "I just wouldn't have guessed that."

We spend the rest of the afternoon drinking, laughing, and hanging out.

Being raised by a single father and moving around a lot, I never really developed friendships or understood what it was like to have a family. The Marine Corps taught me about family, but I still am kind of distant when it comes to making friends.

This is different, this feels natural.

"I am beat," Talia stretches and yawns later that night. "I'm going to head home."

"I'm exhausted as well," Sarah sighs.

"Gia, want to meet up for lunch tomorrow?" Talia asks. "There's an amazing pizza place in town that we can all meet up at."

"I'd like that."

"When do you go back?"

"Not for a few days at least."

"That's great. We'll pack in as much as we can."

"That would be amazing. I didn't expect to have this much fun."

"We're a lively group," Talia teases.

"I should head back to the hotel."

"Are you okay to drive?" Ryder asks me.

"Yeah, I haven't had a margarita or any alcohol for a while."

"Just checking. I should head out too. I'll see you tomorrow," he says as he and Josh do a weird handshake.

Talia hugs us all and heads out of the house. I hug Sarah and Josh before I start out as well. Talia is already gone by the time I leave. Ryder is waiting for me by my car.

"I'm starving. I also am wide awake because of the time changes. Would you like to grab something to eat with me?"I hesitate for a moment then nod.

"I could eat. I'm also in a little bit of a time change rut."

"I assumed. Do you want to ride with me or follow?"

"Follow."

"Got it," he smiles. "There's a great diner on the boardwalk, it's open all night. Josh said you're at the only hotel here and it's within walking distance. We can park there and walk if you'd like."

"Is that Delaney's? I saw it when I was coming into town. That sounds perfect."

"That's exactly where I'm talking about."

He opens my car door for me and then shuts the door when I climb inside. He then trots to his car. He pulls out of the circle driveway, and I follow behind him.

What am I doing?

Why did I agree to go to dinner with this man?

He's way older than me and I'm not looking for anything. I don't even live here.

Ten minutes later, we're pulling into the parking lot of my hotel. He hurries to get out before me and open my door for me.

He's really sweet.

"I'm not sure how you feel about carbs, but this place has the best pancakes in the U.S."

"That's a big claim."

"It says so on the sign, so it must be true," he chuckles as he points at the sign at the entrance to the old building.

"Must be," I laugh.

He opens the door for me and gestures for me to walk in before him. An older woman is running around and tells us to have a seat anywhere. Ryder puts his hand on my back briefly. When I look back at him, he's gesturing to a booth by a window. I follow behind him.

"I'll seat us and get us our drinks, Marge!" he calls out to the waitress.

"You're a saint, Ryder. Do you want your usual?"

"Yes, Ma'am, pancakes and bacon times two."

"I'll let George know. It's so good to have you back in town, sugar," she drawls.

"I see you know the locals well."

"I've been coming here since I was twelve, I think," he chuckles. "I worked here in high school too."

"Wow," I say as I sit down.

Ryder doesn't sit in the booth yet; he walks over to the diner's counter and then goes behind it. He grabs two coffee cups and pours coffee in it, while also grabbing creamer. He grabs two slices of pie from the rotating display case too before walking back over to me.

He expertly handles the coffee and the pies.

That's impressive.

Just as he puts everything down on the table about ten kids walk in the door. He makes eye contact with Marge and then looks down at me apologetically.

"Go," I laugh as I realize that the diner's full and Marge is the only one working.

"It won't take me long," he smiles before he turns to the group of kids and tells them to have a seat.

He grabs menus and hands them out to the table before taking drink orders. He doesn't write anything down, just memorizes them and then goes to fill them. By the time he has them filled and handed out Marge is free enough to take their orders.

"If you ever want to quit everything else and come back to work here, I'll take you in a heartbeat," Marge grins at him.

"I'll keep that in mind," he laughs as he sits across from me.

As I look outside the window, the moonlight is reflecting off the ocean, combined with the lights on the boardwalk it's a surreal sight.

"That's why I chose it," he chuckles.

"Are you originally from here?"

"Yes, born and raised. I'm only here visiting. I live in California part of the year."

"That's pretty cool. Why part of the year?"

"My job. I have a busy period and when it slows down I come back here. There's something about a small town that helps ground you after chaos."

"That's true. This is my first time visiting Ash Cove, it's got a certain appeal to it."

"I'll let the tourism bureau know you think so," he teases. "Are you single?"

"I am. Are you?"

"I am," he grins.

"So, you and Josh have known each other for a while?"

"Since kindergarten."

"That's a long time for a friendship to last."

"Maybe so. It's definitely normal around these parts, small towns and all."

"That means you know the history of my dad."

"A little. I know that he disappeared one day, and people thought he vanished into thin air. I remember for about a month or so no one could believe that such a good, devoted man would just walk out on his wife and children that he clearly adored. I remember my mom saying that a few times."

"And then everyone learned he wasn't what he seemed."

"For a bit, people thought that Josh's mom was in on all of it too. My mom and grandma always said that she couldn't fake that devastation and shock. Josh and I were almost eleven when that happened."

"I think it's when he got my mom pregnant that everything started exploding around him and he left," I murmur.

The waitress comes back through with our drinks and two plates of pancakes for us. We're quiet for a moment while we dig into our food.

Okay, the best pancakes in the U.S. might be right. These are so light and fluffy.

"The timeline would sync that way. He stole a lot of money from a lot of people."

"That's what he did best."

"You two didn't get along?"

"You could say that," I shake my head and he nods slowly.

"What made you join the Marine Corps?"

"Something about getting away where no one knew me or my father and the thrill of getting to travel all over the world. What about you?"

"It was a backup plan to my other career."

"Other career?"

"I play hockey too."

"Vast difference," I laugh. "Are you any good?"

"Not horrible."

We continue eating and talking, getting to know each other. We have a lot in common with both being in the military. Our meals are long finished before I realize that we've been sitting here talking for a while.

I glance down at my phone and realize it's almost four in the morning.

"At this point, I should just stay up until my morning run," I tease.

"Care for a running buddy?"

"I'd like that."

"I have to say, I was hoping I'd run into you again when I went for a run tomorrow morning?"

"Really?"

"Yeah, you're gorgeous. Getting to be around you at Josh's and now, you're pretty incredible. It's rare to find someone who gets all the parts of me, especially the military part."

"Try being a woman in the Marine Corps," I tease.

"I can't imagine that's easy."

"Most men are intimidated."

"I'm not."

"I've noticed. And I appreciate that."

"I'm not here long, it seems like you're not either, but I'd really like to get to know you better."

"Okay."

"Why don't we take a walk on the beach right now? I'm not ready to call it a night."

"That sounds great," I sigh.

He pays for our meal and then the two of us leave the restaurant. Once outside, he puts his hand on the small of my back briefly again to lead me to the beach.

Why does that gesture make my stomach flip?

We're quiet as we walk to the water. We both remove our shoes and carry them in our hands as we let the sand squish between our toes.

"This is extremely forward, but I'm dying to kiss you," Ryder says as stops before a wave crashes over his feet.

My eyes widen in surprise, my stomach flips again. Guys my age wouldn't have been so polite as to ask.

"I'm dying for you to kiss me," I drawl back to him.

"Perfect."

He grins, his eyes locked on to mine before he leans forward and covers my mouth with his.

An electric current races through my body as my stomach flips excitedly. Goosebumps follow as his hand goes to cup my cheek sweetly.

Holy Hell this man can kiss.

My pelvis rocks forward as if searching for him.

Down, girl.

When he pulls away, both of us are breathless and both of us are lost in the other's eyes.

There's something about him.

"Let's get out of here," I say. "This may be forward as well, but do you want to come back to my hotel with me?"

"Perfect," he laughs.

We quickly make our way to the hotel, barely containing our excitement and desire for each other. The short walk feels like an eternity as we steal passionate kisses in between quickened steps.

There's a large crack of thunder just as the skies open up and it starts to pour down rain.

"Oh shit," I giggle.

"Looks like the hurricane is a lot closer than they originally thought."

"Hurricane?"

"Yes, we're supposed to have a hurricane hit land by Sunday night. Let's get you into your room before you're soaked."

I fumble with my key card at the entrance, finally managing to open the door to my room. As soon as the door is closed, he pushes me against it and begins kissing me with such intensity that my knees go weak.

He lifts me effortlessly and carries me to the bed, never breaking our kiss. The storm outside rages on, matching the passion that we are sharing in this moment. Clothes quickly find their way to the floor as we explore each other's bodies with a hunger that can only be satiated by one another.

"I need to taste you," he says gruffly as he gently pushes my thighs apart.

I suck in a breath as he moves downward, making a trail with his mouth before he finds my hot, wet core. I grip the sheets as his finger gently explores my clit, butterfly-like touches so soft that I'm not sure if I'm imagining them.

"Yessss," I moan.

"Beautiful," he breathes before he buries his head between my legs. His fingers and his tongue explore. He's like a starving man at a buffet and I'm the main course.

Yessss, please don't stop.

As he continues to pleasure me, my body trembles with every touch, every stroke, every caress.

I arch my back, my fingers digging into the sheets as his touch sends waves of pleasure coursing through me. My breathing becomes ragged as I feel myself reaching the edge. I desperately grab for him, wanting to feel him inside me, needing to feel his cock in my throat to ground me. Anything to focus on other than the sensations that are rushing through me right now.

He pulls away with a chuckle, moving my hands so that I can't pull him up.

"Be a good girl and let me eat," he drawls with a look that tells me not to argue.

"Yes, Sir," I murmur, surprised by the words as they fall out of my mouth.

He goes right back to between my legs.

Lick, suck, oh damn, that's amazing.

I reach down and grip his head, guiding him closer to me as I feel the sensations pushing me to the edge. He responds to my urgency and increases the intensity of his movements, his tongue delving deeper into me as his fingers speed up their rhythm.

His lips meet my clit again, sending waves of pleasure through me. I can feel my orgasm building, growing stronger with every touch. I moan, arching my back as I cling to him, desperate for release.

I feel him push two fingers inside me, curling them to graze my G-spot. I cry out.

"God, yes!"

He continues the movement, sending me spinning over the edge as my entire body shakes with pleasure.

As I come down from my high, he slowly pulls his fingers out of me and leans up to kiss me gently. "You taste amazing."

I laugh weakly, "That was intense."

He grins, "I'm not done with you yet."

He stands up and reaches for my hand. He pulls me to where I'm sitting up. His erection is hard and throbbing, and I can feel my own desire for him growing even stronger.

My hand goes to his shaft, my mouth following suit.

"Shit, yesss," he breathes as my tongue teases the head of his cock.

His hand goes to my hair, pulling my dark hair into a ponytail so it doesn't distract me.

I bob up and down on his cock, licking and sucking, letting it hit the back of my throat as I moan against him.

He sucks in a breath and groans before he pulls me off him and turns me around so that I'm on all fours in front of him. He stops for a second and I hear him moving around, when I look back he's pulling out his wallet. He flashes a condom at me with a smile.

At least he has his wits about him. Guys my age usually pout when I ask for a condom and I didn't even have to mention it this time.

I hear the wrapper open before he slides it on. He guides his large cock inside me.

"Oh fuck," I moan as he fills me, stretching me to fit his massive erection.

His hands grip my hips, holding me in place as he begins to thrust in and out of me, slowly at first, allowing me to adjust to his size. My body responds to his advances, my hips rocking back to meet his every stroke.

"You feel so fucking good," he growls in my ear. "The way you look at me drives me crazy. Those gorgeous eyes on me make me want to do whatever you ask."

The sound of our bodies slapping together fills the room, our moans and gasps the only other sound. I can feel every inch of him inside me, his cock stretching me wide and filling me in a way I've never experienced before.

His thrusts grow more urgent, his hips slamming into my ass.

"Yes, harder," I urge him, my voice hoarse and needy.

He obliges, slamming into me with reckless abandon. My breasts bounce with each powerful thrust, my nipples scraping against the sheets.

His hand goes forward, his fingers finding my clit.

"Oh shit," I groan as I sit up, my back against his chest.

He kisses my neck as his other hand goes to my breasts, his finger and thumb closing around a nipple. His fingers on my breast and the one rubbing my clit are using the same motion and I've never felt anything more intense in my life.

He's panting and grunting in my ear as I try to focus and stave off all of the sensations. I want to cum so badly, but I also don't want this to end.

"You feel so good," he growls. "You're so damn tight. I don't know if I can hold on much longer. You ready to cum for me, baby?"

"Yes, yes, please, fuck me harder."

He growls as he slams into me faster and harder. His fingers on my nipple and clit move faster, shoving me over the edge.

"Come for me," he growls, thrusting deep inside me as he hits my G-spot with precise strokes.

I can feel the waves of pleasure crashing over me, my body tensing and shaking as I cry out his name.

With one final cry, he comes deep inside me, his cock twitching and pulsing as he fills me with his seed.

"Fuck," I moan, my body still shaking from the intensity of our lovemaking.

He collapses beside me and chuckles before he tugs me into him. I push him away.

"I need a minute," I say as I lay there in the fetal position trying to come down from my high.

"Take your time," he breathes in my ear.

I try to calm my breathing and try to stave off the emotions that are washing over me.

I've never experienced anything that intense before in my life. I feel like I'm floating.

I don't ever want to leave Ash Cove.

The next morning, I'm woken up by the incessant ringing of a phone. It's not mine, so it must belong to the sexy man beside me.

"Ryder, your phone."

He groans and answers it.

"Lafferty," he says into it. "Yes, Sir. On my way, Sir."

He hangs up the phone and looks back at me apologetically.

"Is everything okay?"

"I'm getting called out to help with rescues."

"Oh."

"I need to go," he blows out a breath and runs a hand through his hair.

He stands up and throws his clothes on quickly.

"Okay, well, be safe," I say as I stand up with him.

He pulls me into a passionate kiss.

"I'll see you soon. I'll be back tonight. Can I see you again?"

"Absolutely. I leave on Monday though."

"I'll come back here tonight and take you to dinner."

"Okay."

He kisses me again and is gone within seconds. I fall onto the bed and stare at the door.

***

Ryder never showed back up that night. The following day I meet my siblings for a cookout at Josh's, I expect to see him there.

"Will Ryder be here too?" I ask Josh.

He narrows his eyes and looks back at me with a funny expression.

"No, he got called out to pull people out down south where it's flooding. He'll be there the next few days for sure."

"Oh, we hung out after we left here. I had fun, I was hoping to see him again."

"You did what?"

"We went to Delaney's for breakfast. Both of us are still on different time zones. It was nice to catch up with someone who gets the military part of my life."

"You know he's in his thirties, right?"

"Yes," I laugh. "Will you give him my number? I didn't get a chance to and I'll be gone tomorrow."

"Yeah, yeah, I can do that. But I don't want you dating him, talking to him or whatever. There's too much of an age difference."

"I can't be friends with your best friend?"

"You're not wanting me to give him your number so you two can be friends," he snaps. "I'm not going to enable chaos."

"Chaos?" I repeat as he walks away quickly.

He walks away quickly just as Talia walks up behind me.

"If he doesn't, I will. Josh means well but he basically had to become the adult at the age of ten so he's very overprotective of the people he loves."

"And he doesn't trust me yet."

"I don't think it's you he doesn't trust. It's our father's parenting. You know what, it's probably best if from here on out, you don't let on that you're interested in Ryder. Like, I'm not a big fan of you two dating because there's such an age difference, but I also understand that it's probably nice to have someone who gets your military life."

"I get that," I murmur. "And it is. I don't want to hide something from Josh. That would make me just like our father.

Will I ever stop being punished for the sins of our father? It's not my fault that he had to raise me.

I report to my duty station and get settled in on Monday morning. By Wednesday after a conversation with Josh, I learned that Ryder came back to Ash Cove and he gave him my phone number but Ryder kind of blew him off about it, saying that we hung out and it was fun but nothing worth continuing.

Ouch.

Talia later told me that Josh lied and didn't give him my number, but she did, and Ryder was very weird about the whole exchange.

By Sunday, I hadn't received any messages or phone calls from him.

I guess all he wanted was a one-night stand.

Scan this QR code to get your copy of 'Pucking My Silver Fox"
now!

www.ingramcontent.com/pod-product-compliance
Lightning Source LLC
LaVergne TN
LVHW010542160826
845677LV00013B/2974

* 9 7 9 8 8 9 4 8 0 0 7 0 7 *